The

King

Ian Patrick Kelly

DEDICATION

To my children, thank you for the inspiration, and a special thank you to Macey for encouraging me to knock the dust from The Wooden King and finish writing it.

To Linda (the other half) and all my family and friends for all the support,
To the Grandchildren, Octavia, August, Romany, Arabella, and Axel.

To Bridget Kelly (Ma)
To (Sean) John Kelly (Dad)
To Dave and Peter Kelly (Brothers)

and to
and all of you, the readers.

CONTENTS

ACKNOWLEDGMENTS

To Chiara Girardelli, for the professional design of the Wooden King book cover, you captured the essence of it superbly. Thank you for all you did and helping me through that part of the Wooden King process.
Thank you.

To the proofreaders, your feedback in capturing some blunders was worth the wait, and your honesty is why I trusted you to be a part of it.
Nico McCaffrey.
Bridget Kelly.
Ann Aird.

1. LOST AND FOUND

It all began on a showery morning, raining quite heavily at times and turning very dark and dismal. It was hard to believe today was the beginning of the summer holidays for the kids; living on top of a hill surrounded by sheep and living in this part of the world, this kind of weather has come to be accepted. It was hard to believe that the girls' Holly, who is fifteen years old, Jasmine, fourteen years old & Melody, the youngest, at twelve years old, for they had only been out of bed for a few hours and were already falling out and arguing with one another, over who is able and who isn't able to turn the broken handle of the kitchen's back door. Not forgetting the family's little dog Charlie, whose age wasn't known; however, the girls had decided that he was three years old, for he, like the girls, was also doing his best to join in on the action by barking and whining about being let out.

By the way! Charlie certainly got his paws under the table, for it had only been seven months since Mum, Dad, and the three girls heard scratching on the door at the back of the house late one evening. It was on that dreary, cold December night when they reminded Dad that he was the man of the house and, therefore, it was his duty to investigate the peculiar faint scratching noise.

It must be said! Dad was like a true hero that night; he stood bravely at the kitchen door with the family close behind. He'd armed himself with a brush in one hand and a cup of tea in the other and gave the nod for Mum to yank upon the occasionally jamming handle, which she did. And there he was, covered in dirt, with no lead, no collar, only a message in his eyes, which seemed to be saying, 'I'm a stray; please let me in.' And that was when his introduction was over, and so was Dad's free time.

Meanwhile, the arguing between the girls continued and was about to get a lot worse until Dad walked into the kitchen, and then they vetted their frustration out on him.

'Dad, we've now lived here for almost two and a half years; when can we get a door that opens' exclaimed Jasmine.

'She's right, Dad,' Melody jokingly added, trying to add flavour to stir things up.

'Hey, this house was in a right old state when we first moved here; there's been a ton of renovation work done since then, and that isn't an easy thing to do when it's a house in the middle of nowhere, so, that door remains a finishing job,' replied Dad, having to quickly think and not let the kids get one over on him. 'So, what's the rush? He added whilst pulling hard to open the door before popping his head outside to be greeted with a face full of rainwater. 'Where are you all going? Have you seen the weather?'.

'Take it easy, Dad; we're only going to the garage,' replied Holly.

Incidentally, the garage was different from most other garages; this one was a giant dumping ground of all the things the girls hadn't wanted to get rid of after their big move, it certainly didn't home a car, but it had its purpose on days like today.

'Well, take the dog with you, and make sure you put him on his lead,' said Dad, aiming the responsibility at Holly, the eldest.

Charlie had solid shoulders and knew how to use them to his advantage; he had a happy knack for breaking loose and making the great escape into the neighbouring farmer's field, causing panic for the girls, driving Mum and Dad mad, and the sheep, barmy.

Meanwhile, the girls had been in the garage for only ten minutes when Jasmine came racing back into the house.

'Dad,' she shouts!' Charlies snapped his lead, and he's gone.

'Oh, surprise, surprise,' his reply came bellowing down from the top of the stairs.

All the while, Jasmine stares at Dad, shrugging her shoulders,

'Well, aren't you going to go and get him'? Asked Jasmine.

By this time, Holly and Melody had also appeared and were standing at the foot of the stairs. Both were staring and saying words to Dad, but he couldn't understand a word they were saying, for together, they sounded equally as monotone as each other when something had gone wrong.

'I know Charlie has snapped his lead; what do you want me to do, run around in the farmers' field in only my shorts' Dad replied sarcastically.

'Relax, Dad', laughed Holly; 'we'll see if we can find him.'

'I'll meet up with you all as soon as I'm ready, and remember! If you see Charlie in the farmers' field, ignore him, and don't let the farmer know he's ours'.

'As usual, Dad,' the girls replied while grabbing their coats from the hooks on the wall.

After the girls set off out of the house, Dad set about the bedroom getting dressed; when Mum walked in after stepping out of the shower,

'What's all the commotion,' asked Mum; ah, don't tell me, the lead, the dog, the farm, and the kids.'

'Yup, you guessed it,' replied Dad, then like a modern-day caveman, he, in a strange way of a morning kiss, quickly slavered over Mum's cheek before making his way down the stairs, grabbing his boots and setting off out of the door.

Thankfully the weather had cleared, and the rain had now stopped; this allowed Dad to spot Holly, Jasmine, and Melody from the back of the house, trudging their way up toward the farmers' field, so Dad followed.

In the meantime, the girls had neared the farmer's field; they spotted the farmer fixing a trailer to the back of his tractor. The girls knew the farmer only as Tractor Jack, the grumpy farmer in a Mac. He would suspiciously scowl at the girls whenever he saw an unaccompanied dog running around in his fields, so they decided to bypass his direction and take another route, which would take them through the forest.

Dad should have by now been close behind the girls; only he didn't know that they had gone in the opposite direction to him. So, after saying morning to the farmer, Dad took the usual path leading him directly to the top entrance of the forest, where he thought the girls and Charlie would probably be.

The girls had ventured deep inside the forest, and although it was a place they had visited many times before, it could still be relatively easy to lose direction and become lost. But feeling no cause for concern, the girls raced through the bluebells and began hiding from each other behind the trees and shrubs.

Incidentally, hiding away is one of Melody's favourite games, which was a bit frustrating for the others, for she was dainty for her age at twelve. And with any small nook, it almost guaranteed she would be able to shuffle her way inside them and take some finding, for that's what she did, at the foot of an old tree.

Sitting silently, Melody could hear Holly and Jasmine laughing and sneaking about.

'She's over here.'

'No, she's over there,' Jasmine and Holly said.

Meanwhile, Melody sat content at the foot of the old tree staring at the tops of the other trees which surrounded her; she watched as the rays of sunlight flickered through the peepholes of their branches. And in her little world, she pulled from her pocket a sticky, glittery, and stretchy alien toy that she always seemed to carry with her; she always claimed it was her lucky charm. It had one of its hands missing, caused by Charlie after she had overly teased him with it, and various pockets had covered it in bits of fluff, and it was plain it had seen far better days, but for years it remained her favourite. After bringing out the stretchy alien from her pocket, Melody reached out her arms and held it almost fully stretched before her eyes. She was trying hard to catch it in one of the sunbeams, hoping to watch it reflect and sparkle, when suddenly, from the corner of her eye, she spotted Charlie just before he disappeared behind the mound of a small hill.

'He's over there,' shouted Melody as she hurried onto her feet.

The three girls then chased toward the area Melody had pointed to, but still, they could not see Charlie. So, Jasmine tried to whistle while the other two began to shout his name.

'He's probably too far away; he won't be able to hear us.' Jasmine said.

So, the girls sped up the small but steep hill until they finally reached the brow.

Together they all peered over with smiles, hoping and expecting Charlie to greet them, but unfortunately, he wasn't.

The girls stood looking and shouting beyond the thickness of the trees; he was once again spotted, and this time, all three girls had seen him. Ever so disobedient, Charlie just stood with his ears pricked up, staring upwards and in the direction of the girls, cocking his head from one side to the other while they coaxed him over by calling his name.

'What is he doing?' asked Holly, with a hint of annoyance.

'I don't know,' answered Jasmine in a similar tone.

'Come on; he isn't listening; we'll have to go further,' demanded Melody.

Just as the girls began to move in on Charlie, he too began to move, but not in the direction they'd hoped; he just casually sniffed around the surrounding area before jumping up onto a pile of moss-covered rocks.

The girls shouted for Charlie to stay, but before they knew it, he'd trotted off and disappeared behind a vast leafy ivy wall. The great ivy wall seemed to swing across the hillside like a giant theatrical curtain, making it difficult for the girls to keep sight of the area where he'd gone.

Judging by the look on Holly and Jasmines' faces, trying to catch Charlie wasn't much fun; it was apparent; they were increasingly becoming fed up, but Melody remained optimistic and wasn't about to give up hope in capturing him.

'Come on; we'll try for five more minutes,' exclaimed Melody while moving closer to the foot of the swinging ivy.

'I don't think we should; we've been ages, and anyway, Dad will be wondering where we've got to,' replied Jasmine.

'That's a thought,' cried Holly; 'Dad should have caught up with us ages ago; come on, Melody, we'll have to go and let him know where we are'.

'She's right! We better get off,' added Jasmine. Melody agreed, but before she did, she bent towards the ground and picked up a rotten old stick; she then threw it into the air and toward where Charlie had gone. The girls watched for a second as it sailed through the air, spinning several times before fluky making its way through the same gap Charlie had made.

'What a shot,' yelled Melody as she threw her arms up.

'Shush, Melody,' said Jasmine in a harassed tone.

For a moment, the girls stood in silence, watching and hoping Charlie would come racing out from beneath the foot of the ivy, but nothing happened. The girls could only see movement made by the breeze blowing and rustling at its leaves.

'Come on; it's no good; we'll have to leave him and get Dad.' exclaimed Holly.

Melody thought for a second and decided that she was staying put and wasn't leaving Charlie, and it took much persuading that Charlie would be fine before Holly convinced her that leaving him and going to find Dad was a better idea.

The girls had only managed to walk twenty yards up the hill when Jasmine suddenly stopped and threw her arm across the chest of Holly.

'I think I can hear Charlie barking,' she said.

Melody and Holly then also stopped to listen.

'I can't hear anything,' said Holly.

'Listen, be quite a minute,' replied Jasmine.

And there it was three or four faint-sounding yaps; although they were faint, they heard them.

'It sounds like his barks are defiantly coming from behind all that ivy; I wonder if he's trapped or something,' exclaimed Melody.

Hearing Charlie's barks made the girls feel less worried, for at least he sounded fine, and they knew where he was. Suddenly his barks were now less muffled and more frequent, but the girls couldn't understand why his barks seemed happy; it was almost like he was playing. So together, they decided to go and investigate.

After they reached the foot of the hill, they clambered over a few rocks, which brought them to the gap in the Ivy where Charlie had gone. The ivy didn't look as lush or green and nowhere near as lovely as it did from a distance. For up close, they saw vines entwined with one another, masses of spiders' webs with what seemed like every species of fly and bug imaginable trapped in their snares.

'Eww,' cried Jasmine in dislike at what she could see, 'I can do without this', she added.

The crawlies have never bothered Holly, and as for Melody, it was impossible to know what her dislikes were, for she always seemed to do whatever she felt like doing.

'Well, don't just stand there, Jasmine, pull back the ivy,' asked Holly.

'No way, I'm not touching that,' replied Jasmine, taking a few steps back.

'I thought things like this didn't bother you, Holly,' asked Melody while rolling her eyes and shaking her head, pretending to disapprove.

'Erm, no, they don't bother me,' replied Holly hesitantly.

'Well, if that's the case, you pull back the ivy and stop trying to get me to do it,' scowled Jasmine.

Melody couldn't be bothered waiting anymore, so she again picked from the ground a long stick, but she didn't throw it; she used it to whack aside the thick vines.

'Take that and that,' she yelled as she whacked away at the ivy with each swing she took.

Jasmine and Holly were mortified and began screaming for her to stop, but by the time Melody had even bothered to listen, it was too late! And all the matted webs and bugs wrapped up in the spiders' silvery silk and ended up all over Jasmine and Holly's hair and clothes.

'There we go,' said Melody, nodding and carrying a cocky look of achievement.

But while Melody gloated in triumph, Jasmine and Holly were frantically jumping around, trying to shake out the bugs from their hair and clothes.

'That's it; we're off! Demanded Holly, 'We're not staying here one second longer,'.

Jasmine managed to get over the shudders and began following Holly, but before Melody joined them, she moved closer to the hole she'd made and began peering into it. A frown fell across her face, and curiosity at what she could see caused her to push that bit further until she stood inside what looked like a cave, and to her surprise, she muttered the words' wow, to herself.

'Hey, you two, come here and look at this,' she shouts.

Before answering Melody's call, Holly and Jasmine turned, looked at each other, and rolled their eyes.

'What now, Melody?' replied Jasmine.

'Just come here a minute,' she asked.

'Come on, we better see what she wants, and this had better be good,' Holly muttered while clambering back onto the moss-covered rocks.

On approaching Melody, she was standing beneath the threshold of the hole she'd made; before elegantly waving her arm and welcoming them into what she jokingly called her hillside suite.

Standing before the girls were almost indescribable; a large cave-like room seemed carved from the side of the hill. From the ground to the top, and from side to side, was covered with thick shoots of weed, each carrying thorns the size of the girl's fingers.

The girls couldn't believe what they were looking at; the cave looked like a miniature jungle, and they could hear trickling water falling from behind the weeds. As they ventured inside, the air suddenly grew heavy with the smell of dampened soil. A noticeably cool draft began to circle the ankles of the girl's feet, causing them to cast their attention away from the clambering thorn-filled weeds to the ground below. Upon the earth, they noticed a small clearing of dampened soil, and dotted around within the clearing were tracks, and from where the girls were standing, they could only see some of the tracks; the others had fallen into a shadow on the other side of the cave. They began to edge their way further into the shadow in the hope of being able to follow the tracks, but as they got closer, the jitters took over, so they decided to leave. Then, just at that moment when the girls turned to walk away, a ray of sunlight strangely shone through the opening Melody had made and lit up the somewhat dimly lit cave.

'Hey, look, they're paw prints; you can see them,' cried Jasmine.

'Where do they lead? Can you see?' asked Holly excitedly. Quickly all three girls began to scurry around the cave, and it wasn't long before the paw prints led them to the foot of yet another wall covered with weeds and ivy.

'Not again,' Melody muttered while firmly standing with her hands on her sides.

Holly didn't have to pretend anymore about not being afraid of the crawlies, for this time there weren't any, so with great confidence, she used both hands and prized open a gap in the wall of weed. Then, as soon as she pulled the weeds apart, they could hear Charlie's barks echoing in and around yet another cave they had uncovered.

Whatever darkness lay behind the wall of weed was soon chased away by the brilliant light of the sun shining in from the outside. For no sooner than the girls popped their heads through the gap, the light was there before them. And with it, the light lit up a strange weed-filled tunnel, which careered off to the far right and rose slightly upwards before eventually disappearing out of sight into another shadow.

Although the girls couldn't see Charlie, they could still hear him barking, but as far as Holly was concerned, Charlie would have to carry on barking until they had gone and come back with Dad. So it was with that thought in mind that she interrupted Jasmine and Melody's shouts for Charlie; by sternly telling them that, this time, they had to go.

The girls then hastily made the short journey back to the top of the hill, leaving Charlie and the sound of his barks alone in the weed-filled tunnel.

'This doesn't seem right, leaving Charlie alone,' muttered Jasmine.

'Jasmine, we've been trying to get him for over an hour now; Dad is going to go mad when he sees us,' replied Holly.

Melody suddenly took off across a small forest clearing

with a daft, mischievous look.

'Charlie's here,' she yelled.

Jasmine and Holly quickly turned to see, only to find Melody with her tongue sticking out, her eyes cross-eyed, and a daft, screwed-up expression on her face.

'Oh, what's the point, Melody?' yelled Jasmine.

'Come on, let's get her,' whispered Holly as she leaned towards Jasmine. They quickly set off for Melody, who was by this time happily walking away in a world of her own, unaware they were chasing her. But just as Jasmine and Holly were beginning to gain some ground on Melody, she glanced over her shoulder and spotted them, and at once, stopped walking and started running.

'Get away,' shouted Melody while running towards a bunch of trees, where she hoped to hide and catch her breath. Then, after almost skidding to a halt, Melody began tiptoeing around one of the big trees while constantly keeping a watchful eye on them as she peered between the trunks of the others. The nearer they approached, the further round the tree Melody tiptoed until suddenly, a hand landed on her head.

'Gotcha,' a deep voice said.

Melody jumped and let out a scream; she then lost her footing and fell onto her backside; no sooner had she landed on the ground than she could hear howls of laughter coming from Jasmine and Holly. When Melody looked up, Dad stood with his hand over his mouth; it was apparent that he was trying not to laugh at her misfortune.

'Shut up, you two,' scowled Melody while Dad reached out to pull her up from the ground, only for her to refuse, jumping onto her feet as though nothing had happened to her ego. The argument about who started what shortly followed was soon interrupted when Dad seemed keener to hear about Charlie and his whereabouts. And the girls were very keen on telling him all about it. So much babbling took place, with each girl telling Dad their version of events. But, somehow, Dad managed to get a

gist of the tales the girls were telling but didn't for
one second believe them.

'So, let's get this straight; you're telling me that our dog
Charlie is barking inside a cave that looks like a jungle with
weed-filled tunnels? It all sounds a bit far-fetched to me!'
exclaimed Dad.

'What? Far-fetched,' the girls replied, shocked that he
didn't believe them.

'Well, all we can do is show you,' said Jasmine.

So off they went, with the girls leading the way and Dad
in close pursuit. They ventured back down the small hill,
across the short valley at the bottom, and back up over the
moss-covered rocks, until, eventually, they had arrived
back at the ivy-covered hillside and to the opening Melody
had made.

'There you go, Dad; well, what did we say,' said Melody
while pulling aside a lone dangling piece of ivy.

'Wow, this place is weird!' Dad replied while stepping
further inside to investigate, and he was lost for words as
he stared open-mouthed at the surroundings of the weed-
covered cave.

Meanwhile, outside, the sun had shifted in a different
direction and was now lighting up even the darkest corners
of the cave. The girls had been slightly surprised, for the
once dampened, dimly lit, cold, and spooky cave seemed
to transform into a more enchanting and less dangerous-
looking place.

'Have you seen enough yet, Dad?' asked Holly. Because
there's more here, pointing her finger toward the weed-
filled tunnel.

'Yeah, you'll like this bit, Dad,' added Jasmine as she took
him by the hand and ushered him towards the hole which
led to the tunnel.

As Dad bent down and began to peer through the hole,
he heard Charlie barking.

'I can hear Charlie,' exclaimed Dad.

'Far-fetched, eh, Dad? We did try telling you,' replied Melody.

Weeds somewhat blocked the hole Dad peered through, and the view of the other tunnel had fallen into semi-darkness, for the shadow that the sunlight once banished had now silently crept its way back across the cave walls toward the tunnel's far end.

'Well, girls, said Dad, 'here's the idea; I'm not entirely sure this is the best thing to do, but if Charlie doesn't come out, I'd better go in, or we leave him to find his way out'.

'No way, Dad, we can't just leave him,' cried Jasmine.

'And I'm not standing outside; I'm going in with you,' claimed Holly.

'And if she's going in, then I'm going in,' added Melody.

Dad stood in silence, scratching his head whilst the girls watched as he contemplated what he should do next when suddenly! Without any warning! He shouted at the top of his voice, 'Charlie,' almost making the girls jump out of their skin.

Despite Dad's best efforts, and between those screams from the girls telling him to stop yelling, Charlie continued to bark and yap.

Dad's quest still had yet to finish, though! for he was now about to use the most unsuccessful approach anyone could have on this dog.

'Come on, boy; it's dinnertime,' He yelled.

'Oh yeah, great stuff, Dad,' Melody sarcastically added.

'Well!, If he isn't coming out, then we're all going in', said Dad.

'Yes, finally,' yelled Melody, throwing her arms up.

After taking from his pocket a small penknife, he began cutting through the shoots of weed, and surprisingly, they weren't as tough as what Dad first thought, so after a few short minutes or so, he'd managed to pull down a whole load of weed from the makeshift wall. Then, with a bigger and broader opening now carved out from the wall of weed, the sun's light was again able to travel down through the tunnel and lighten up again the very bottom of the tunnel.

But before venturing up through the tunnel, Dad tried to take a good look at the surrounding they were about to climb, but the light didn't reach, and it was too dark to continue. The girls immediately knew that Dad was about to mutter something disappointing; they knew this by how he sighed through his puckered-up nose.

'We're not going any further, girls; it's too dark and looks too dangerous, so we'll have to see if Charlie makes his way out'.

With their loud shouts of disapproval, it was a miracle that the girls didn't cause the tunnel to come crashing down around them. Still, Dad was adamant about his decision, so the girls reluctantly began to make their way down through the tunnels; they had only taken a few steps when Charlie seemed to have other ideas, for once again, he suddenly began to bark.

Dad and the girls instantly turned and began to call his name, but as always, Charlie ignored them and just continued to bark; it was as if he was trying to tell them something.

Time was running out, for the sunlight against the tunnelled wall was slowly ebbing its way back outside. And it wouldn't be long before the whole tunnel would again be in complete darkness. The time had arrived for Dad to decide what he would do, but stupidly he wanted the girls to help him make up his mind.

'Right, we must make our minds up now. Do we go in and get Charlie before it gets too dark, or shall we leave him and hope he follows us?'.

'Not a chance, Dad; we can't just leave him! And anyway, we have already made our minds up; and it's you who can't decide.' replied Melody.

'Yeah, we agree with Melody; we've come this far; we may as well go the rest of the way,' Jasmine exclaimed.

'Right, come on then, keep up, girls; this time, we're going in.'

It hadn't taken long before Dad and the girls had nearly reached the top of the corkscrew-like tunnel when he noticed daylight growing brighter and brighter the closer he got to the top.

At the top, there was a small faint shadow forcing him to squint his eyes as he tried to make out what it was when suddenly he let out a startled shout.

'Charlie,' he yelled after realizing it was the dog.

Charlie seemed to appear from out of nowhere and was standing just a short distance ahead of Dad. Charlie was yapping, and his tail was wagging with excitement; he came running down through the tunnel to greet Dad, only to stop just out of his reach to start barking again; he then turned and ran back toward the top.

'Is he there, Dad? Can you see him?' the girls eagerly asked.

'Yeah, he's just there,' Dad jolted his head in Charlie's direction; 'I almost had him; he's run to the top of the tunnel, wagging his tail, and it looks like he's been treating this like a game'.

Finally, Dad was now able to tell the girls that they had made it to the top, and eagerly they raced up and shoved past him to hopefully greet Charlie, instead greeting them were twinkling bright beams of daylight which seemed to dance out from behind a long and leafy curtain like a laser show.

Aching, Dad had managed to clamber to the top and was about to stretch when he was interrupted by Charlie's barks.

'Dad, it came from behind here,' Holly cried as she pointed towards the bright curtain.

'Shush', Dad replied as he made his way down the short

tunnel towards the lights. 'Don't move a muscle; I'm getting him this time'. "Charlie, are you in there"?.

It fell silent for three or four seconds as they tried to listen for his exact whereabouts when suddenly Charlie raced out through the bright leafy curtain and towards them. Then, screaming, they all jumped up! Dad panicked and hopped up into the air, frantically stomping from one leg to the other, trying desperately not to stand on the dog as he raced beneath their feet; unfortunately, he couldn't maintain his balance and stumbled into Jasmine, landing on her foot.

'Ouch,' screeched Jasmine as she stumbled back into Dad, knocking him off balance again and sending him flying through the long flickering leafy curtain and in through the other side of it.

Dad then came crashing down with a thud, skidding across the earthy ground on his backside before finally coming to a halt.

Between their fits of laughter, the girls were trying desperately to ask Dad if he was OK, but the excitement of seeing Charlie again, their words just never came out.

Meanwhile, Dad wasn't too concerned with the lack of care the girls had shown him, for he was too worried about his problem, rubbing a sore elbow and backside simultaneously.

'That is it, Charlie! No more, I've had enough of you,' yelled Dad from behind a cloud of settling dust that had surrounded him.

Unfortunately, the mere mention of Charlie's name had only caused him to come charging back into where Dad was sitting, where Charlie then greeted him with a big sloppy wet lick to his face.

'Err, get off,' said Dad as he struggled to push Charlie's head away and escape from his flickering tongue, which seemed to have a life of its own.

Charlie then tucked his wagging tail firmly between his back legs and began charging around the cave, and it didn't matter where he was; if he felt the need to do it, he'd do it.

'Can someone get a hold of that dog before he disappears for another, however many hours?' yelled Dad.

'I'll get him,' Melody replied, 'Charlie boy, what have I got here?' She added. Melody then shoved her hand deep inside her pocket and rummaged around, searching to bring out her favourite glittery alien toy. Melody's actions caught Charlie's attention, causing him to stop what he was doing, and he quickly approached her.

'Quick, grab him,' yelled Jasmine.

Surprisingly, Holly got a hold of Charlie with minimal effort, but only because he was more interested in what Melody was doing.

Melody continued to rummage from one pocket to the other, desperately searching for her lucky charm, hoping to tease Charlie with it simply because he loathed it. However, unfortunately for Melody, her little game was not even about to start after realizing! she had gone and lost it.

Her attempts to get Jasmine and Holly's help searching for the glittery alien were in vain, for they were far too interested in pampering and making a fuss over the dog.

Meanwhile, Dad was still sitting in the cave-like room, brushing himself down and nursing his lumps and bumps. His face

was all tacky and wet with spit from Charlie's tongue, so in his attempt to wipe it dry, he turned his head to one side and began to use his shoulder to dry himself. While patting his cheek, Dad noticed a peculiar object at the far end of the cave, so he decided to go and investigate. Dad then crept across the cave floor, crossing through more bright beams of daylight and towards a giant-like object, standing, large, and still.

'What on earth is that?' yelled Dad.

'What is it, Dad'? The girls replied as they moved further

into the cave and gasped in surprise at seeing an amazingly old-looking and decrepit giant tree trunk.

The girls lightly held on to each other and nervously began to laugh when suddenly the giant tree trunk began to creak and groan, giving Dad and the girls the impression it was about to fall over.

'Come on, girls, it's not safe here; we'll return now. That thing looks like it could topple over at any time,' exclaimed Dad.

However, the girls were intrigued by the shimmering light that trickled in through what looked like an ivy-covered window, which seemed carved out from the cave wall. A slight breeze then suddenly and steadily blew as it gently moved the ivy, causing the lights behind it to flicker and dance around the cave walls, leaving the girls to wonder what they may see by peering behind it.

'Get your knife out, Dad, and cut that away so we can just look behind it,' asked Melody as she pointed to the flickering light.

'Yeah, Dad, cut it down,' added Jasmine.

'We'll never get out of this place, will we,' replied Dad with a sigh. 'Stay away from that thing,' he added, nudging his head toward the giant rickety old wooden trunk; 'It could topple over at any minute'.

When Dad had made his way toward the sparkling beams of light, he suddenly caught a slight glimpse of something to the back of the old wooden trunk, but whatever it was, it was just too far out of sight for him to determine what it was. Intrigued, Dad steadily moved closer and edged his way around to the far side of the vast, old wooden trunk; he'd not needed to walk much further, for he had seen all he needed to see, and that was enough. A vast, seemingly endless, dark, hollowed hole stood before him, three times his size, and its hollowed depth seemed endless. Dad suddenly began to feel a strange eerie feeling, which caused him to move quickly away and head back toward the sparkling beams of light.

There was a little more urgency in how Dad moved around now; it was almost as if he'd had enough of being there. So, he quickly pulled out his penknife and began cutting away at the stems of ivy to reveal what lay behind.

The more that Dad had cut, the brighter was light that shone through into the cave, and more significant was the relief on his face as the brightness grew clearer.

'Oh, wow! Come over here, girls, you've got to look at this; we've made it back outside,' exclaimed Dad as he cut, snapped, pulled, and tugged at the last remnants of ivy.

Every nook inside the cave lit up and gleamed like a new coin; the girls raced past the giant old wooden trunk and across to the opening. Upon reaching it, Jasmine, Melody, and Holly just stood and stared out in splendour at the view before them.

Busily, the girls began talking about the birds they could see nesting in the treetops, the squirrels jumping between the trees, the streams they could see far across the valley, and the forest paths they had recently walked.

While the girls were talking, Dad was busy thinking about the tunnels, the cave, the old wooden trunk, how it had come to be, and why it seemed that Charlie was the one to have led the way.

Dad had put his thoughts aside and decided that enough was enough!

'Come on, girls; it's time we were off,' he said after spooking himself again by staring into the eerie darkness of the wooden hollow before reaching out to take Charlie out from hollies arms.

'I'll walk him home,' he said while placing Charlie on the ground. But before Dad managed to take the dog's lead out of his pocket, Charlie quickly ran straight between his legs and through the same entrance he had unfortunately fallen through.

'Oh no, not again,' yelled Jasmine.

Before Dad realized what had happened, Charlie had again disappeared.

'Where's he gone?' Yelled Dad frantically.

'He's run back through there,' replied Jasmine, frantically waving her finger towards the makeshift door hole.

Dad rushed in close pursuit of Charlie and quickly followed him out of the cave when the strangest thing happened. Dad had suddenly stopped moving, frozen to where he was standing! It was the oddest thing to see, and looking at him, he didn't look any different; for he wasn't like that of ice or anything like that; he had the same gleam in his eyes, for even the sweat on his forehead was still wet.

Meanwhile, unaware of what had just happened, the girls began calling Dad from inside the cave.

'Did you manage to get him, Dad?' shouted Holly as she and the others made their way towards the door hole.

The girls had only managed to walk halfway across the cave when another strange occurrence happened, for a somewhat quirky old voice echoed out to them.

'Children, wait, don't go,' It spoke.

2. THE OLD WOODEN MAN

Suddenly, silence fell; there was no noise, and the air inside the cave seemed hollow and somewhat empty; it was like a giant vacuum had sucked the atmosphere out, and all the girls could do was stand at the spot from where they stood. Then suddenly, the loud, strange voice called out to the girls again, 'Please don't go,' this time, it was louder than the previous call, though more desperate, yet more sincere; still, it did cause the girls to jump in fright.

Clinging onto one another, they slowly turned around to look, but neither could see anything unusual other than the vast giant tree trunk.

'What do you think it is?' whispered Holly.

'I don't know; it came from that thing,' replied Melody, wafting her finger toward the wooden trunk; What do you think it was, Jasmine? she added.

'I don't know, and I don't care,' replied Jasmine, slowly edging towards the makeshift door hole and quietly calling Dad's name, tugging at Holly and Melody's coats for them to follow her. Then, huddled together, the girls nervously managed to make their way across the cave floor; they had almost reached the door hole when they heard rustling from outside.

'Dad, is that you? Jasmine. And no sooner she asked, Charlie came cheerfully racing back into the cave, passing the girls, and running straight to the foot of the old wooden trunk, wagging his tail, barking excitedly at the girls before turning his attention towards the old wooden trunk.

'Strange! What's he doing? Charlie come over here, boy,' asked Holly.

'I don't know, but all this is getting far too weird; I'm going to get Dad, and then I'm getting out of here,' replied Holly.

'Wait for us,' exclaimed both Jasmine and Melody.

No sooner had they taken their first step did the quirky old voice call out to them again.

'I need your help; please stay for a moment longer,' it said.

'Will you stop doing that? It made me jump again,' scowled Melody; 'who or what are you anyway? And where are you,' she added.

Meanwhile, Charlie lay at the foot of the old wooden trunk with his head resting on his two front paws, never moving a muscle and never flinching once at the loudness of the strange voice. Although his tail was slightly wagging, and he seemed happy and content to be there, the girls couldn't help but notice a sorrowful look in his eyes.

'It's alright, Charlie, you're a good dog,' said the old voice. Then immediately following his words came faint creaking noises and, with them, a lot of very tired huffing and puffing sounds until the old wooden trunk began to move, steadily rocking from one side to the other until it slowly began to turn.

The girls could only watch as they tightly held on to one another; neither of them didn't make a sound; they were too stunned by the sight they saw before them.

'It'll be wise of you to move well out of the way, Charlie boy,' said the loud, quirky old voice as the old trunk continued to rock from side to side, creating dust clouds with every shudder. Eventually, it turned almost half a circle before suddenly stopping, and with it came a loud thud on the ground, which sounded like something hard and heavy had fallen.

Holly, Jasmine, Melody, and Charlie all stood in silence and watched inquisitively, waiting for the dust around the old trunk to settle. And before long, it was almost visible enough for the girls to see another strange sight.

'What is that? Asked Melody.

'I'm not sure,' replied Jasmine, her eyes squinting and a frown on her face.

'Where's dad, dad? Are you out there?' yelled Holly, with a worried tone in her voice.

The dust inside the cave finally settled, and Charlie immediately sensed something, for his actions were like one of those moments where he would run towards the house door before the visitors had even arrived. This feeling had caused him to set off across the cave and back towards the trunk to investigate what looked like a mound of slightly golden-coloured wood piled high at the base of the old wooden tree trunk. The pile was significant in size and appeared like the texture of a giant dried raisin hanging out from the inside of the trunk's hollow.

Upon reaching the old wooden trunk, Charlie sat and stretched out his paw before tentatively placing it upon the strange-looking mound, and no sooner had Charlie done this! There were loud creaking noises, to which Charlie whimpered softly before moving his paw away and sitting down to wait. Then a strange calming feeling suddenly fell upon the girls, who were now edging further away from the makeshift door hole and back into the cave, for they were now beginning to feel less about wanting to leave and more about wanting to stay.

Between the silences of the girl's concerned whispers
came more creaking noises and more movement from the
strange-looking mound, which now looked like old bark
on closer inspection. Again, the girls suddenly stopped and
stared as they watched in astonishment as the pile suddenly
sprung into life, and from it sprouted two massive wooden
arms, complete with hands and branch-like fingers which
stretched across the cave's ground before they slowly
heaved upwards, pushing hard against the ground until a
bark-like torso became visible. The sounds of creaking,
cracking, snapping, and breaking filled the cave when
slowly but surely shoulders began to form, then a chest,
until finally a neck and head; it was at that point when the
old wooden man heaved himself up and into the hollow of
the trunk.

Meanwhile, Charlie was still sitting in the same place; he
raised his head high and stared at the old wooden man
whose appearance was just that. An old wooden man of a
slightly golden colour with bark-like skin, whose main
features were of a square chin, and eyes of a lovely green
colour, he was bald and had no beard, his torso and arms
were slender thou very muscular and strong, looking. In
the meantime, Charlie continued to stare before letting out
a little bark; Charlie's little yap attracted the wooden man's
attention away from longingly gazing through the
makeshift window at the scenery and to that of a hearty
and brave-looking robin perched on a branch, inquisitively
watching on from outside.
The old wooden man's head creaked and turned as he
looked down towards Charlie with a smile,
'Ah, hello Charlie boy, and hello girls,' said the old
wooden man while turning his head towards Holly,
Jasmine, and Melody, who was still holding tightly onto
one another and not saying a word.
'Forgive me! Please, don't be afraid; I'm sorry,' said the old

wooden man; I've probably frightened you all, it's not surprising that all this will have come as quite some surprise to you, but I had to try and prevent you all from leaving because I'm very much in need of your help!'.

The girls stared at the old wooden man bewildered, astonished, and unable to say anything.

'I'd almost forgotten how beautiful the views were; it has been a long time since I have seen them', said the old wooden man as he glanced out of the makeshift window.
'The little bird with the red breast, I've never seen before; what's their kind'? The wooden man asked.
'That'll be a robin,' Muttered Holly, somewhat confused with herself by answering the wooden man's question.
'A hearty fearless little thing, it seems,' replied the old wooden man.
'Can we forget about the robin? What are you?' stuttered Jasmine.
'Yes, what are you? Is this magic? Should we be scared? Because I don't feel afraid? I must admit, though, none of this makes any sense, and how did you know Charlie's name,' added Melody.
Melody seemed to have already made her mind up about the strange old wooden man, for she managed to shrug off the grips of Jasmine and Holly, and much to their disapproval, they watched her make her way closer to the trunk and the old wooden man.
'What are you,' asked Melody again while trying to get a closer look without getting too close; what do you think dad will say?' She added While turning to Holly and Jasmine and interrupting the old wooden man as he was about to speak.

Not until Melody had mentioned Dad's name did Jasmine and Holly almost forget about him being outside the cave. So, in somewhat of a panic, they began to call out his name while quickly making their way back toward the makeshift door hole.

In the meantime, the old wooden man was trying to interrupt them; he had been trying to explain what had happened to their dad to save them from the sudden shock of seeing him.

'Stop and look outside; please take a look outside,' he frantically asked; 'there is something I need you all to see'.

'We need to see where our dad has gone; we'll come back as soon as we get him,' replied Jasmine.

'No, there is something outside you all need to see first, and then I can explain everything; but first, please, look outside.'

After a short discussion between the girls about what they should do, they surprisingly decided to go ahead and look.

'Ok, we'll do it; we're not sure why you need us to look outside, though; what is there to see out there we haven't seen already?' asked Holly.

'Please, I promise it'll only take a short time,' replied the old wooden man, pointing his long branch-like finger towards the opening.

Holly and Jasmine glanced at the opening, then turned and looked at one another with uncertain expressions. Holly then told Jasmine and Melody to stay close by and to walk on the other side of the cave so that they would be well out of reach from the old wooden man.

However, Melody hadn't bothered to pay any attention to Holly's concerns, and off she went, straight down the middle of the cave, smiling at the old wooden man as she passed.

If anything, Melody's attitude seemed to have eased the nerves of Jasmine and Holly, for passing the old wooden man, they did manage to nervously look up, stare him in the face, and smile. Although, they
still weren't overcome with gallant bravery and still

played it safe by shuffling their way past, brushing up close against the dusty, weeded wall of the cave.

'Holly, Dad's been gone for ages; I wish he were here with us; I'm getting worried,' whispered Jasmine.

No sooner had Holly said this did the old wooden man slump further back into the darkness of his hollow, sorrowful at the thought of what he was putting the girls through.

'Sorry, I overheard that whisper Jasmine, said the old wooden man; don't worry; your dad is fine, as you will soon see, but first, there is something I desperately need to explain,' said the wooden man. 'I have had to do something only you three can see, it's something you may not like, but it's the only way I can explain! Let me show you.'

'Come on, you two, everything's fine; I'm sure Dad won't be long! He's probably outside calling mum or something,' said Melody as she stood waiting near the makeshift window.

'Yeah, come on, Jasmine,' remarked Holly.

Finally, after reaching the opening, the three girls rested with their elbows down on the rocky ledge, resting their chins into their hands.

'What exactly is it that you want us to see' said Holly.

'If you all take a very close look at everything you see outside, you'll notice something odd indeed,' replied the old wooden man.

The girls looked, then they looked closer, and then closer still.

'Wait a minute,' cried Jasmine, shaking Holly with one hand and pointing with the other.

'What is it, Jasmine? I can't see anything,' asked Melody.

'Will you get on with it, Jasmine, and tell us what you can

see? Replied Holly.

'It's, it's everything; look both of you; look all around the outside! Everything has stopped; nothing is moving,' exclaimed Jasmine.

Finally, they could see what the old wooden man had wanted them to see, for Jasmine, Melody, and Holly stared out in astonishment at a world that was somehow standing still. The birds had stopped mid-flight; the rain droplets had tumbled from the forest leaves but hadn't continued their journey. Butterflies, Bees, and other insects were interrupted in the skies, cattle hadn't finished grazing, and the winds weren't blowing, even high and far into the distance; an aircraft was hanging from the clouds above, silent and still.

Dumbfounded, the girls naturally turned to the old wooden man with questions.

'How has it happened, is everything still alive? Is it magic? Will it all move again?' were just some of the questions they asked.

'Yes, everything will return to normal, and what you all see will be seen as magic, and more significantly to that, nothing will be hurt, and life on your planet will resume, with not even a second of its time lost, for I have requested for time to stop'.

The old wooden man suddenly looked happier; like he had a great weight of burden removed, he seemed delighted that the girls had finally seen what he had wanted them to see. But still, a cloud of uncertainty overshadowed his appearance, for he knew there would be no turning back once he'd explained everything to the girls, for they had yet to learn something that would forever change their lives.

'We'd like to ask you a question! You say you have

requested time to stop; who is it you have asked, and why?' asked Jasmine.

'Well, please allow me to start with the most important,' replied the old wooden man. 'Whom I requested for time to stop will all be revealed later. And I have requested time to stop because only you three can see what I have shown you, and only you three can hear what I must tell you, and unfortunately, that includes your parent.'

It immediately dawned on the girls what the old wooden man had just said to them and that Dad had also been stopped, along with everyone and everything else.

'Dad, dad,' the girls shouted as they raced towards the makeshift door hole across the cave.

The old wooden man's face suddenly looked fraught with worry at the thought of the girls seeing their dad unable to move so silently; he began to ask for time to start again; however, just as he began to speak the words, he heard all the girls laughing outside the makeshift door hole. Surprised that the girls didn't seem distressed at seeing their dad in this peculiar state, the old wooden man continued to listen.

Meanwhile, outside the cave, the girls were poking fun at their dad's funny-looking face; he looked cross as though he was about to say something. It was evident that when the time had stopped, he was left standing in a strange kind of monkey pose, as though he was just about to grab hold of Charlie.

Suddenly Melody spotted Charlie moving around the back of Dad's leg; Melody began pointing frantically but could hardly speak through her laughter.

'He, he's having a pee on dad's leg,' she shouted.

When Jasmine and Holly turned to see, they laughed as they watched the wetness seep into the bottom of Dad's jeans.

The old wooden man hadn't seen what had happened, but he had heard, which caused him to bellow some almighty laughter. His laughter was so loud and meaningful that it caused the girls to stop what they were doing to peer around the corner of the makeshift door hole, from where they watched for several seconds as the old wooden man laughed from within the insides of the hollow, when suddenly he stopped laughing, for his laughter soon turned to sadness.

'Why are you upset,' asked Melody.

'Don't be upset; what's the matter?' asked the others reassuringly as they moved to try and comfort the old wooden man.

What looked like a single tear was slowly running down one side of the old wooden man's cheek, so Jasmine tugged at her sleeve and wrapped it around her hand as she surprisingly moved to the foot of the trunk.

'I can't reach you; can you move closer?' asked Jasmine.

The puzzled old wooden man creaked and groaned as he bent and lowered his big wooden head toward Jasmine. It was the closest any of the girls had come to the old wooden man, and it wasn't until Jasmine came face to face with him that she or the other girls realized just how big he was.

Still, with her hand wrapped inside the sleeve of her coat, Jasmine reached out to wipe the old wooden man's cheek but momentarily became distracted by a bright, beautiful wave of colours that quickly flashed in his green eyes. Jasmine wasn't sure what she had just seen, so she looked closer. Suddenly the colours returned once more, long enough for her to see what they were, and she had seen images of a sunrise, a sunset, moonlit skies, lush green forests, meadows, and a rainbow that stretched as far as her eyes could see.

'It's beautiful,' muttered Jasmine beneath her breath, but no sooner had the vision appeared than it was gone.

For a short time, Jasmine seemed in a trance and had forgotten what she'd been doing; it was only for the faint voices calling her that she remembered.

'Jasmine, your sleeve,' yelled Holly while nodding towards the old wooden man's face.

Jasmine turned to look and noticed that her sleeve was somehow attached to the old wooden man's cheek; she stared at the old wooden man with a confused, worried look on her face, and equally confused was the old wooden man, for he too was staring back at her.

'What's happening? Let me go? Demanded Jasmine in her panic as she tugged and pulled at her arm, jolting the old wooden man's head several times before finally breaking herself free and stumbling backwards during her final tug.

'What's so funny? You saw what happened; he wouldn't let me go,' scowled Jasmine.

'Jasmine, the tear you were trying to wipe away was sticky resin; it's not like our tears; you've ended up getting stuck to his face,' laughed Holly.

'Oh, yeah, what was I thinking? I panicked,' she embarrassingly replied.

'But why did you get upset? You seemed very sad about something,' she asked the wooden man.

'Hearing you all laughing has brought me hope, for what lay ahead are troublesome times, and that's my worry, for unfortunately, I need to share those troublesome times with you', the old wooden man replied. 'But firstly and before I do, I need to explain how all this has come to be and what it all means,' explained the old wooden man while gesturing to his surroundings with his open hands.

'The old wooden man you see before you is not what I truly am; yes, you see that I am old, and that's because I am old, or at least my memory is, for that is older than you could dare to think. If you could, I would like you to pretend for a moment that I am not here,'.

At that moment, the old wooden man took refuge inside the darkness of the hollowed-out trunk, purposely setting a sorrowful scene for the story he was so desperate to tell.

'You see,' said the Wooden Man, his voice softly echoing from inside the hollow. 'I am nothing more than a broken dead tree, with a hollow void torn out from the inside, but this isn't how It started, nor how it should end,' he added as the girls cast their eyes around the lifeless old trunk standing before them.

'So, what happened to you?' asked Holly inquisitively.

'One step at a time, Holly,' replied the old wooden man. 'One step at a time; I can't tell you everything today; it's too soon, and it's complicated, but I shall briefly share with you what I was and where I came from.'

I was born into a world very similar to this; the name for that world is the Green Planet; it was a vibrant world full of natural energy and an abundance of life with countless animal species roaming freely upon it. The rivers fed the streams and, in turn, fed the meadows and forests surrounding them; the woods were home to thousands of species of trees where they grew to a magnificent size, and none more so than those of the rare oak species, with each one living for hundreds if not a thousand years. Still, there was one exception: the Rare Golden Oak, for it had lived for thousands of years and was the only surviving Rare Golden Oak.

During the Rare Golden Oak's life on the Green Planet, it saw many wonderful things, enjoyed many beautiful years, was blessed with health, and still had many years to give. However, unfortunately, the Rare Golden Oak's time had arrived, and through no fault of its own, it had no choice but to stop living and sacrifice itself so it could pass its seed to the next generation of oaks after it. But sadly, that seed could never be left to grow on the Green Planet, so instead, it was brought here to the safety of your world and left to grow. However, no sooner had the first shoots of the new rare oak risen from the soil; is when something was about to happen on your planet, which meant the new oak needed to be protected whilst it grew, and so to give the last surviving rare oak a chance at life, its growing time was significantly hurried and increased by over two hundred years so it may have been strong enough to protect itself from what was about to unfold. But sadly, that wasn't enough to save the rare new oak from what happened, and its life was also barbarically cut short; however, a slight chance of hope remains to make good all that is bad, and that is why I am here and why you need to hear what I have to say. Suddenly the old wooden man fell silent! He lowered his head and closed his eyes. At that moment, the girls no longer saw a giant old wooden man full of character and wisdom but a frightened, lonely creature fraught with despair.

'It's ok if you don't feel like telling us anything else; we understand,' said Jasmine.
'You're right; I shalt continue today,' replied the old wooden man; 'there is so much to get through, so much to understand; it's complicated with so little time to explain! And that is something we don't have, for if we don't use the short remainder of the time we have left, then everything we have come to know and love is in terrible danger, and I can't allow that to happen again'.
'But what happened? What could happen,' asked Holly, frustrated at not knowing anything.
'The Green Planet witnessed the arrival of a new breed of species not seen before is what happened, Holly,' replied the old wooden man, 'It is because of that species that the danger remains'.

At that point, the old wooden man suddenly grew tired, his eyes sorrowful and distressed.

'I cannot continue; it's time I stopped; you must all go now, but could you promise to come back tomorrow? I must tell you the whole story, and after you hear it, the decision is yours.'

'What decision is that' asked Melody, looking at the other two for answers.

'Deciding whether or not you are willing to help me,' explained the old wooden man. 'It's time to go; I must request time to start again,' he added.

'Just before you do,' asked Holly; can you tell me who you ask for time to stop and start? And why do I feel that you and Charlie know each other?'

'I'm sure you will all have many questions you need answering, but I cannot tell you now; in time, I will tell you everything,' replied the old wooden man.

With that, he retreated into the wooden hollows' darkness before requesting time to start.

'Wait, just one more minute,' cried Melody shouting to the old wooden man.

'Yes,' he replied, looking a little confused.

'Do you have a name?' asked Melody.

'A name,' answered the old wooden man pausing for several seconds to think.

'Well, Melody, no, I don't, but why do you ask?'

'Oh, no reason, I just wondered, that's all,' she replied before walking away.

A tad puzzled, the old wooden man again retreated into his hollow, and suddenly, without any warning, the girls could hear their dad outside the makeshift door hole. Then as though nothing had ever happened, he popped his head from around the corner and asked the girls to grab hold of Charlie. The girls stared at Dad, then at the old wooden trunk, then at each other. Although the girls had an idea of what to expect, it all surprised them; all they could do was shrug their shoulders at one another.

'Well, girls, what's the matter with you all? Dad said.

'Hello, Dad, do you feel ok' asked Holly while walking across the cave and greeting him with an awkward smile.

'Stressed out because of that dog,' he replied, slightly puzzled by her question. Still, before he could correctly answer, he paused for a moment, interrupted after suddenly feeling slightly uncomfortable down the left side of his leg.

'Wait a minute, what's happened here? My leg is wet through,' he remarked while feeling the damp patch of his jeans; 'that smells so bad; come on, I've had enough of this place; let's get out of here,' he added whilst marching off back through the weed-filled tunnels, occasionally flicking his leg in an attempt to dry it off before getting the girls outside and eventually back home.

After arriving home, the girls spotted their mum standing by the back door, her arms folded and a not-very-pleased look on her face.

'She doesn't look too pleased, does she?' whispered Jasmine.

'Hello, mum, we finally got Charlie,' shouts Melody.

'Well, it's about time, but where did you all have to go to get him? Replied mum, looking them up and down at their state; you look like something has dragged you through a field; go and get yourselves cleaned up, and where's Dad?' she added.

'Oh yeah, Dad, well, he's on his way up with Charlie, but go easy on him; he's had a stinking day,' replied Jasmine laughingly.

The girls kicked off their boots and raced upstairs, and while Mum was busy knocking the dirt from the girl's boots, Dad arrived with Charlie at the foot of the garden path, equally looking like they'd just appeared from a swamp.

'Hello love, you wouldn't believe what we had to endure to get him back,' said Dad, pointing and trying to pass all the blame onto Charlie.

'I can't begin to imagine,' replied Mum with a strong hint of criticism.

'I did try calling you, but I had no signal on my phone!' exclaimed Dad; we were deep inside a hill, crawling through weed-filled tunnels and trying to avoid being crushed by this giant old wooden tree trunk; the girls loved it; they thought it was a great adventure.

Mum had been listening while Dad babbled, but the tale of weed-filled tunnels and wooden effigies wasn't Mum's thing. It seemed the only way Mum could get him to shut up at this point was to hurdle a piece of mud she'd scrapped from the boot she was cleaning, gleefully watch as it flew through the air before coming to rest dead in the middle of Dad's already mucky forehead.

'That's for having me worried, putting the girls in danger, and allowing them to get in such a state; make sure you and that dog clean each other down before you come into the house; there's a good boy' she added before patting Dad on the head and walking off into the house.

Throughout the evening, Jasmine, Melody, and Holly stayed in their bedroom and reflected on the day's strange events; it was all they could do. It'd left them dumbfounded, with all kinds of unanswered questions and more appetite to revisit the old wooden man and to hear the whole story. Still, they needed a plan that wouldn't raise any suspicion from Mum or Dad about where they'd go the next day.

3. A TITLE BESTOWED

Crash, bang, wallop were the first noises; Dad heard that morning, alarming him so much that he sat straight up in the bed like a scene from some scary movie. While sitting there trying to distinguish whether he was awake or asleep, he heard the girls charging downstairs and Charlie doing his usual race around the house in sixty seconds. Dad dropped back into his pillow and tried desperately not to look at the clock, fearing it would be time for him to get up.

Then, just when Dad thought he was beginning to fall back to sleep, Charlie came racing through the bedroom door. No sooner had he leapt onto the bed, hurried across the duvet, and dashed back out of the bedroom than he almost woke Mum, causing her to shuffle around in the bed. Firstly, she would begin by pulling the blankets off Dad, kicking her legs, and throwing her arms around before finally bringing one arm down directly into the path of Dad's awaiting face.

'I don't believe that dog,' Dad muttered while leaping like a madman out of bed, 'It's happening to me all over again'. The morning didn't start too well for Dad, but it was much different for the girls than any other. Everything seemed to be going to plan; they were up earlier, dressed quicker, and even had breakfast, which was most unusual. The morning soon rolled on, and noon was fast approaching; Mum was about to set off to visit a friend, and Dad was busy emptying the garage, desperately trying to find the lawn mower.

Meanwhile, finally, a morning of waiting arrived for the girls; after waving to Mum as she set off in the car, the girls raced through the living room to the kitchen, where they could hear Dad singing along to the 'Impossible Dream' playing from the garage. And while he was preoccupied, singing away, the opportunity was too good to miss, and Holly took full advantage by peering out from the kitchen door and spying on Dad while he rummaged around in the garage.

'Dad', shouted Holly, over the loudness of the music playing in the background; 'we're just going for a walk up the lane; we might even call into the village,' she added, slightly popping her head around the kitchen door, to peer across at the garage. 'We won't be too long'.

'OK, but don't forget your phone, and leave the dog in the house, replied Dad.

'Yeah, will do; bye, Dad,' said the girls as they marched down the path.

Excited, The girls raced through the forest in a hurry to meet the old wooden man; before they knew it, they were standing at the foot of the hillside, ready to journey back through the tunnels.

'Well, here we are again. Are we all sure we want to do this?' asked Holly.

'Well, I don't know about you,' replied Melody while popping her head through the hole in the ivy, 'but I'm sure'.

'Yep, I too.' replied Jasmine rubbing her hands together in readiness.

There was no messing around; Jasmine, Melody, and Holly were soon through the corkscrew-like tunnels, and once again, they found themselves standing outside the makeshift door hole. But once again, Holly began to feel nervous and unsure about what they were doing.

'Well, what's the problem? Go on through,' said Melody, wondering what Holly was contemplating.

'Is it such a good idea' asked Holly, still uncertain.

'What! 'Well, I'm going in,' shouted Melody while shoving past Holly and into the cave. 'Come on and look for yourself; it is the same as yesterday'.

'Yeah, come on, Holly, it'll be fine,' said Jasmine.

Holly didn't have time to think, for suddenly, out from the old trunk hollow, came a very slight whistling sound, like that of wind. It was a subtle sound and reassured Holly and the others of doubts, for they had oddly vanished.

'What is it? What is that noise?' asked Holly while she and Jasmine entered the cave.

'I don't know; I can't see anything,' replied Melody while edging toward the old wooden trunk; 'hello, are you in there?'.

The whistling sound suddenly stopped, and a pulsating green light appeared in its place, and with each pulse, the green light shone brighter and brighter until that also suddenly stopped.

'I don't know what's happening, but that's a beautiful colour,' said Jasmine.

'Look, it's fading,' exclaimed Holly.

Amazed, the girls could only stand and watch while the sight of the old wooden trunk gradually became visible from behind the brilliant green light.

'I think I can see the old wooden man,' said Melody; is that you behind there,' she called.

The green light began to fade more and more, and while it did, the girls could undoubtedly see the wooden man behind it. He was smiling at them, but there was a change in his appearance; he somehow looked different. The girls watched hard, waiting impatiently for the view of the old wooden man to become clearer. Then, eventually, the girls could see what had happened when the green light had gone.

'Oh wow, you're younger, yelled Melody in astonishment; you look terrific she added while shaking her head in disbelief.

The girls stared across at each other, surprised at the old wooden man's transformation.

'Well, say something,' cried Jasmine ecstatically; how have you managed it?

The girls watched on, waiting for a reply, for the old wooden man they left behind the day before just looked back at them with a smile.

'Well, thank you all for returning,' he said.

The girls suddenly burst out laughing.

'Your voice, it sounds, how can I put it? Handsome,' screamed Holly.

The old wooden man laughed,

'Well, I'm happy you like it, but none of this my doing; it was yours', replied the wooden man.

Amongst all the questions Jasmine and Holly were asking the Wooden Man, Melody stood silent at the foot of the old wooden trunk and waited until they had finished.

'Right, listen, everyone, I have an announcement to make, but first, I just want to say something,' exclaimed Melody, surprising Jasmine, Holly, and the Wooden Man.

'Wooden Man, everything about yesterday was extraordinary, and it seems that today will be much the same; we can't begin to understand how any of this is possible, and we don't yet know if we can help. But, when we learn about what happened to you and what happened on the Green Planet, we'll know for sure because it sounds like something terrible has happened that seems very

wrong and worrying for us all, and we want to help.'
'That's nice, Melody, but can you get on with the
announcement, or whatever it is' laughed, Jasmine.
'I'm getting to it,' replied Melody before continuing.
'When you told us yesterday about the Green Planet and
how things were, I imagined the place as magnificent and
you as majestic, and suddenly it popped into my head, and
that's why before we left, I asked if you had a name, but
you said you hadn't. So, I have one for you,' laughed
Melody while awkwardly ruffling at her hair before saying,
'The Wooden King, there, what do you think?'.
'Mm, the Wooden King?' he replied while thoughtfully
rubbing his chin with a branch-like finger.
'Well, Melody, what can I say to that? I'm honoured and
gladly accept the name, the Wooden King replied.
'We'll give you that one, Melody; it's a good name,' said
Jasmine while looking across at Holly, who also agreed.

Meanwhile, time was moving on, and the Wooden King
was now ready to explain everything from the time on
Green Planet to the present.

'Before you sit comfortably, I have requested time to stop,
and it won't start again until I have told you everything and
some of that may worry you. But before I do, I want you
all to think carefully about your answer at the end, for this
will be the only time I get to tell you what you need to
know.'

In between searching the ground for somewhere to sit,
the girls had listened carefully to what the Wooden King
had to say, and surprisingly they didn't seem worried about
what they were about to learn. Instead, they seemed more
concerned about finding somewhere clean and
comfortable to sit, and the Wooden King looked on with a
broad smile.
'Well, if neither of you is going to ask me where you can

sit, then perhaps you'll all have to continue standing!' said the Wooden King.

'OK then, could you find us a comfortable place to sit?' asked Jasmine.

'Yes, of course; how about you all sit on these', the Wooden King replied.

Looking confused, the girls watched while the Wooden King stretched out his arms and opened his branch-like fingers wide from within the hollow.

'Your joking, right? Do you want us to sit there?' cried Holly while waving her finger at the Wooden King's hands.

The Wooden King suddenly clicked his branch-like fingers, and a green haze appeared before their eyes. The girls watched intently as the green mist steadily started spinning, and the longer they watched, the faster it became. The girls watched on for as long as they could, but it was moving at such speeds it made them feel slightly disoriented, and they were about to turn away when it suddenly stopped spinning. Then, the haze came to rest, like wet liquid above them, before separating into three bubble-like pieces.

Jasmine, Melody, and Holly watched in amazement as the three brightly green objects slowly moved around the cave, occasionally bouncing from one to the other and whirring as they did. Then, suddenly, the green objects stopped moving, and the noise ceased before coming to rest just above the girls' heads, before falling and bursting as they hit the cave floor, creating three giant-sized leaves that seemed to hover just above the ground.

'Please, go ahead and make yourselves comfortable,' said the Wooden King with a pleased look.

There were no words, only nervous giggles that could describe what the girls had just witnessed.

Then, after stepping onto the hovering leaves, they each gingerly sat down, fearing their weight would cause them to fall on the floor. After seating, the green leaves began to vibrate steadily and curl at the edges to cushion and support the girls while they sat. Then, with a gleeful eye, the Wooden King watched Jasmine and Holly chatting about how magical it was before being quietly amused at watching Melody hanging out from the side of the leaf and pushing at the ground, causing it to spin. Suddenly the Wooden King took a breath and carefully blew towards the hovering leaves, causing enough breeze to lift and carry the girls higher and higher until they were high enough to look him in the face.

The Wooden King gave the girls a moment to settle themselves before explaining everything they needed to know.

4. ONCE UPON A GREEN PLANET

The passage of time brought many wondrous things to the Green Planet; it was a beautiful place to live, with so much beauty and abundance of life, and for thousands of years, the Rare Golden Oak was a part of that life. It had taken hundreds of years for the rare oak to mature fully, and once it did, its fantastic golden colour would brighten the skies from the hillside from where it once stood. The Rare Golden Oak was a giant in stature and, with its glowing colour, acted as a beacon of light, protecting everything around it by using the earth's frequencies above, beneath, and around it. Until one summer season several hundred years ago, that all changed when the Rare Golden Oak began to feel an uncertain sense of change, for that summer season had brought with it the arrival of a new species, something that no life on the Green Planet had ever met.

The sudden uncanny appearance of the new species was instant and had made things seem strange and slightly worrying for the Rare Golden Oak, for it sensed that their presence had created an eerie feeling within the valleys below the hillside from where it stood.

Many wildlife living in the surrounding area of the Rare

Golden Oak had sensed the same feeling, for immediately after the new arrivals, most of the animal kingdom who had homed themselves across the hills and valleys of the surrounding area had suddenly left or never returned.
 The arrival of the new species' to the Green Planet's woodlands went almost unnoticed, for they lived and looked like many other land mammals; they were small, like rodents. But as time went by, and while they were still in their infancy, their bodily fur, although it was at the time, short, began to turn a slightly yellow colour; they quickly gained strength and speed by hurrying in and around the shrublands of the forests of the Green Planet. The new species spent an equal amount of their time scurrying on both their hind legs and all fours, and by using their long thorn-like claws, they were able to move fast above ground also. Their eyes were small, dark, and round, and they didn't seem to favour the sun's light, for they often squinted, which was why they weren't around in full daylight. And that made it hard to know what the new species ate, for their yellowish teeth were long, sharp, and strong looking, and they seemed well equipped to tackle most things, but that still needed to be discovered. However, it wasn't long before the Green Planet witnessed a darker and more sinister side to the new arrivals.

 Three seasons had now passed, winter approached the lands across the new planet, and the new species had lost almost all their bodily fur and had grown considerably in size and strength. Not only had their appearance changed, but there was also a recognized change to the surrounding areas of the Green Planet, where some small pockets of forestry were suddenly beginning to die out and disappear. The new species were, for the first time communicating, for faint clicking noises could be heard when daylight began to fade, and they had ventured out from wherever they came. It wasn't until several seasons had quickly passed, bringing the time of the species' arrival to almost a year since they first appeared. It was around that time when the new species suddenly began to show a more complex form of communication; it started with them standing side by side until a line of around thirty Neplèns had formed, and this continued until another line of thirty had created, and so on, until an amass of lines appeared, it was then that they began to communicate with one another, and this would become known as a 'gathering.'

Using two fleshy-looking sacs beneath their jawline enabled the new species' communication, like that of a fish; these sacs would open and close but also create a mixture of snorts and loud ticking noises. This menacing-looking behaviour continued throughout the darkness of night and every night for several months after. It was the turn of the spring season when for the first time, the creatures appeared in full daylight; throughout those days, the species began to display other strange behaviours; for they had once again come together to form a gathering; however, this was not like the times before, for this time they were holding objects in their mouths. In turn, some creatures began to break free from their lines; those that did were carrying small rocks, sticks, and other debris? and before placing them down onto a clearing of earth, the creatures would scrape at the soil to drop the objects in.

This strange behaviour only had significance once the Neplèns placed down the objects and were then viewed from a distance, for they left a diagram with a hidden message, and there seemed to be a somewhat sinister motive behind it. It was plain to see that the creatures had developed a way of communicating, not just for themselves but also for others. For the message they left seemed intended as a claim of territory and show for the first time just who they were, for the diagram read the words of 'the Neplèns.'

Time soon went by, and like the seasons, the years had also quickly passed, for it was now exactly twenty years to the day since the arrival of the Neplèns. Throughout these twenty years, there was further damning evidence that something terrible was happening to the areas of the Green Planet. Many trees and wildlife were dead or dying, and the area surrounding the Rare Golden Oak became unrecognizable. Although the scale of destruction seemed to be caused by the Neplèns, they hadn't yet shown themselves to be the cause; however, suspicion had always surrounded them; However! The twenty-year mark, which brought their arrival, also brought about their sudden disappearance.

And the reason for that was not at the time known. However, as the seasons went by, and the Neplèns remained unseen, it was thought that the climate on the Green Planet may have been responsible and that it could no longer support their needs, and that they had left the area or perished. However, it was unfortunate that proved incorrect for precisely two years after the Neplèns first left the area of the Green Planet; they returned bigger and bolder, for even their mannerisms had changed, for they now seemed evermore fearless and daring.

As time moved on and throughout many years of watching and learning about the Neplèns, things became more apparent, and the reasons behind the Neplèns' continued disappearance became clear: for every twenty years that the Neplèns spent awake, they spent a further two years in hibernation. It wasn't clear at the beginning where the Neplèns were spending their hibernation time; still, a pattern had emerged, and their resting place was tunnelled deep beneath the surface of the Green Planet, where they had created a refuge to hibernate and grow. This period of rest became known as the 'Year of Two.'

It was over some time that the Green Planet became more accustomed to the Neplèns' behaviour, for after several years, it became evident that the forests were the Neplèns' primary source of food, but why the forests were dying in such significant quantities and how they continued to fall was still unclear, for the surrounding areas of the Green Planet became more desperate with each day, with each of those passing days, the Rare Golden Oak grew more concerned, for it was clear that the Neplèns did harbour a darker and more sinister side to their existence. And that proved correct when another year of two had ended, and chaos ensued when they re-emerged from their slumber, for they had again grown more significant in size, reaching that of two men; their features had considerably changed also and were more savage-like; their skin looked like that of hardened wood and covering their back, and the head was a yellowish resin-like shell, which careered to a point just above their eyes; that was the moment that the Neplèns had re-emerged from their year of two, as an army of Neplèns. And from that moment on, barrages of vicious attacks took place every day, every night, within every season of every year, and continued until virtually nothing remained of the Green Planet.

The sheer scale of carnage that the Neplèns had inflicted throughout hundreds of years was so dire that the Green Planet didn't stand any chance of healing itself and had entered its final years. However, hope remained that this wouldn't necessarily be the case; but time for the planet was still running out.

As time crept by, all seasons upon the Green Planet had turned chaotic, and it no longer seemed to matter what season it was, for they were now much the same as the last. However, something was happening for three days had passed since, and shockingly the majority of Neplèns and their onslaught of the last remaining forests had suddenly stopped. Instead, they seemed preoccupied with their newly discovered wisdom, for attempts at engraving into the soiled earth were diagrams and different map-like drawings of the surrounding areas of the Green Planet, for it now seemed that the Neplèns were planning to search for alternative food sources elsewhere. During this time, a lone Neplèn of giant stature and much bigger than most other Neplèns had quietly observed the others; it seemed to watch at their failed attempts keenly and their noticeable lack of leadership. While watching them, the lone Neplèn suddenly began sniffing keenly at the air of the Green Planet; this continued until a satisfied expression fell across its face, but why it did this wasn't yet known.

Meanwhile, disagreements between the Neplèns about maps and diagrams suddenly interrupted the thoughts of the lone Neplèn, and this caused the two fleshy sacs beneath its jawline to vibrate slightly and sound a ticking noise.

Until this moment, the Neplèns had lived and worked in unison; during that time, it had seemed that they had one common aim, one interest! But something had changed, and that was no longer the case. Fractures within the group of Neplèns became more violent, and within less than three days, violence erupted and became so rife that the Neplèns were now killing one another.

Days went by, and the Neplèns became evermore ruthless, for groups of the strongest Neplèns had begun to form, which eventually led to an even greater divide between them; it was now about dominance, control, and power, and so it was inevitable that fighting and unrule within the groups had become ever more widespread.

Throughout that time, the lone Neplèn continued to observe the divide within the groups quietly; for the lone Neplèn was conjuring up a plan which would inevitably decide the Neplèn army leader, but at the time, it seemed fruitless and pointless given that the Green Planet was dying. Nevertheless, through the darkness of that winter's night, loud frenzied snorts and loud ticking noises came bellowing up through the tunnels. They echoed across the desolate valleys of the Green Planet above, for the 'lone Neplèn had excited the others by rampaging through the tunnels, calling for a gathering of all other groups and their leaders to challenge it for the ultimate dominance and leadership of all Neplèns.

It was on the surface of the Green Planet where the Neplèns had gathered, and standing in the middle of a clearing at the foot of the hill from where the Rare Golden Oak stood was the lone Neplèn, surrounded by the loud sounds of stomping Neplèn feet as they crashed down against the hard frosty earth. The stomping noises had grown louder as challengers from different Neplèn groups had stepped forward to challenge the lone Neplèn. The loud noise from the excited Neplèns then suddenly began to ebb away. Eventually, the sounds had become nearly silent after several leaders from various groups had gathered in the centre of the clearing to accept the lone Neplèns challenge.

The on-looking army of Neplèns hadn't waited long for the battle of the leadership to begin, for the Neplèns groups of onlookers immediately watched as the lone Neplèn savagely killed two of the biggest Neplèns in a violent and quick attack; the third one eventually fell was severely wounded and struggling to breathe its final breath, and the fourth and fifth had escaped almost certain death by submitting and laying humbled against the earth of the Green Planet before the thousands of others followed their lead, by submitting to the lone Neplèn.

Meanwhile, time moved on, and the infighting and division within groups of Neplèns almost ended, and for now, feeding from what remained from the forests of the Green Planet continued. In the meantime, the lone Neplèn had gained the full respect of the others and was now titled 'The Great Neplèn.'

It was during the dawn of the day and the eve of the Neplèns' year of two when the fearsome sight of the Great Neplèn emerged from the tunnels of the Green Planet; beneath its heavy muscular frame, it confidently paraded its way between the army of Neplèns and across to the hilltop from where the Rare Golden Oak stood!

Before the Great Neplèn began sounding to the others with a call for them to feed before the arrival of their 'year of two, it began sniffing hard at the air of the surrounding areas; and by using its menacingly blackened eyes, it scoured the valleys of the Green Planet. At that moment, the Great Neplèn noticed a strange, yellow-coloured mist carrying on the breeze; this made it splutter and slightly choke with every breath it breathed, but this again seemed to please the Great Neplèn for a contented look fell upon its face. Meanwhile, the army of Neplèns below was a fearsome sight as they spread out in the valleys like locusts, tearing through what remained of the fallen and dying forest, and the Rare Golden Oak could only stand as it felt the earth's vibrations scream as their onslaught drew them closer to where it stood. Still, the Rare Golden Oak would already have fallen if it were not for its sheer size and the interruption of the Neplèns' year of two.

5. A MOTHER'S MESSAGE

The Great Neplèn and its Neplèn army had finished scavenging what remained on the land and were buried deep beneath the Green Planet, where they settled for their arrival of the year of two.

During this time, Mother Nature visited the Rare Golden Oak, and she blew her whispering message within the winds. The words she said to that of the Rare Golden Oak were of the most significant urgency. She told how the Neplèns did not only inflict destruction upon the surrounding areas, but others had also created the same widespread destruction throughout the entire Green Planet. Mother Nature's message continued to say that she could seemingly do nothing to prevent the eventual deaths of both the Green Planet and of itself, the Rare Golden Oak.

Mother Nature continued by telling how hundreds and thousands of Neplèns across the Green Planet had perished because of the damage they had inflicted upon themselves and their world. But the Rare Golden Oak could feel only a little pity for them, for through their greed, they hadn't only killed themselves, but the Neplèns had also destroyed everything else. And the little bit of

sympathy the Rare Golden Oak had disappeared altogether
when Mother Nature explained what she had learned
about the Neplèns and how they had tunnelled far beneath
the earth, from where they would drink the life force out
from the roots draining the trees above, before severing
their roots and causing the forests to fall. Mother Nature
then explained how drinking from the tree roots would aid
the Neplèns' mental ability, the wood they consumed
would help their physical and skeletal strength, and the sap
likened to that of their blood. She then went on to say how
very little was known as to where or what the Neplèns had
originated from and why they would create an
environment in which they could never survive, and that
she believed that the Neplèns had evolved from minute
spores of fungi and how the Neplèns purposely destroyed
the Green Planets climate so they could live. She also
remarked on how she believed that the Neplèns had
already been living beneath the surface of the Green Planet
for a thousand years before they were ready to surface on
the land above.

Whether the Neplèns had sown the seeds of their demise
or whether it was part of their strategy remained to be
seen.

However, Mother Nature wanted to explain why she
couldn't intervene sooner and went on to tell the Rare
Golden Oak of the two rules she was forbidden to break
for all of eternity!
The first and most crucial rule she was forbidden to break
was one that she could never purposely become the
destroyer of any life, no matter if it was friend or foe, evil
or pure, and the only exception to that rule would be? If,
for the greater good, the life she intended to take agreed,
she could take it.
The second rule was never to intervene with the Green
Planet's natural evolution, even if its existence was in

danger.

Since the creation of the Green Planet, Mother Nature has nurtured everything' she has seen all the extraordinary events which shaped the green earth and made it what it was. Still, for countless years, and since the Neplèns' arrival, she has had to bear witness to the brutal slaying of the Green Planet, a planet she loved, a world she swore to protect. Those reasons alone made her encounter with the Rare Golden Oak a tough, challenging time, for Mother Nature knew that the end of life was in sight and that nothing could save the Green Planet, for everything depended on the plants and forests to survive. However! she had one option and one plan to try and save the Rare Golden Oak from inevitable extinction without breaking any of her two rules.

The plan Mother Nature had in mind would have to be hurried, for the time was now of great urgency, although the Neplèns' year of two had just started; if she did nothing before their year of two had ended, then the Rare Golden Oak would inevitably fall without grace. So, Mother Nature first had to ask the Rare Golden Oak for self-sacrifice to ensure it wouldn't become extinct and that the legacy of the oaks would survive. She then told of her plan, of how she would create a fierce lightning bolt, one of which to be thrown at great force from the skies above to then strike the belly of the Rare Golden Oak, which would then create a vast hollow deep inside the middle of its trunk, which in turn would display an 'Emerald Green Acorn?

The Rare Golden Oak knew nothing about the Emerald Green Acorn to which Mother Nature had spoken; still, it continued to listen and try to come to terms with what she had said. Mother Nature continued to explain. How hundreds of years ago, and not long after the Neplèns had appeared on the surface of the Green Planet, how she had predicted the unfortunate circumstance, and it was during that time that Mother Nature requested an exception from nature. And that exception would allow the Rare Golden Oak to carry an Emerald Green Acorn deep within its trunk, and while the Emerald Green Acorn was growing inside, it would hold untold amounts of magic. And that the magic the Emerald Green Acorn would possess could only protect the rare oak from other unfortunate circumstances, such as what had happened in present times or any other similar instances after that.

Mother Nature stressed and added that the strength of the magic that the Emerald Green Acorn possessed would depend only on how big and how long the rare oak which carried it lived, for the longer it lived, the more power the acorn would hold.

She continued to explain that after the lightning bolt had created an enormous hollow in the trunk of the Rare Golden Oak, the hollow would become a 'Woodlock' and that the Woodlock would serve as a passageway through to another world. She continued to tell how, after the lightning bolt had exposed the Emerald Green Acorn, the acorn would immediately gather up and store all the memories of the Rare Golden Oak's life before it was taken through the Woodlock to the closest, most habitable planet and planted in a secret location. Then, after planting the Emerald Green Acorn, it would grow to become a sapling before beginning its young life as a 'Rare Silver Oak,' which would be indicated by its colour and, more significantly, within the trunk of the Rare Silver Oak, another Emerald Green Acorn would grow inside, and continue to store every memory of that life also.

It was at that moment that Mother Nature gently whispered the words, which pained her greatly, for she had to ask of the Rare Golden Oak and the last of its kind if it agreed for its life to end. Although the Rare Golden Oak was fully aware that its time on the Green Planet was about to end, it was still hard to accept and overwhelmingly sad to feel the words of Mother Nature.

There was an immediate lull in the air and silence for the briefest moments. At that moment, the Rare Golden Oak had agreed to its sacrifice and, ultimately, its death in favour of Mother Nature's plan and the chance to save its kind from extinction.

Mother Nature didn't want the Rare Golden Oak to suffer from its decision any longer than necessary. Still, before she began to take the life of one of the most fabulous creations on the Green Planet, she spoke briefly about that of the Great Neplèn and the title it had bestowed upon itself. She told the Rare Golden Oak how the title was one of respect and that! From that day forward, its legacy, its name, the Great Neplèn, would never be heard of again, and therefore! It will only be known as 'The Woodhunter'.

6. ONE SACRIFICE FOR ONE CHANCE

The tunnels beneath the Green Planet were now almost silent as the Woodhunter and its Neplèn army began their' year of two. Meanwhile, Mother Nature wasn't about to take any unnecessary chances and didn't want to waste precious time. So, she suddenly created a loving, warm breeze that flowed around the foot of the Rare Golden Oaks trunk. The loving flow steadily began to make its way upwards until it reached through and across the branches. A strange tingling feeling travelled around the insides of the Rare Golden Oaks frame, and the flow of loving air the Rare Golden Oak could feel could only be that of a tender goodbye kiss from Mother Nature.

The Rare Golden Oak stood firmly on the hillside, fearless, proud, and strong, and in one final moment of love, its huge strong branches, which had once stretched out towards the skies, began closing in, twisting, and bending around its gigantic trunk. Then in one instant, clouds gathered in the sky, darkening the whole hillside; winds of rage blew violently around the valleys below, lifting and throwing the wreck of the forests that once was. Thunder crackled greatly in the heavens above, and lightning sped across the skies in different directions like thousands of shooting stars. Then with one crash of thunder so strong, it shook the earth of the Green Planet, causing the made-up hills of soil, rock, and stone to come crumbling down. The lightning continued to light up the skies as it swirled and spread from every direction until suddenly! The lightning amassed together in one giant orb of light.

The light from the orb shone down and illuminated the Rare Golden Oak in bright white silver. Then, with another loud crackle of thunder never before witnessed on the Green Planet, the Rare Golden Oak unwrapped all of the branches from around its gigantic trunk. It then stretched them out fully until they had touched the violently swirling clouds above, and for one last time, the Rare Golden Oak could feel the power of the wind as it gushed through its branches.

Still standing ever so tall, strong, and proud, the Rare Golden Oak sensed the silvery orb of lightning as it powerfully hovered above the hillside. Hanging like that of the moon, it then, without warning, seemed to pour like molten lava down from the skies, and with an almighty blast, lightning sped across the whirling black clouds before crashing down into the belly of the Rare Golden Oak.

The sheer lightning force which struck down at the Rare Golden Oak caused millions of leaves to fall from its branches, and only after all the leaves had fallen to the earth below a giant Woodlock and that of the 'Emerald Green Acorn seen glowing from within.

Once again, Mother Nature created another lightning bolt to strike the millions of fallen leaves, instantly turning most of them to ash.

Although the Emerald Green Acorn now stored all the fondest memories and feelings of the Green Planet, the sight remained desperate, sorrowful, and sad. For surrounded by a great pile of ash was that of the Rare Golden Oak' silent, bowed, and broken, a creation of wonder was now only a relic of a time gone by.

Meanwhile, beneath the Green Planet, the Woodhunter and its army of Neplèns couldn't help but hear the thunderous din echoing down through the tunnels. The noise at once interrupted their 'year of two', causing them to charge through the tunnels and toward the surface of the Green Planet.

With no time to waste, Mother Nature quickly continued with her plan to ensure that the Emerald Green Acorn would have a safe passage through Woodlock and to the new planet. Without warning, Mother Nature displayed her magnificence by creating a soft blowing breeze; the breeze she had made had silently and slowly begun by circling its way around the foot of the hillside, from where the Rare Golden Oak was standing. Then, without lifting any other debris off the ground, the breeze suddenly gathered pace as it drew closer and closer to the top of the hill.

Then for only a moment, the wind suddenly stopped before gathering up more speed as it sped like a miniature tornado across the ground, gathering up the great pile of burnt and blackened ash surrounding the dead golden oak.

Meanwhile from the tunnels below, the Woodhunter and the Neplèns appeared and witnessed the burnt, blackened ash being taken high into the sky before spinning at incredible speeds toward the Woodlock. While the burnt foliage and blackened ash drew closer to the Woodlock, it began to create a slight but high-pitched whistling sound, and then like a whirlpool, the ash started to get sucked into the Woodlock faster and faster until it had disappeared entirely? However, no sooner had the blackened ash been sucked into the Rare Golden Oaks Woodlock did the rest of the ash pile begin to shake and turn red? Suddenly there were muffled screeching sounds from beneath the red-coloured ash, and with the sounds came many brilliantly bright gold and orange beams of light. The colourful rays of bright lights, which now shone, had lit up the Rare Golden Oak and most of the hilltop surrounding it. Causing the Woodhunter to open its piercing black eyes wide as it tried hard to cast a closer look at what the strange beaming lights were. It could not understand what it could see, so it stretched out its head further from inside its yellowish-looking shell and began sniffing frantically at the stale air while it moved ever closer, up the hillside and towards the Rare Golden Oak.

Suddenly! The Woodhunter stopped to listen, for it could now hear a faint screeching sound coming from over the brow of the hilltop! Immediately the Woodhunter stood upright and pulled back its head until it was fully back inside its bark-like shell. While there, the Woodhunter listened carefully while the faint screeching sound echoed inside its cover. At that moment, the Woodhunter viciously snarled, for it could now clearly hear that the screeching sound was that of a threat. The noise caused the Woodhunter to fiercely charge up the hillside, where those of its Neplèn army closely followed it.

Meanwhile! The reddish-looking ash pile suddenly burst into a great cloud of red and gold embers, creating a ball of fire that filled the sky with flames. Then from behind the flames came a high-pitched screeching noise so loud it blanketed the valley, causing most Neplèns to stumble and fall as they made their way up the hillside. Then without warning, the ball of fire vanished, and out from behind it flew a giant phoenix with red-and gold-coloured wings, which spread out to cast a significant shadow over the Woodhunter and the Neplèns below.

The dazzling bright colours of the phoenix, and the loud screeching sounds it was making, had caused the Woodhunter and the Neplèns to momentarily stop and watch, mesmerized as it flew at incredible speeds, high into the night sky.

The Woodhunter watched as the phoenix suddenly

stopped in mid-flight before turning its head to glare directly down into the direction of the oncoming Neplèns. The phoenix then opened its huge yellow beak and bellowed out yet another screeching noise, so loud it again echoed in and around the valleys of the Green Planet. The Woodhunter viciously stared back at the phoenix before glancing across at the Rare Golden Oak; only then had it noticed the giant hollow and the attractive glowing Emerald Green Acorn inside it. The Woodhunter glanced again at the phoenix before looking once more at the shining green light of the acorn.

The Woodhunter instinctively knew there was something special about what it could see, for there was something profound inside itself, saying 'it must have it'.

The earth shuddered beneath the weight of the Woodhunter as it fell to the ground, slamming its front legs hard into the dusty surface before racing up the remaining part of the hillside at a fair speed.
After witnessing this, the phoenix pressed its wings tightly to its sides and dived through the air! to leave only a trail of colour behind it.
The Woodhunter then, in a terrible rage, kept one eye on the 'Emerald Green Acorn and the other on the screeching phoenix as it continued its charge. The earth was dusty and dry, causing the Woodhunter to keep losing its footing as it slipped and fell onto the dry land beneath it. Then, through the dust-filled air, the phoenix, with its bright colours of red and gold, pushed out its great talons from beneath its chest and stretched out its claws.
The Woodhunter was almost within touching distance of the Emerald Green Acorn when the phoenix flew straight past, loudly screeching over the top of its head as it disappeared through the swirling ash-filled Woodlock.
Immediately after, the phoenix had picked up the Emerald Green Acorn and flown through the Woodlock of the

Rare Golden Oak's great trunk; its branches instantly
began to wither, therefore causing its golden colour to fade
from that of gold to that of grey.

The Woodhunter was a few moments too late, so in a
violent rage, it lunged itself inside the Woodlock, where it
began crashing its massive body against the heartwood
structure, trying frantically to understand where that of the
phoenix and the 'Emerald Green Acorn had vanished?

After a short time, the Woodhunter reluctantly retreated
from inside the Woodlock, only to scale the enormous
trunk. Then, through its brute strength, it began smashing
down what remained of the lifeless branches from that of
the Rare Golden Oak.
After finally giving up its savage attack, the Woodhunter
ordered its army of Neplèns to continue where it had left
off! To tear down the Rare Golden Oak's limbs and save
the hollow part of its trunk.

After leaving the army of Neplèns to scavenge around the
remains of the Rare Golden Oak, the Woodhunter
continued rummaging around the vast pile of ash and
burnt foliage! as it searched the area for some explanation
as to what may have happened.
During the darkness of night, the Woodhunter continued
its search but still hadn't managed to understand any part
of the Woodlocks mystery. Frustrated and reluctant to
leave the area, the Woodhunter rested while the Green
Planet's hazy early morning sun began to rise; the
Woodhunter watched as the sun stretched its light across
the valley and peered its head above the surrounding
hilltops. The earth the Woodhunter sat upon was dry, and
each day, the sun's heat seemed more intense than the last,
scorching the already arid landscape and vaporizing the last
of the remaining stagnant pools of water. But the
Woodhunter remained unfazed by the dying planet before

its feet; instead, it sat tasting the air with its tongue. And all Mother Nature could do was nurture what remained of the green earth, for she had now accepted that the uncertain future ahead was no longer in her hands but in fate itself.

Mother Nature's plan to protect the rare oak was now safely placed in the hands of another Mother Nature who governed from somewhere else on another planet. And the hope was that she would ensure the survival of the Emerald Green Acorn and the future oaks which are born from it.

Meanwhile, the Neplèns now brought the remainder of the Rare Golden Oak to the ground and laid among the ash-filled ruins was that of its trunk and the seemingly endless dark pit of the hollow. The Woodhunter then returned to its frantic search of the area, still hoping for an explanation as it rummaged in and around the strewn debris from that of the Rare Golden Oak. The Woodhunter was unsuccessful again, and its anger grew as it moved back to where the Rare Golden Oak had once stood and aggressively began kicking at the enormous golden oak's trunk; as it lay among its fallen debris, the Woodhunter angrily kicked and pushed hard before eventually rolling it down the hillside where it came crashing to rest at the foot of the hill.

Before ordering the Neplèns to take the trunk to its tunnelled cave, the Woodhunter briefly stopped to bitterly glare toward the empty hilltop void before heading toward the tunnels below.

Meanwhile, the Woodhunter sat in the blackness of its cave, and throughout that night, it searched its mind while staring at the wooden trunk for clues, but still, it remained unsuccessful. Again, frustrated at not knowing, the Woodhunter kicked two hard kicks against the enormous trunk, causing it to topple and crash against the weed-filled rocks to the far side of its den. The Woodhunter then seemed to settle, for it shuffled around the hard surface of its cave until it had found a suitable place to lie. Then, while lying on the earthy ground, it turned to face the trunk and glared deep into the blackness of the hollowed Woodlock until, finally, the Woodhunter rested before returning to the surface of the Green Planet.

Meanwhile, through the Woodlock, the phoenix was flying majestically amongst the clouds of the new planet, where it searched for a suitable resting place for the 'Emerald Green Acorn.

The new planet looked similar to the Green Planet; it homed everything from the heavens above to the earth below! With one exception? Living among its inhabitants in the new world were humans, so the phoenix continued its search in the utmost secrecy, far from any prying eyes that may have been. It wasn't long before the phoenix had eventually found the ideal place to plant the Emerald Green Acorn. But before planting, the phoenix had hovered high above the hilltop from its chosen location; where would it wait? Suddenly blackened ash and burnt foliage belonging to the Rare Golden Oak appeared like a vast swarm from over the brow of a hill; the blackened ash spun and swirled high into the skies before abruptly stopping and coming to rest among the clouds and high above the chosen hilltop.

After only a short moment, the vast cloud of burnt, blackened ash began to pour from the skies like sand before landing, creating a huge mound, blanketing the hilltop from where it came to rest. No sooner had the last flake of ash fallen than the phoenix let go of the Emerald Green Acorn and watched as it fell from the sky until it disappeared into the mound of ash and foliage below. The phoenix's work was over, for it, once again, folded its wings tightly against the sides of its vast body and dived swiftly and silently from the skies into the pile of burnt, blackened ash from which it first came, and then it was gone.

The sudden arrival of the Emerald Green Acorn from the Green Planet was an unsuspecting gift for Mother Nature, which left her with many unanswered questions; still, she instinctively began to nurture it. And in doing so, she quickly learned that it held all the memories of the Rare Golden Oak and everything she needed to know about the Green Planet.

Visions of the Rare Golden Oak's life and its time spent on the Green Planet had quickly begun to flow between Mother Nature and the Emerald Green Acorn, and it hadn't taken long before Mother Nature understood some of the reasons why she had received the gift. After reading from the Emerald Green Acorn's memories and seeing the Rare Golden Oak's life end, Mother Nature was sorrowful. Nevertheless, she wanted to ensure that the Emerald Green Acorn would flourish and that the rare oak to be born from it would have a far less dramatic start to its life than the one that had just ended.

Mother Nature wasted no time requesting a strange and freakish event to ensure that the Emerald Green Acorn would get the best start to its life on the new planet. Immediately she gathered up tiny dew drops of the purest water from the surrounding grassy hillside and made a protective transparent dome like the firmament before placing it over the top of the newly planted acorn. Then, within its dome, she produced weather of all types and tremendously sped up the miniature seasons from within it; within seconds, a root appeared from within the Emerald Green Acorn and began to push its way out of the earth above. Seconds soon turned into minutes, and with every passing minute, the shoot grew stronger and stronger, taller and broader. Then, when the hours passed, the characteristics of a Rare Silver Oak could be seen, but its glowing silvery colour could not.

What would have taken several hundred years had only taken less than a day, for already that of the once small root growing from the Emerald Green Acorn had now almost fully grown to that of a Rare Silver Oak, and within the belly of its trunk the Emerald Green Acorn grew. From that moment, Mother Nature removed the protective transparent dome from around the Rare Silver Oak, and by removing it, time returned to normal.

The Rare Silver Oak and Mother Nature quickly learned what life on the Green Planet was like; the memory, for the Emerald Green Acorn, had shown them all they needed to know. Everything from the Neplèn arrival to the Rare Golden Oak's unselfish sacrifice to the Green Planet's almost certain death and destruction. However! Life now had only just begun for the Rare Silver Oak, and all had seemed well, but Mother Nature had held close her concerns regarding the colour of the Rare Silver Oak, explaining that something had interfered with it.

Mother Nature quietly searched her thoughts before inviting the Rare Silver Oak to share any strange memories or feelings that the Emerald Green Acorn may have shared. And no sooner had Mother Nature asked for this had the Rare Silver Oaks trunk begun to glow brightly, and beneath the thickness of its bark exterior, the Rare Silver Oak felt a slight humming-like vibration before being shown visions. The Rare Silver Oak shared with Mother Nature the distorted dreamlike images and flashbacks from the Green Planet, for they showed the trunk of the Rare Golden Oak destroyed and then dragged through its remains and into darkened tunnels. Immediately after seeing the worrying visions, Mother Nature warned the Rare Silver Oak that the Woodlock must have somehow been left open. Still, she could not explain nor understand how that could have happened.

7. A MISSING LINK FOUND

Daylight arrived on the Green Planet, but the night before had seen most of the larger Neplèns not return to their tunnels, for they were still feeding from the remains of the Rare Golden Oak; other lesser Neplèns were becoming agitated and confused with missing their 'year of two and found themselves trying to fight for what food remained.

The second day was much the same as the last, the food was becoming scarcer, and disorder was becoming more frequent. The Woodhunter had, on three occasions, managed to control the Neplèns, but the situation quickly became uncontrollable, making it increasingly difficult for the Woodhunter to keep its leadership status.

The third day brought some Neplèn deaths, leading to further bloodshed and more Neplèns killed that night. Unable to control its army any longer, the Woodhunter returned to its cave! Upon returning, it at once made its way to where the Rare Golden Oaks trunk had fallen days earlier. Unconcerned about what was unfolding above the tunnels, the Woodhunters' primary focus was to find out what happened during the falling of the Rare Golden Oak. And so, the Woodhunter again began searching for answers by pulling great clumps of wood and bark from inside the trunk's hollow, but its search for answers again proved fruitless. Frustrated by this, the Woodhunter shunted its shoulder hard against the Rare Golden Oak's great trunk, where it fell from the weed-filled rocks and rolled onto the ground of the Woodhunters den! only for it to display more of the hollow. The Woodhunter then found itself staring out from its den's darkness into the Woodlocks' blackness, from where it could see a small green light shining out from deep inside.

Reacting instinctively, the Woodhunter reached into the Woodlock to take hold of what it had seen but could not take hold of the object, for it was too far from its reach, so it decided to heave the great trunk upright and climb inside. No sooner had the Woodhunter put its head past the threshold of the Woodlock than a slight humming sound echoed in and around the inside; this startled the Woodhunter, causing it to panic and quickly pull its head out. Then, from the outsides of the trunk, the Woodhunter began banging hard, trying to dislodge the green object from inside.

After several attempts, the Woodhunter remained unsuccessful.

Pondering for a moment, the Woodhunter snapped a thick stalk from the weeds that had grown in and around its den; using the thick stem, it reached back into the Woodlock, and by doing so, the humming sound returned, only this time! The Woodhunter had ignored it and tried to dislodge the green object by jabbing and prodding at it. However! The more jabs the Woodhunter delivered, the stranger the Woodlock became, for the sound it made was not only that of humming but also that of whistling, and no sooner had the whistling occurred had a green mist appeared.

Suddenly the Woodhunter quickly removed the thick stalk from the Woodlock and watched as the green mist suddenly disappeared; the Woodhunter then gave out a loud crackle of a snort, which echoed through the tunnels, and alerted the other Neplèns to its den.

Only twenty or so Neplèns had heeded the call, and the first Neplèn to arrive at the den's entrance was quickly pounced upon and forcibly taken across to the trunk of the Rare Golden Oak. At the foot of the Woodlock, the Woodhunter pointed at the green object and ordered the bewildered Neplèn to climb inside and retrieve it. No sooner had the Neplèn stepped inside the Woodlock that the humming sound returned; as the Neplèn drew closer to the green object, the stranger that of the Woodlock behaved; for again, the humming noise grew louder, and with it came the whistling, and then that of the green mist was soon to follow. It was at that point when the Neplèn partly disappeared. The terrified Neplèn noticed this and instinctively pulled back to distance itself further from the green object. Still, by doing this, the panicked Neplèn stumbled out from inside the Woodlock and began to kick its way past the Woodhunter. Once again, the Neplèn stumbled; only this time, it had fallen into the path of the other Neplèns, but they were keen to see the outcome of this strange event. The onlooking Neplèns wasted no time in pushing the terrified Neplèn back into the direction of the Woodhunter; the Woodhunter then swiftly lunged forward and firmly dragged the kicking Neplèn back to that of the Woodlock. No sooner had the Woodhunter done this had the Neplèn been forced back inside the Woodlock to retrieve the green object.

The glistening object had now captured the attention of the onlooking Neplèns, and fascination grew as they eagerly watched and waited for the unknown outcome, and as for the Woodhunter! Its desire was fast becoming an absolute obsession.

Meanwhile, the Neplèn was again back inside the Woodlock; it waited a moment before plucking up just enough courage to take hold of the green object. The Neplèn quickly began twisting and pulling hard at the green piece in a desperate attempt to try and dislodge it, but at once, the loud whistling returned, as did the pool of green mist. In that instance, the Neplèns arm again began to disappear, only this time the Neplèn tried to ignore it by fast closing its eyes shut. Eventually, and after a struggle, the Woodlock fell silent as the green object suddenly broke free and bounced several times before falling out from the Woodlock and landing at the foot of the Rare Golden Oak's trunk.

The Woodhunter looked slightly puzzled as it moved to where the green object had fallen, for it was now no longer green in colour. But instead! it had turned dark and grey' like that of a small rock.

The Woodhunter didn't seem too concerned about the green object losing its colour, for it quickly scooped it up from the dusty ground and held it up triumphantly for all the watching Neplèns to see.

From that moment, the Woodhunter sensed it had discovered something unique and extraordinary, and those watching Neplèns shared the same feeling.

The excitement of the Woodhunter was brief, for it tightly clasped the grey object in its fist and ordered the Neplèns to protect the trunk with their lives; they were then to carry it to the top of the hill and place it back into the hole from where the golden oak once stood.

The Woodhunter had soon made its way to the top of the hill, from where the Rare Golden Oak once stood; there it sat perched, staring at the grey object, trying to understand what it was. Soon after, other Neplèns joined it, carrying with them the trunk of the Rare Golden Oak; several Neplèns at once started to dig out the oaks' fallen debris to uncover the hole and to put the trunk of the Rare Golden Oak into it. Other curious Neplèns had also begun to gather around the foot of the hill and had, for the time being, stopped scavenging and fighting among themselves.

Meanwhile, the Woodhunter stood to its feet and ordered the Neplèns to place the trunk of the Rare Golden Oak back into the earth; no sooner had the Neplèns done this than the grey rock-like object that the Woodhunter was tightly holding began to vibrate within its tightly clenched fist? The Woodhunter immediately unclenched its fist to watch the grey object shake; by doing so, the grey object was notably moving across the Woodhunters palm, across its fingers into the direction of the Woodlock. The Woodhunter tightened its fist and clasped it hard around the grey object.

The Woodhunter then ordered the Neplèns to protect the trunk and decided to distance itself from the Woodlock, and in doing so, the grey object stopped vibrating. The Woodhunter had now retreated to an isolated area some distance away, where again, it sat perched on the dusty earth and stared strangely at the grey object. Some time had passed, and the Woodhunter had remained fixed in what looked like a trance-like state when suddenly something happened which caused the Woodhunter to awaken. The Woodhunter then immediately looked across to the hilltop from where the trunk of the Rare Golden Oak was standing, and without warning, the Woodhunter wasted no time in quickly making its way back.

Upon reaching the trunk, the Woodhunter stopped and briefly stared directly into the Woodlock; it now seemed that the Woodhunter was not acting solely on instinct but on something it had subconsciously now learned. It reached out its arm, and from its tightly clenched fist, the Woodhunter dropped the grey object into the Woodlock, and by doing this, it turned from grey back to its original colour of green! More so, it was now much brighter than before and had brightly illuminated the inside of the Woodlock.

Meanwhile, it was three days since the Rare Silver Oak had its growing time sped up. Still, there was no way Mother Nature on the Green Planet would know this; however, she still, in her haste, created a silent, strong gust of wind to carry a message and send it through the Woodlock in the hope that it would reach the Emerald Green Acorn on the new planet. The wind quickly blew as it travelled across the baron valleys and then passed the hordes of Neplèns surrounding the hill; there, it swiftly and silently swept in and around their bodies before reaching the top and passed the unsuspecting Woodhunter, as it stood menacingly at the entrance of the Woodlock.

Surprisingly, Mother Nature from the new planet had also taken advantage of the opened Woodlock and quickly sent her message, telling all about the Rare Silver Oak's life and how she had sped up the growing time of the Rare Silver Oak to give it a less dramatic start to its life.
Meanwhile, the message from the Green Planet now reached the Rare Silver Oak; the news was a warning and an explanation of how the Woodlock had remained open. The words told how a fragment of the Emerald Green Acorn had broken off and wedged deep into the heartwood of the Rare Golden Oak's trunk; the news also described how it had happened when the phoenix had taken hold of it. The message then told how the Rare Silver Oak had been grown from a broken Emerald Green Acorn and that a fractured acorn may affect how it develops while it grows. The message continued by encouraging the Rare Silver Oak to learn all it could and, if a time arrived when it needed to protect itself, it should

use whatever magical powers it owned. The final part of her message warned that the Woodhunter was now in possession of a broken piece of the acorn, and it could still provide the Woodhunter with all the same qualities as the Emerald Green Acorn itself.

The end of the message was Mother Nature's direst warning yet, for it spoke about the broken piece and how significant the part was; she told how the Woodhunter wasn't only in possession of a broken piece, but it was now holding part of a key to open the Woodlock and that it is known as the 'Emerald Key. And with the Emerald Key, the Woodhunter could learn from it and become the bearer of unknown amounts of magic, knowledge, and power by reading all the same memories from the Emerald Green Acorn, and furthermore! Adding that the Emerald Key is one with the Emerald Green Acorn, and they are spiritually connected. Therefore, the Emerald Key would unwillingly lead the Woodhunter to wherever the Emerald Green Acorn was.

8. THE LEARNING

Meanwhile, the Woodhunter seemed unfazed by the brightness of colour the Woodlock was now omitting, for it was now more eager to learn more about the Woodlock, the Emerald Key, and, more importantly! Why and where did things disappear when they came into contact with it? And with those thoughts, the Woodhunter reached back into the Woodlock and placed its hand directly over the Emerald Key, and once again, the rippling pool of green mist appeared, and with it came the whistling sound. The watching Neplèns frantically began to push and shove one another in their bid to take a closer look; they watched as the Woodhunter lowered its hand, touched the Emerald Key, and then watched as the arm of the Woodhunter disappeared. A twisted expression suddenly fell upon the face of the Woodhunter as it peered gleefully into the Woodlock, only to watch its arm reappear when it pulled it back out.

The Woodhunter wasted no time selecting and ordering one of the Neplèns to touch the Emerald Key and place its head into the green pool of rippling mist to see whatever lay behind it. Although reluctant, the Neplèn climbed into the Woodlock and touched the Emerald Key, and with the Neplèns claw-like hand now placed firmly over the bright object, came the green pool of rippling mist, into which the Neplèn put its head into it.

Through the Woodlock and onto the new planet, Mother Nature and the Rare Silver Oak they had now, for the first time, borne witness to the coming of the Neplèns! For out of nowhere, and hanging motionless above the grassy fields, appeared the bizarre sight of the Neplèns ugly head. The bizarre sight of the Neplèns head had, for a moment, hung motionless and still, until suddenly it began to move erratically from one side to the other as it struggled to adjust its piercing black eyes to the brightness, and clarity of the colourful sights which surrounded it. Then the Neplèn began to breathe hard and heavily as it sniffed briefly from the air of the new planet. The sudden appearance had no sooner started than it had already finished, for the Neplèn suddenly disappeared from the 'new planet' the instant it pulled its head back out from the pool of rippling green mist. The Neplèn then stepped out from the Woodlock, fell to the ground, and praised the Woodhunter for leading it to a new place of plenty. After the Neplèn had relayed its findings to the Woodhunter, the Woodhunter became ecstatic. However, its jubilant showing was briefly interrupted when the Neplèn began to tell of an unfamiliar smell carried with the winds.

After hearing the tales of this strange planet, the Woodhunter was eager to take a closer look, and with that, the Woodhunter climbed into the Woodlock and touched the Emerald Key. No sooner had the green mist appeared had the Woodhunter peered through it, and like the Neplèn before, the bright shining light and all the colours made it feel slightly disoriented. Only after the Woodhunter had managed to focus its piercing black eyes could it see the full size of what it had achieved. The magnificence of the new planet, and the different smells carried on the winds, only fueled its curiosity and encouraged the Woodhunter to climb further into the green pool of rippling mist. With the Woodhunters claws now deeply embedded into the heartwood of the Woodlock, it leaned forward, stretching half its body into the new planet, displaying a tormented and hideous-looking sight of only its head, broad shoulders, and muscular chest, hanging menacingly in mid-air, and into that of green pastures and forests of a new planet.

The reaction to this bizarre intrusion was instantaneous and likened to that of the Green Planet when the Neplèns first appeared, for most wildlife from that surrounding area had already begun to flee in countless numbers. Nevertheless, the Woodhunter remained unconcerned about what was happening around it, for it only concentrated on what it could see, especially what it could smell. But the smells blowing in and around the area that the Woodhunter preyed on were hard to detect. The Woodhunter soon became overcome with the number of different scents made from those of the fleeing animals and creatures it had already disturbed. After a short while, the Woodhunter fell still, its eyes fixed on a particular part of the dense forest; it became evident that the Woodhunter had now detected the unusual smell that the Neplèn had previously expressed.

The Woodhunter remained for some time but could not detect precisely where the unusual smell was coming from or what the unique smell was, angered and frustrated at not knowing! It began to inhale deeper and fuller breaths to identify what it could be. The Woodhunter eventually gave up, but not before pushing itself further onto the new planet and bellowing out a battle-like cry, which seemed to be a warning to whatever species lay undetected.

Daylight was steadily fading on the new planet, but before

returning, the Woodhunter spied through the depths of the forests, a familiar-looking sight with a faintly glowing light at the top of a hill. The Woodhunter stared for a short time but wasn't fully aware of what it was staring at, which was that of the Rare Silver Oak. Still, subconsciously this encounter would play heavily on its mind.

After seeing and witnessing plenty, the Woodhunter eventually pulled itself back through the green pool of rippling mist and was once again standing inside the Woodlock; the Woodhunter stepped out onto the dried-up surface of Green Planet.

After seeing a new planet full of colourful sights and bursting with life, the view the Woodhunter was looking at made the picture look even more desolate than it already was! However, and surprisingly, Woodhunter seemed to relish that it was back and instantly began to suck deep into its lungs, the hazy yellowish mist which hung still in the air.

A short time later, the Woodhunter ordered its army of Neplèns to the foot of the hill for a gathering; the Woodhunter briefly revealed its findings to them. It began by telling them that the land it had seen was rich and plentiful in food but that they would need to be patient before being led to the new planet to feed. The Woodhunter continued by saying they would have to save their much-needed energy until a plan was ready, for the new world could only provide them with food and not at the moment offer them the right environment they needed, which would allow them to stay.

Mother Nature listened intently, for the Woodhunter was about to give the first clear indication of why the Neplèns had rid the Green Planet of its entire splendour. And would also explain why they have created an environment in which they could not survive.

Meanwhile, standing at the top of the hill, the Woodhunter detailed why they could not leave the Green Planet and permanently cross the Woodlock, for the Woodhunter feared that crossing over to the new world would leave them with no Woodlock and no way of returning to the Green Planet. The Woodhunter reminded the Neplèns how it had taken thousands of seasons to shape the environment purposely and that it would be needed when the time came for many of the chosen Neplèns to spore. The Woodhunter then also reminded them of their purpose, which was to create the conditions they were now seeing on the Green Planet, and that those conditions were almost ready for the next new breed of Neplèn.

Lastly, the Woodhunter then briefly told of the new smell it had smelt; it described how the scent belonged to a creature they had not encountered before.

No sooner had the Woodhunter finished revealing to the Neplèns its findings; it had then ordered them to their tunnels, where they were to wait and save what little energy they had. With that, the Woodhunter turned and looked towards the Woodlock, where it stopped and stared as it thought hard about what to do next.

The Green Planet was, for the moment, silent. However, the Woodhunter still had to appease the other Neplèns before they soon became restless and took the matter upon themselves. And so, the Woodhunter instinctively searched for answers by stepping inside the Woodlock and placing the Emerald Key down.

It was now dark on the new planet and was only partly lit by that of a half-moon; the moon had only managed to illuminate the ground somewhat as the winds broke the passing clouds from beneath it. There was a silent hush that was sadly interrupted by the faint calls from the many recently abandoned young creatures, for the arrival of the Neplèns had already made an unfortunate impact. However, the Woodhunter was again unconcerned, for the only decision it had returned to the new planet was not out of pity or remorse but to learn from the sights, sounds, and smells it had to offer. It wasn't long before the Woodhunter quickly realised that the strange smell it had recently smelt had disappeared, and no trace of it remained. Nevertheless, the Woodhunter continued to spy on its surroundings, studying the area from where the Rare Silver Oak was standing. During this time, the Woodhunter realised the oak it had seen previously shared similar characteristics to the Rare Golden Oak and that the darkness of the new planet now showed this to be correct, for a very faint silvery colour could now clearly be seen emitting from it. A menacing expression fell upon the face of the Woodhunter; its eyes widened in surprise at what it had suddenly thought, which made it speedily step out from the Woodlock and hastily down towards the tunnels of the Green Planet.

The Woodhunters' spontaneous decisions seemed again to be one of instinct, but the truth was! It was the inherited yet reluctant guidance of the Emerald Key upon which the Woodhunter was now acting. And it was now apparent what Mother Nature told in her, for she had warned, amongst other things,

how the Woodhunter may become the bearer of unknown amounts of magic, knowledge, and power, for the Woodhunter was already learning from the Emerald Key, without even realising it.

After arriving at the tunnel's entrance, the Woodhunter gathered all Neplèns at the foot of the hill; it was there that the Woodhunter spoke of its second visit to the new planet; it eagerly told them of the tree it had seen. It told them how the tree reminded it of the Rare Golden Oak and how it was likely to be connected to the Emerald Key and all that happened to it. The Woodhunter then spoke of its plan, telling the Neplèns that it would cross through the Woodlock while the new planet was in darkness. And with it, it would take fifty of the strongest Neplèns to carefully tear open the belly of the tree and see if it holds another Emerald Key and how it may open a passageway back to the Green Planet.

With no time wasted, the Woodhunter and the Neplèns prepared themselves for an attack on the Green Planet.

Upon the Woodhunters' visit, Mother Nature had sensed the apprehension within the Rare Silver Oak; she constantly reminded it of its magical powers, saying to use them if and when the time came. But unfortunately, the time was coming, and for as long as the Woodlock remained closed, the Green Planets Mother Nature couldn't send a message through, and therefore she could not warn the Rare Silver Oak of the Woodhunters plan.

9. THE FALLING OF THE SILVER OAK

The Woodhunters call came when it ordered all fifty of the strongest Neplèns to make their way to the trunk of the golden oak, for the time had now arrived for them to cross through the Woodlock and to tear down the Rare Silver Oak. A fierce stampede ensued, and only the strongest Neplèns had managed to make their way to and around the top of the hillside, where they gathered, hoping that the Woodhunter might choose them to cross through the Woodlock and to the new planet. Others could only stand by and watch as the Woodhunter confidently paraded itself between the mass of Neplèn bodies to boast of its plan and choose which Neplèns would follow it. While making its way toward the Woodlock, the Woodhunter briefly stopped to look from where it was standing and saw the countless Neplèns who never made it past the foot of the hill, for many of them were too weak to take part, some that did become injured, and others died in their bid to escape the stampede.

The sight before the Woodhunter was again a reminder of the frustration building within some of the Neplèns, for the Woodhunter was still fully aware that if the Neplèns chose to attack, they could easily overpower it and take the

Emerald Key for themselves. But the Woodhunter had one thing which the others hadn't, and that was its knowledge, for that was fast becoming far superior to that of the Neplèns.

Meanwhile, the Woodhunter made its way to the trunk of the golden oak, and throughout that time, it held tightly onto the Emerald Key, and only then did it leave its tight grip to place inside the Woodlock. The Woodhunter then selected fifty of its strongest Neplèns to prepare to travel through to the Woodlock and onto the new planet.

However, no sooner was the Woodlock opened, and without the Woodhunters' knowledge had Mother Nature hastily sent a message to the Rare Silver Oak on the new planet.

The news Mother Nature sent was one of the utmost urgencies! For it pleaded for something to stop the Woodhunter and its fifty Neplèns from taking the Emerald Green Acorn from within the Rare Silver Oaks trunk. However, the news of the Woodhunters plan had arrived too late, for neither the Rare Silver Oak nor Mother Nature was ready to try and prevent this from happening, and the Woodhunter would soon reaffirm this.

Meanwhile, the Woodhunter began to send the first fifty Neplèns through to the new planet, each with their order to wait in silence until it followed.

From the distance of the Woodlock, the Woodhunter took one last look around the desolate valleys of the Green Planet, and then it turned its eyes to those of its dead and injured Neplèn army. For a moment, the Woodhunter seemed thoughtful before choosing one Neplèn to watch their progress from the Woodlock and ordering fifty more Neplèns to prepare to cross through to the new planet, and with that, the Woodhunter then stepped through the Woodlock and was gone.

The air on the new planet was warm, and the night was calm and still. But the mood instantly changed upon the arrival of the Woodhunter and the Neplèns, for no sooner had the Woodhunter appeared than it then gathered all Neplèns and was about to tell them where to start the attack when suddenly the Woodhunter smelt at the air, for once again it detected the strange scent? Although the smell was faint, the Woodhunter Immediately ordered all the Neplèns to hide beneath the tall shrubs and foliage areas.

The Woodhunters' concern was that of its plan, for until it could figure out what the creature was, or indeed what it was capable of, the attack of tearing down the Rare Silver Oak may have to wait. Still, the reality was that the Woodhunter was aware that this might be the only chance it had, and that the opportunity was far too great not to take.

Meanwhile, the Neplèns awaited instruction as they watched silently at the seemingly undecided Woodhunter while it pondered its next move. Still, their wait wasn't to be long, for suddenly, in the air and above the ground, a Neplèn appeared from the Woodlock, where it peered through the green mist to check on the progress of the Woodhunter. The Woodhunters' immediate reaction was to reach out and touch the watching Neplèn; likewise, the watching Neplèn reacted to do the same. Although they both were within reach of one another, their grips couldn't take hold, and finally, after several attempts, the Woodhunter realized there was no way back to the Green Planet, for their attempts to touch one another passed through as though neither of them was there.

With no possible way back for the Neplèns, the Woodhunters' plan would have to succeed, for the

Neplèns could leave the Green Planet and never return for their time to spore. Or the Neplèns could choose to stay and die of starvation before they had time to spore.

Either way, if the Woodhunter failed in its plan, the new breed of Neplèn would cease to exist.

The Woodhunter realized its limited options, and despite the unknown outcome, the prize of discovering another Woodlock was too great not to take. Hence, the Woodhunter then gave the fifty Neplèns the order to attack the Rare Silver Oak. Unlike before, the Woodhunter chose not to charge up the hill towards the oak; instead, it and the Neplèns crept silently in amongst the foliage like giant insects.

The unseen Neplèns were a worrying time for Mother Nature, for she didn't know their whereabouts, so in an attempt to identify them and protect the Rare Silver Oak, she created a blazing fire that surrounded the foot and surrounding hillside. The blazing fire soon took hold and lit up most darkened areas around the foot of the hillside, and it was then that Mother Nature then spied a glimpse of the Woodhunter and the Neplèns trying to fight back the fierce flames of the fire.

Similar to the times of the Rare Golden Oak on the Green Planet, the Woodhunter began to realize that something powerful must also be protecting the Rare Silver Oak; its only thought was to work faster and smarter for its plan to work.

Meanwhile, the flames continued to blaze as Mother Nature tried keeping the Neplèns in sight, but this was proving difficult, for the Woodhunter reorganized them and moved them away from the flames and back into the darkness the shadows until Mother Nature eventually lost all sight of them altogether.

Mother Nature was left confused at their sudden disappearance and warned the Rare Silver Oak to prepare itself and try calling upon the powers of the Emerald Green Acorn to help thwart the Woodhunters' attack.

Meanwhile, Mother Nature continued to seek out the Woodhunter by desperately trying to chase it out from the shadows, for she then created and scattered in every direction many forks of lightning, which crashed down to the ground and onto the area from where Mother Nature hoped it would be.

Beneath the crashing bolts of lightning, Mother Nature remained unsuccessful and couldn't force the Neplèns out of the shadows from where they were hiding.

A thought suddenly crossed the mind of Mother Nature, for she was now beginning to think she may have killed the Woodhunter and the Neplèns in her rage and, by doing so, breaking one of her vows. But then the Woodhunter appeared from the earth and within the inner circle from where the blazing fire raged. And from there, the Woodhunter and the Neplèns charged up the hillside and towards the Rare Silver Oak.

Mother Nature acted quickly by creating a freezing wind and spinning it rapidly into the dark clouds above. She then promptly gathered all the moisture from the surrounding areas until a great water whirlpool had amassed and met with the freezing winds in the sky. The combination of icy winds and water created giant hailstones never seen before.

A noise of rumbling boulders began echoing in and around the valley and crashing around the night skies. Then, and with great wrath, Mother Nature again spun the winds and created a tornado in the clouds above. The tornado turned at incredible speeds; it pulled and collected all the giant hailstones into one vast funnel and was directed down towards the Woodhunter and the Neplèns as they continued their charge up the hillside.

It appeared that Mother Nature had forgotten or was no longer concerned about the two rules she had sworn to uphold, for it now seemed that what she had created wasn't only to slow the Woodhunter and the Neplèns down but was intended to stop them.

Meanwhile, the funnel from the tornado spun violently toward the ground, hurling giant hailstones in every direction. They were now falling fast and heavy as they crashed through the boughs of the forest trees; the force of the impact caused the giant hailstone to shatter into many small fragments that sped out across the hillside like spears. The winds pulled hard and strong, causing the Neplèns to be dragged back down the hillside and towards the tornado's funnel. There was no escape, for giant hailstones grew ever closer and were now crashing down around the Neplèns, many of which were now lying still on the ground, unable to move as the tornado dragged them ever closer to the entrance of the funnel.

The relentless winds and giant hailstone had slowed the Woodhunter and the Neplèns to the point of giving up, for they were now battered, bleeding, and bruised. The Woodhunter could only watch how the remaining battered Neplèns had fallen to the ground in sheer exhaustion; and how they had to retreat within their bark-like shells in the hope of gaining some form of protection from the ongoing onslaught.

Meanwhile, on the Green Planet and from the safe distance of the Woodlock, the watching Neplèn had seen the Woodhunters failing plan. So, at once, it sent fifty further Neplèns through the Woodlock and to the new planet hoping they would continue raising the Rare Silver Oak to the ground.

The Woodhunter continued to resist the tornado's power, but its grip was fading fast as it tried to bury its claws further and deeper into the sodden earth; with each passing moment, the funnel entrance of the tornado grew closer and closer. At that moment, the Woodhunter spied out at the Rare Silver Oak while buried inside its wood-like shell. Through sheer strength and determination, the Woodhunter had somehow not only managed to clamber back onto its feet, but it had also managed to make a final attempt at racing up the rest of the hill and towards the Rare Silver Oak. There, it spied an opportunity through the gaps of the falling hailstones to take several leaps before pouncing up and onto the trunk of the Rare Silver Oak.

With very little strength left, the Woodhunter only had enough energy to hold onto the trunk but didn't have enough power to attack, so it could only watch and wait. And during the wait, the Woodhunter spotted in the distance the faint flickering green light of the Woodlock, and to its surprise, the Woodhunter watched as the newly arrived Neplèns began to charge towards the hillside. Mother Nature tried desperately to stop their charge by directing the winds and giant hailstones toward them, but the Neplèns had been rested for too long and were too fast to slow them down.

Meanwhile, the Woodhunter regained its strength and frantically began to smash great clumps of bark out from the trunk of the Rare Silver Oak, and in doing so, it called out to the charging Neplèns for them to join it. One after another, the Neplèns pounced on the Rare Silver Oak and quickly began tearing it down.

There was nothing more Mother Nature could do for the Rare Silver Oak, for it was just too young and didn't have enough time to learn from the magic of the Emerald Green Acorn. It wasn't long before its silvery colour soon disappeared beneath the hefty mass of Neplèn bodies surrounding it.

The tornado winds now passed, and the giant hailstones stopped falling; the area surrounding the Rare Silver Oak was in ruins, and the sodden earth and ice now covered the forest and fields, and among them were strewn with broken down boughs, branches, rocks, and boulders. More so, the Rare Silver Oak was a solemn reminder of what the Woodhunter could achieve, for what was left was destruction on a significant scale.

The Neplèns' attack on the Rare Silver Oak had only lasted for a short time; Mother Nature had hoped that the Rare Silver Oak could have learned how to use its magical powers, and between them both, they may have prevented what happened, and more importantly! What was to come could be far worse than she cared to imagine.

10. MEMORIES OF THE GREEN PLANET

Daylight was now slowly creeping over the hills and ebbing away the darkness of the surrounding forest. Silhouettes made from the light across the hilltop were those of the Neplèns as they tore down the Rare Silver Oak's last remaining branches before uprooting it. The Woodhunter eagerly watched but was soon interrupted by the daylight, which was now approaching. A nervous urgency to move more quickly suddenly fell upon the Woodhunter, for it didn't know what other battles the day may bring. So, it promptly ordered the Neplèns to carefully carve open the trunk of the Rare Silver Oak without damaging whatever they found inside.

A short time had passed, and the Neplèns had carved out a vast hollow from the trunk of the Rare Silver Oak, but they still found nothing inside; the Woodhunter then became agitated and began ordering the Neplèns to stand the trunk upright. From there, the Woodhunter stepped into the carved hollow, and by using its teeth and claws, it began to frantically scrape out various sides of the heartwood walls from within. The light outside the hollow was now getting brighter, and with it, the Woodhunters' frustration grew, for it was now trying to find something that it wasn't sure existed, but it continued anyway.

In desperation, the Woodhunter lashed out several times more at the heartwood from within the hollow when suddenly it could hear a slight humming sound. The Woodhunter recognised the sound, similar to that of the Rare Golden Oak Woodlock. Excitedly the Woodhunter began scraping in and around the area from where it could hear the humming sound. While carefully removing one large splinter after another, the sound grew louder until a pulsating green light finally shone out from behind.

The Woodhunter then suddenly stopped what it was doing, for it had a flashback to those final moments of the Rare Golden Oak and how the phoenix took the Emerald Green Acorn through the Woodlock and out from its reach. Because of this memory, the Woodhunter called out to the Neplèns and ordered them to surround the Rare Silver Oak trunk and watch the skies.

It was now daylight on the new planet. In the distance, the morning summer sun had fully risen above the hills, warm sunlight had fallen upon the tops of the forest trees, and sounds from the planet's wildlife had briefly made things seem normal. Still, daylight showed the full-scale devastation from the previous night, for it was now in full view. Around forty or so Neplèns lay injured and trapped beneath large rocks and fallen debris, and a mixture of large swathes of shattered melting ice and soddened earth fell like a blanket across the fields and hills from where the Neplèns had made their charge. The hilltop was no longer a once grassy hill with a giant oak standing in full view of the valleys, but an empty area full of Neplèns, and laying at their feet was the trunk of the Rare Silver Oak.

Meanwhile, the Woodhunter pulled away the last remaining heartwood splinters, fully revealing the pulsating green light from behind. For a moment, the Woodhunter looked puzzled, for it instantly recognised the shape of an acorn, but its size and colour were not something it had seen before. Nevertheless, while the acorn remained encased in the heartwood wall of the hollow, the Woodhunter reached out and touched it. Then, like the Woodlock before it, a rippling green mist appeared, and the Woodhunter peered through it; no sooner had the Woodhunter done this had it found itself staring out from the Woodlock and onto the Green Planet. With that, the Woodhunter stepped back from the green mist and took the Emerald Green Acorn out from the heartwood cast surrounding it.

No sooner did the Woodhunter place the Emerald Green Acorn into its hand than it suddenly began to display visions of the memories of past times on the Green Planet. The images to which the Emerald Green Acorn had shown were swift and appeared nothing more than a flash through the Woodhunters mind. The strange occurrence was so sudden and over so quickly that it left the Woodhunter little time to understand what it was.

Meanwhile, the Neplèns eagerly gathered around the trunk hollow, from where they waited for the Woodhunter to tell them of its findings. The Woodhunter appeared beneath the threshold of the Woodlock and stared out at the Neplèns and then across at the valleys of the new planet; it was at that moment the Woodhunter triumphantly threw its arm up and showed the Neplèns the Emerald Green Acorn it was holding. The Woodhunter quickly shared the news, telling the Neplèns about the plan's success. It described how the Emerald Green Acorn displayed the green mist allowing it to see through to that of the Green Planet.

The Woodhunter then told the Neplèns that more work

was needed before they knew if the plan was a real success and that they would only know this by travelling back through the hollow and back to the Green Planet. The Woodhunter then turned and ordered all but ten Neplèns to go and free the ones trapped from beneath the debris, then hide within the dense forest and wait; then the Woodhunter called the other Neplèns to plant the Rare Silver Oak trunk deep into the darkest recess of the woods.

The one thing the Woodhunter had purposely kept from the Neplèns was that of the visions it had seen, for it was now feeling a great sense of power, and until it had learned all it could, then the Neplèns would never hear about it.
  Meanwhile, while the Woodhunter sat amongst the ruins of the Rare Silver Oak, it watched the silhouettes of the Neplèns carrying the trunk down towards the shadowy parts of the forest; when out of sight, it took the Emerald Green Acorn and held it close to its face to study it.
  The Emerald Green Acorn was familiar in sight, like that of any other acorn, but this felt strong in the Woodhunters hand, and to the touch, it was like that of a smooth stone; the colour was vibrant and pulsating, and its size and weight were like that of a large rock. As the Woodhunter studied the acorn, there was a sudden cold silence around the hill and from where the Woodhunter sat, which made the Woodhunter feel slightly uneasy about its surroundings, so it decided to leave and follow the others into the forest. But before doing so, the Woodhunter suddenly clenched its fist and drove it hard into the new planet's soiled earth, pulling out a long piece of root belonging to the Rare Silver Oak, which it used to tightly bind the Emerald Green Acorn before placing it over its head. The Woodhunter then made its way to the density of the forest below and the trunk that awaited it.
  Upon reaching the densest part of the forest, the Neplèns were already gathered and had surrounded the trunk of the

Rare Silver Oak, for it now stood upright and purposely placed into a ditch. While walking towards the Rare Silver Oaks trunk, the Woodhunter lifted the Emerald Green Acorn from over its head and stepped into the hollow, where it placed the Emerald Green Acorn back into the heartwood cast from where it first took it.

The Woodhunter ordered one of the Neplèns to touch the acorn and step through the rippling green mist; the Neplèn acted quickly, and no sooner had the mist appeared than it stepped into the Woodlock and through and into the Green Planet.

Immediately after the Neplèn stepped through the rippling mist, it arrived standing inside the Woodlock on the Green Planet, from where it looked out at the onlooking Neplèns before turning back around to step again through the green mist and returning to the hollow.

Upon returning inside the hollow, the Neplèn received a pleasing acknowledgement from the Woodhunter, for the Woodhunter knew it had found a new route back to the green planet, which would become known as the 'Silverlatch'. Still, there were no celebrations, for even in the densest part of the forest, the Woodhunter wasn't taking any chances and immediately ordered the Neplèns to collect large boulders and foliage to secure the Rare Silver Oaks trunk. After that, the Woodhunter called the Neplèns, including the injured, back through the Silverlatch to return to the Green Planet.

The Woodhunter was last to arrive on the Green Planet. After stepping out from the Woodlock, the Woodhunter paraded itself for the first time at the top of the hill, displaying the Emerald Green Acorn hanging from its neck like some trophy for all the awaiting Neplèns to see. It was from the hilltop where the Woodhunter wasted little time and spoke of its next plan. It told of the times on the new planet when darkness had fallen, telling the Neplèns that several hundred of the weakest would be the first to cross through the Woodlock to feed quickly, and several hundred more Neplèns would then follow after they had returned. The Woodhunter went on to say that this feeding pattern would continue until all Neplèns were eventually fed and made stronger until, finally, all Neplèns were strong enough to create the army of Neplèns it wanted and to make the new planet their own.

What the Woodhunter spoke of next was still unknown, for it spoke briefly about the Neplèns' and their time to spore; it reminded them that those chosen to spore, including itself, would not know until that time arrived and added that the chosen ones; would remain on the Green Planet and that they would receive their food through the Woodlock. The Woodhunter then finished by ordering several hundred of the weakest Neplèns to prepare to cross through and feed from the new planet.

While the Neplèns prepared themselves, the Woodhunter left the hill and retreated to the tunnels beneath the Green Planet and its cave below; the damp cave-like burrow was in near total darkness, but for a glowing light that came from the Emerald Green Acorn and partly illuminated the area from where the Woodhunter sat. From there, the Woodhunter took hold of the Emerald Green Acorn and stared directly into its pulsating light; suddenly, the Woodhunter felt
drowsy, and its eyes became heavy as it fell deeper into a dreamlike state. So many different dreamlike visions of past times and places were suddenly beginning to appear through the Woodhunters mind; at first, the Woodhunter couldn't make sense of what the memories were, for the visions that the Emerald Green Acorn was showing were blurred, nonsensical and confusing. The Woodhunter soon began to realise that the more it tried to see an image, the clearer it became; it was also aware that it had to mentally challenge the Emerald Green Acorn for it to show what memories the Woodhunter wanted to see.

The longer the Woodhunter remained in a dreamlike state, the more precise the memories that the Emerald Green Acorn was showing, for they had now become almost as real life. The memories were old, and from a time before the Neplèns' arrival, they showed the Green Planet as it used to be, how peaceful and beautiful it was. The memories then began to flip back and forth, showing the Woodhunter things it didn't understand; and whispers it had never heard before.

The Woodhunter was quickly learning from the Emerald Green Acorn as it continued to win the challenge to see what memories the acorn held. And by winning the challenge, the Woodhunter soon realised that the Emerald Green Acorn would grant whatever memory the Woodhunter requested to see. For a moment, the Woodhunter sat and thought about what vision it wanted to see when suddenly it remembered the scent of the other species from the new planet. And so, the Woodhunter thought hard and eventually won to be shown the memory that the Emerald Green Acorn had of the unknown species.

Within moments the Woodhunter was shown visions of the new planet, and within those images were two humans, one man and one small boy. The Woodhunter watched from the images, and it saw: a man hunting and fishing for food and a boy collecting wood and placing it on a small fire within a forest.

After being shown the visions of the humans, it wasn't clear how the Woodhunter was feeling, for the Woodhunter didn't show any signs of anything. The hope was that it may have been fearful of the memories it had seen, but that wasn't to be! The Woodhunter dismissed the visions, seemingly viewing humans as inferior, irrelevant, and not worth the time spent. However, the Woodhunter did request to see how many humans there were on the new planet, but the Emerald Green Acorn had no memory of this, for it simply had yet to see any other.

The Woodhunters' next challenge was to see memories of the Rare Golden Oak and those seemingly magical powers which aided it throughout its final moments on the Green Planet.

The challenge to request memories from the Emerald Green Acorn was getting harder to fight; Still, the Woodhunter did see the memory of the Rare Golden Oaks' final moments.
The memory that followed was not of visions but of feelings, whispers, and emotions, for these were the messages that the Rare Golden Oak had received from Mother Nature, where she had warned the Rare Golden Oak of the Woodhunter and the Neplèns plans of attack. The Woodhunter listened intently for quite some time and had learned most of what it had wanted. But when the Woodhunter heard Mother Nature telling the Rare Golden Oak why she first created the Emerald Green Acorn and its magical powers, it became strangely excited and immediately broke free from its trance-like state.

For some time, the Woodhunter remained weary and weak, for the challenge for the Emerald Green Acorn's memory had taken its toll, leaving the Woodhunter knowing that it would have to be strong and fight hard to learn all that it could learn from the acorn's memory.

The Woodhunter then placed the Emerald Green Acorn over its head and made its way through the tunnels to the Woodlock, where it eagerly waited for the light of day to fall on the new planet.

11. THE WOODHUNTERS CHALLENGE

Feeding from the new planet was well underway, and hundreds of Neplèns had passed through the Woodlock for several nights. During this time, the Woodhunter held a brief gathering but hadn't shared with the Neplèns the memories it had seen. Instead, it spoke about the Humans on the new planet by telling the Neplèns they needed to be watchful when feeding from the new world until it had learnt more about them and how many humans were living there. The Woodhunter went on to tell how it wanted to build hundreds of tunnels within different parts of the forest's woodland, that they would serve as a battleground and how building them would begin immediately. Lastly, it said work on the tunnels would only occur when the Green Planet was in total darkness.

During the build times, the Woodhunter continued to leave some of its most favourable Neplèns with the orders to watch over the others while they fed and worked within the forests so it could further study the Emerald Green Acorn. And it was during the darkness of one particular night when the Woodhunter learned more of the memories from the Emerald Green Acorn, and it was from that moment when things were about to change. For it was while the Woodhunter had fallen into a trance-like state that it requested the Emerald Green Acorn to show more from its memory of Mother Nature, and no sooner had it asked for that whispers of Mother Nature's voice swept through the mind of the Woodhunter.

The request the Woodhunter received had brought it back to the precise moment when Mother Nature had spoken to the Rare Golden Oak before its death. The Woodhunter heard Mother Nature's whispering message telling the Rare Golden Oak about the Neplèns, telling how she had seen countless more Neplèns scattered across the Green Planet, how the earth was dying, and how she was allowed an exemption from nature to create the Emerald Green Acorn. The Woodhunter continued to listen, and for every whisper it could hear, it became plainer that the acorn had stored away everything the Woodhunter had ever seen or done since it had owned the acorn. Moreover, the Woodhunter also realized that each time it opened the Woodlock, Mother Nature had passed the acorns' memories through to the Rare Silver Oak, warning it of all the Woodhunters' plans.

The final part of the message that the Woodhunter listened to was how Mother Nature explained to the Rare Golden Oak that she was forbidden to become the destroyer of any living thing on any planet and that she could not intervene with the planet's evolution. After hearing this, the Woodhunter became ecstatic and broke free from its trance; for now, it had realized that no matter its plans, however, brutal Mother Nature battled with it, nothing could stop it.

It was through into the night, and the Woodhunter wanted to learn what magical powers the Emerald Green Acorn possessed. Still, the request failed, and the Woodhunter grew tired of challenging the Emerald Green Acorn and made its way to the Silverlatch and the Green

Planet. Then, reaching its cave, the Woodhunter sat and thought about what to do next! Then, it suddenly spied a sudden movement from the corner of its eye at a chrysalis attached to its arm. The Woodhunter flicked at it, and the chrysalis fell to the ground, where it began moving.

The Woodhunter was intrigued and watched as the insect struggled to break free from the tomb that encased its body. The insect began awkwardly to push hard against a small opening it made at the end of the chrysalis. With that, the Woodhunter moved forward to watch more closely as its curiosity grew until the insect finally managed to push its body halfway out from the chrysalis.

The Woodhunter sat motionless, expressionless, and almost statue-like, fascinated as it watched the red wasp-like insect finally break free from its chrysalis and begin its first short journey across the dusty ground of the Woodhunters den. Then, in an attempt to dry off its dampened wings, the wasp-like insect began fluttering them softly against the sandy surface, which created a small dust cloud from which it became hidden, and out of sight from the Woodhunters' view. The Woodhunter had been so intrigued with watching the newly hatched insect that it hadn't noticed the Emerald Green Acorn, which hung from around its neck, beginning to glow a faintly green colour.

After the small dust cloud had settled, the Woodhunter shifted its eyes in all directions to see where the wasp-like insect had disappeared! When suddenly, it reappeared and flew instinctively toward the direction of the slightly glowing emerald-green acorn. Its swift and sudden flying manoeuvrers annoyed and pestered the Woodhunter, which was unfortunate for the insect, for the Woodhunter lashed out, instantly killing it.

Almost immediately after killing the insect, the Woodhunter fell to the ground grasping hard at its throat! While trying to catch its breath, it rolled across the earth of its den, kicking and banging itself hard against the rocky walls surrounding it. Suddenly the kicking stopped, and the sprawled body of the Woodhunter lay almost lifeless on the ground. Its breaths were fast and heavy, and this continued until the Woodhunter had taken several gasps of air, then after its final gasp, the breathing suddenly stopped, leaving nothing but silence from within its den.

 The Woodhunter may have momentarily lay dead for several seconds when its eyes suddenly began to flicker and open. Disorientated, weak, and bewildered at what had happened, the Woodhunter lifted itself off the ground and stood to its feet. After composing itself and catching its breath! The Woodhunter decided to leave its lair, but only after clambering to a more upright position and only managing to focus its sight did its whole body begin to shake and tremble. Confused and not knowing what was happening to itself, the Woodhunter called on the others to make their way towards its den. The Woodhunter was now shaking so violently it was hard to tell what was happening, and only after the violent shakes had stopped could two deep cuts be seen splicing their way open to the sides and just below the pits of the Woodhunters arms. At the same time, the Emerald Green Acorn glowed an ever brighter green! Suddenly, four massive veined transparent objects appeared out from the sliced openings from the sides of the Woodhunter.

 While the Neplèns charged down through the tunnels and towards the Woodhunters lair, a wall of sound greeted them; the sound seemed to be that of giant heartbeats, pounding to that of the same beat.

 Approaching the Woodhunters lair, they met another wall, only this time it was one of dust and debris which sped past them and out from the tunnel's entrance. The Neplèns watched from the threshold of the Woodhunters' den, bewildered at a strange silhouette flickering from behind a wall of dust surrounding it.

 The puzzled on-looking Neplèns stood and watched as

the dust began to settle inside the cave, and as it did, the monstrous sight of the Woodhunter kneeling on the ground began to emerge, for now, the Woodhunter had changed, and in its changing, it had acquired four giant-wasp-sized wings.

It had taken some time for the Woodhunter to recover from the shock, and only after that could it move somewhat more freely. The first thing the Woodhunter had noticed was an uncomfortable weight seemingly resting on its back, and as it awkwardly turned to see! Four giant-sized wings as they silently fluttered of their own accord.

Typically, the Woodhunter wasn't shocked at seeing its body's new addition, for it had already prepared itself and had requested that the Emerald Green Acorn grant it the same means of flight as the insect it had killed. And although the Emerald Green Acorn was unwilling to give such a request, the Woodhunter had fought hard, and unfortunately, through severe pain and near death, it won its most difficult challenge.

Meanwhile, the Woodhunter steadied itself just enough to shove its way past the shocked on-looking Neplèns and hastily make a somewhat cumbersome move towards the tunnels, stumbling and occasionally crawling in a desperate effort to make it outside and to the open baron land of the Green Planet above.

On appearing through the tunnel's threshold, the Woodhunter looked, moved, and crept like a giant insect; its wings began to flutter almost instinctively each time as it moved further and further toward a small mound or hill. The Woodhunter staggered as it eventually made its way to the hilltop from where the trunk of the Rare Golden Oak stood. In full view of countless Neplèns and the Green Planet's hazy moon, the Woodhunter knelt to catch its breath before wafting its wings, slightly raising itself and the sandy earth from the surface and into the air; after many failed attempts at trying to fly the Woodhunter suddenly began to ride higher and higher until it finally disappeared beyond the yellowish haze, leaving the watching Neplèns on the earth below watching the darkened silhouette of the Woodhunter fading from the light of the moon above.

12. THE GATHERING OF THE NEPLÈN ARMY

Several days passed, and the Woodhunter began to believe that it wasn't just the master of the earth but also the sky above, for it was several days since the Woodhunter had acquired wings. Within that short time, it had remained mainly in the skies, mastering its flight and furthering its plan by readying itself to search the vast areas of the Green Planet for what Mother Nature had spoken about, being those of the other Neplèns.

It wasn't until the tenth day that the Woodhunter eventually called all Neplèns for a short gathering around the hillside and tunnels of the Green Planet. From there, the Woodhunter told them of the things it had seen in the skies, saying how it believed it had seen thousands of Neplèns strewn across areas of the Green Planet. The Woodhunter told how it would need more journeys to be sure of what it was seeing and that it could be gone for some time, adding that work and feeding from the new planet would stop until it had returned.

On day eleven, the Woodhunter had finished feeding

from the forests of the new planet. Before taking the Emerald Green Acorn out from the Silverlatch, the Woodhunter ordered all Neplèns to return to the Green Planet, where it also briefly joined them before taking to the smog-filled skies, hoping to further whatever plan it had conjured up.

Several days later, the Woodhunter eventually returned from its journey across vast areas of the Green Planet. On reaching the Woodlock, the Woodhunter called for an immediate gathering of all Neplèns to tell them of its findings.

The Woodhunter wasted no time telling the Neplèns that it had seen in some parts of the ruined planet many thousands of Neplèns aimlessly making their way across the land in search of food. The Woodhunter then briefly spoke of another female breed of Neplèns who had already spored and were known as the 'Carriers, adding that there were few in numbers; lastly, the Woodhunter added how it planned to lead those other Neplèns and Carriers to the new planet, where they could also feed from its forests until they had grown strong enough to add to its army.

With that, the Woodhunter ordered all the Neplèns to take as much food as possible from the new planet's forests and that the trunk of the Rare Golden Oak would be needed and its Woodlock used elsewhere.

Another several days had passed, and the Neplèns finished feeding from the new planet, and the Woodhunter called all but fifty of its most trusted to return to their world; before ordering the other fifty Neplèns to stay close to the Silverlatch and, await for what could be the arrival of hundreds more Neplèns and Carriers to the Green Planet. So, after leaving its fifty most trusted Neplèns, the Woodhunter stepped into the Silverlatch, out onto the

Green Planet. The Woodhunter wasted no time preparing to go; still, before doing so, it had taken the Emerald Key out from the inside of the Woodlock; and bound both the key and the Emerald Green Acorn tightly together before placing them both over its head.

Since the acorns' separation, it was the first time that both had met, and by being bound so closely together, they touched, and a golden mist silently appeared from them and silently drifted unnoticed into the skies.

Meanwhile, the Woodhunter and several Neplèns wasted no time toppling the trunk of the Rare Golden Oak onto its side. The Woodhunter then grappled hard with the trunk of the Rare Golden Oak, which stood four times its size, and twice its width of itself, before taking it to the skies. At first, it didn't seem possible, but unfortunately, the Woodhunter had the strength to hold it, its wings had the power to carry it, and soon the Woodhunter had gone.

In a seemingly short time, the Woodhunter had flown a fair distance before seeing hundreds of the wondering Neplèns and Carriers. The Woodhunter could see they were already too weak to continue their fruitless journey, so it would have to act fast to save them.

The Woodhunter circled many times in the hazy skies above before choosing its moment and swooping toward the feet of skeletal-looking Neplèns and Carriers. The Neplèns were too frail and hungry to run from the sight of the Woodhunter, whose wings sped out, casting a flickering shadow across many of them as it came to land. Instinctively, the Neplèns fell to the ground submissively, but unexpectedly, the fearsome-looking Carriers remained standing stubbornly bold. The Woodhunter disregarded the Carriers' behaviour and began to speak to the submissive Neplèns. Still, while doing so, a few Neplèns crawled across the ground towards the trunk, mistakenly thinking it was a food offering. The Woodhunter noticed this and wasted no time teaching them a lesson, for it opened up its fleshy sacs and warned them to move back and away from the trunk. Two Neplèns took no notice, but one did not and continued making its way toward the trunk of the Rare Golden Oak, so with the quickest of movements, the Woodhunter pounced and plucked it up from the ground. In a lesson for the others to learn from, it flew it into the skies before dropping it to its death, and before returning, the Woodhunter waited from the skies to watch if any other Neplèn wanted to make their way to the trunk; the Woodhunter waited until it was satisfied with the Neplèns submission. The Woodhunter flew back to the ground, lifted the Rare Golden Oaks trunk from the ground, and stood it upright; from there, it explained the Woodlocks' importance and showed the Neplèns and Carriers how it worked. The Neplèns and Carriers stood nervously aside and watched while the Woodhunter placed the Emerald Green Acorn inside the Woodlock; in a hurry, it stood aside and began ordering each of them through to the new planet.

The first nervous Neplèns made their way through the green pool of rippling mist and fell from the Silverlatch and onto the New Planet, where the Neplèn guards were waiting. The Neplèn guards watched the decrepit sights of the Neplèns and Carriers as they toppled out from inside the Woodlock. Squeals of fright echoed around the new planet's dense forest as each one Neplèn toppled out on top of another, their eyes burning from the glare of the sun, to which their hardened shells had served little cover as they tried to use them as cover. The awaiting Neplèns that stood menacingly in size compared to their fellow breed at once began to usher them out of sight and into large dug-out holes, which would eventually become tunnels, from where they would stay until the daylight had fallen.

One after the other, the Neplèns continued to spill out from the Woodlock until the last one finally arrived, and the Woodhunter achieved the first part of its plan. However, its most challenging task still lay ahead, for its goal would take around one season to complete, but the worrying thing was that the Woodhunters' plan certainly looked achievable.

Meanwhile, after several journeys and hundreds of Neplèns saved, the Woodhunter, for now, had ended its mission by returning to the top of the hill and placing the Rare Golden Oaks trunk back into its rightful place! And from there, it immediately opened the Woodlock, allowing the waiting Neplèns to cross through and feed from the new planet.

With an ever-increasing number of Neplèns, the Woodhunter called upon its fifty most trusted for a gathering before selecting and adding one hundred and fifty other Neplèns to join.

It was on the Green Planet where the Woodhunter spoke to the two hundred Neplèns, telling them of its plan, and that being how for the next several weeks, it would continue moving back and forth across the Green Planet to gather as many more Neplèns and Carriers as it could, it told them to expect large numbers crossing through the Woodlock. It went on to say how the forest on the new planet would not be big enough to sustain the amount of Neplèns it expected. Lastly, the Woodhunter mentioned how it would find another forest of more significant size; the Woodhunter then left them with the order to watch over the rare golden and silver oak.

Some weeks passed, and the Woodhunter returned with

countless more Neplèns and Carriers throughout that time! And as each day passed, the might of its army unfolded before its eyes.

The Woodhunters plan had been meticulous and far exceeded its judgment, for it had now managed the impossible task of gathering hundreds of Carriers and tens of thousands of Neplèns, and only when the Woodhunter was satisfied that any remaining ones were either near death or dead, had it given up its search.

It had taken the Woodhunter less than two seasons to achieve all it had reached; to accomplish that, the Woodhunter sacrificed the Neplèns' year of two. Nevertheless, it continued progressing and soon witnessed its most significant achievement.

Upon returning the Rare Golden Oak trunk, the Woodhunter didn't take any rest, for, after yet another gathering of the two hundred Neplèns, it quickly left them with the order of protecting both trunks, telling them that they would remain open for some days. With that, the Woodhunter immediately opened the Woodlock, stepped through to the new planet, and flew into its night skies to learn what it could from its vast areas.

Two days later, the Woodhunter returned with another sinister scheme that would involve preparing its Neplèn army for an invasion of the new planet. The Woodhunter wasted no time and called for a gathering of the entire Neplèn and Carrier race.

Meanwhile, while The Woodhunter waited for the Neplèns to appear from the tunnels of the Green Planet, it sensed a strange lull of quietness, and the surrounding areas seemed void of Neplèn life. It momentarily paused while squinting its eyes to look closer around when suddenly plumes of reddish-looking spores began steadily rising from the ground. The Woodhunters tongue began to spontaneously flicker as though trying to taste something from the surrounding air. The Woodhunters' bizarre behaviour didn't last long, nor did the plumes of reddish-looking spores, which seemed to disperse in the winds rapidly, and quickly soon after, the Neplèns appeared from the tunnels. Still, the Carriers remained, and the reason behind this would quickly become clear.

Although the strange event hadn't lasted long, it seemed to gratify the Woodhunter, for it seemed to know that their time for sporing was soon to arrive. Nevertheless, the Woodhunter called all Neplèns from the hilltop to assemble, and this was the only time it had done this since first finding them wandering the vast areas of the Green Planet. And what unfolded was of a shocking size and was enough to send a chill down the spine of the Woodhunter itself, for The Woodhunter hadn't waited long before it heard loud stomping, snorts, and ticking noises as the Neplèns made their way through the tunnels. As they grew closer, so did the vibrations of heavy movement, which caused the earth and stone to begin to fall from the hills of the surrounding valleys.
Surrounded by the incredible noise, The Woodhunter moved closer to the edge of the hill before taking to the skies to see its achievement.

A long time had passed when the Neplèns finally stopped marching, and with it, the loud noise they had created ceased. The dusty air swept away from beneath the Woodhunter as it flew around the smog-filled skies, and the incredible sight of what it had achieved was of grave concern.

The Woodhunter came to rest at the top of the hill and began telling the Neplèns of the vast journey it had taken across the new planet and how it had brought it to a new forest of the most extraordinary size. The Woodhunter went on to tell them how the arrival of the new Neplèns and Carriers had now caused them to outgrow the forest on the new planet and that it was too small and not purposeful enough for the plans it had. The Woodhunter continued by telling them more about the enormity of the forest it had seen, how dense it was, and how it would supply vast amounts of food and shelter, which would serve them well until the time came to make the new planet their own. The Woodhunter went on to say how the forest would become known as the 'forest of a million trees' and how, beneath it, it planned to build what would become known as the 'Tunnelled Kingdom. Lastly, before the Woodhunter ordered all the Neplèns back to the tunnels, it spoke briefly of the humans on the new planet; it told how it needed to know how many dwelled upon it and how not knowing could ruin its plan. It then spoke highly of its army of Neplèns and how it would repay them for their loyalty and that it would be shown to them soon.

After ordering the Neplèn masses back to the tunnels, the Woodhunter stepped through the Woodlock and took to the skies of the new planet in search of the humans.

Meanwhile, the Woodhunters' journey took it across vast land and sea areas before it noticed from the darkened skies small flickering lights from the valleys below. Intrigued by what it could see, the Woodhunter decided to watch from a ridge of a mountainside from where it spied down at the dark valley below. From what it spied were many small flickering lights of flame, and the light from the fires cast shadows of several silhouettes of the human species. The Woodhunter recognized the shapes as those of humans from the memory it had previously seen of the man and young boy. Still, while it continued to spy on them, a thick heavy fog approached, blocking the light from the fires and making the Woodhunters' view unclear, so it decided to leave the area and return later for its next and most crucial part of the plan was to repay the Neplèns for their loyalty.

The Woodhunters' obsession with the human species was playing heavy on its mind, and it became clear that it wanted to know more about them. Still, for whatever reason, the Woodhunter wanted a lone human to learn from and was already thinking of another plan to achieve that.

Soon after returning to the Green Planet, the Woodhunter standing at the top of the hill, hastily called upon all Neplèns to join it; from the mass of Neplèns, it again called out to its most trusted to stand alongside it so the army below could watch how the Woodhunter paid their loyalty.

The two hundred most trusted Neplèns watched bewildered in silence while the Woodhunter took from over its head the Emerald Green Acorn. Shortly after, the Woodhunter passed it to the first Neplèn in line and ordered it to request from the Emerald Green Acorn to be granted wings for flight. Nervously the first Neplèn took hold of the acorn and requested its wings for flight, and no sooner had the Neplèn asked that it fell to the sandy earth and began squealing in extreme pain. The Neplèns body soon became disfigured and twisted; its neck swelled, its breathing choked, and its eyes bulged from its head. Suddenly the Neplèns back then arched, and through its oak-like skin, four wings sprouted out from beneath its yellowish fur-like shell. While the Neplèn lay unconscious, the Woodhunter dragged it to one side before taking from its clenched fist the Emerald Green Acorn. The Woodhunter passed it to the second Neplèn in line, then the third, and forth; this continued until all two hundred had their turn! And in their battle to win their request, many Neplèns did not survive, for they weren't strong enough to win the fight.

Throughout the battle of requests, there was a total of twenty-three of the Woodhunters' most trusted Neplèns to die. But that seemed to make no difference to the Woodhunter, for it showed no sign of pity or remorse for those that had died, for it told its watching army of Neplèns that they must learn to understand what happens to the weak.

While the winged Neplèns rolled upon the ground, desperately trying to catch their breaths and struggling to stand, the Woodhunter walked to the hill's edge and held up the Emerald Green Acorn. There, it addressed the army of Neplèns below to tell them that the winged Neplèns would now be known as the 'Terror Flights', and thousands of others would eventually join them in the skies of the new planet.

It was the dawning of the Terror Flights' first day, and they were already learning the skills to master the skies above.

Meanwhile, The Woodhunter waited for them to learn their skills before it would choose twenty Terror Flights to share the responsibility of flying the trunk of the Rare Silver Oak on its long journey to the forest of a million trees.

13. HIDDEN TO SEEK

Several days had passed, and the Terror Flights had learned to master the skies and had already flown the trunk of the Rare Silver Oak and hidden it deep inside the dense forest of a million trees and a great distance from where it once lived.

Meanwhile, the Woodhunter was about to embark on a journey to find a lone human. Still, before it did that, it ordered the Terror Flights back through the Woodlock and to the Green Planet; and left them with a message that it may be gone for several days; with that, it removed the Emerald Key and placed it around its neck along with the Emerald Green Acorn.

The Woodhunter didn't know where its journey would take, but it was evident that it had a plan, and nothing would stop it from achieving it.

Throughout the darkness of night, the Woodhunter embarked on its long journey across the skies and back to the mountainside ridge from where it first spied the humans and the flickering flames. The Woodhunter climbed around the cliff face to see if it could see the humans again, but they had moved on. The Woodhunter then waited a while longer, moving backwards and forwards in an agitated manner while trying to shelter from the heavy rain, which suddenly began to hit hard against the slated rock of the mountainside.

The rains continued to hit hard, and the winds that carried them were also unforgiving; this left the Woodhunter no option but to leave the wind-swept ridge and hastily make its way to the shelter of a small collection of trees, near where the Woodhunter had spied the humans.

After finding a welcomed rest bite from the brutal winds, and heavy rains, the Woodhunter sat menacingly on a large trunk beneath the foliage from one of the trees and began to sniff hard at the air, but the heavy rains washed away any smells there might have been. The Woodhunter had little choice but to leave the tree and investigate the area from ground level. While moving around the ground, the Woodhunter made its way creepily across to a mound of ash that the human species left. Silently sifting through the ash pile, it was evident the ash was cold and had only left the Woodhunter in doubt about how long the human species had left the area.

Unsuccessfully the Woodhunter spent the remainder of that night and most of the following night searching far and wide for a human species, but with no sign, it decided to journey back to the forest of a million trees. However, some distance into its flight, the Woodhunter suddenly spied from the darkened skies, a lone human sitting in among a small patch of grassed woodland and again by the light of a small fire flame. They're from a secluded area on a cliff; the Woodhunter menacingly spied upon the lone human throughout the night.

The sunlight slowly edged in on a new day, and the Woodhunter had already decided that the lone human it had spied on would be the one it would learn. The Woodhunter had waited for this opportunity and had prepared itself to fight a long hard battle to request from the Emerald Green Acorn to become a human. And so the Woodhunter held the Emerald Green Acorn from around its neck, tightly clasped it in its hand, and began to stare longingly at it, and soon after, it fell into a trance, and the expected long and dangerous battle for the request started.

It was a hideously slow, painful, and disturbing transformation, but the Woodhunter again became victorious.

Meanwhile, the sun was near rising when the Woodhunter awoke from its unconscious state damp, cold, bruised, and cut at the bottom of a rocky hillside from which it had fallen while battling the Emerald Green Acorn for its request. As it did, it found itself lying naked, but for the Emerald Green Acorn and Emerald Key hung loosely and heavily from around its neck and was now awkwardly large for the Woodhunter to carry openly. Still, it didn't want to hide it until it had made closer contact with the human.

While lying among the rocks, the Woodhunter uncomfortably tried shielding its eyes from the rising sun; in doing that, it also was trying to look and make sense of its new human form. At the same time, the sun rose higher into the skies, and its brightness was getting stronger and was piercing through breaking gaps between the Woodhunters' unusually slender fingers while it tried to shield itself from the glare. The shock of everything caused the Woodhunter to panic while it tried hiding away from the brightness of the skies and the colours surrounding it. Confusion became too much and caused the Woodhunter to scurry around the ground, burying its head beneath the grass until it finally found a hiding place behind some rocks.

The Woodhunter sat for a moment, familiarizing itself

and occasionally peeking from over the rocks at its new surroundings, where it was to wait until the clouds blotted out the brightness before venturing out. Steadily the Woodhunter crawled out from behind the rocks, but unsteadily it tried to stand, for its new skeletal frame made it uncomfortable to travel on all four limbs. Eventually, but unsteadily the Woodhunter managed to walk around the hills and valleys for some time. Still, it had to stop many times, for the soft tissue beneath its feet was punctured by the hard stones, adding more discomfort to the already battered body of the Woodhunter. In addition, the Woodhunter compared its usual self as a Neplèn to that of a human, and suddenly it began to feel very small, weak, and pathetic; that only made the Woodhunter feel more meaningful than ever before.

It was approaching three nights since the Woodhunter had left the Green Planet, and it knew that it would soon have to make its way back to open the Woodlock and allow its army of Neplèns through to feed. Hastily, although still in discomfort! The Woodhunter began to speed up and soon managed to trek out a course, which led it to where it had spied the lone human. Again, the Woodhunter stopped, thus briefly, to check the surroundings before it began to edge its way further and further down the side of the hill, occasionally stopping to peer through the branches at the lone human while watching him wade in and out from the water's edge. The Woodhunter was now close enough to the human and near enough to where the human had made camp, so it took the opportunity to bury the Emerald Green Acorn and the key to hide them from view.

The surrounding areas were tranquil, and the fisherman was knowledgeable and had a keen sense of his surroundings. So, when he heard the faint rustling of bushes and snapping of twigs that lay on the ground, he realized he was not alone, which caused the fisherman to stop what he was doing and call out in the direction of that of the dense shrublands. So, he listened again and waited a brief moment before calling out for a second time, and with no reply other than a faint rustling sound coming from beneath the shrubs, he'd decided that the fish he'd caught may have attracted the forest animals. Then, with a slight shrug of his shoulders, he bent down to pick a rock from the ground and take his fish knife out from the side of his boot, but in doing so, the fisherman caught an unmistakable glimpse of bloodied feet from beneath the shrubs. The fisherman was shocked at what he'd seen, and cautiously he called out again while steadily walking towards the shrubs with his knife pointed at arm's length. Just as the fisherman reached out to begin sifting through the dense shrubbery with his knife, the human-looking Woodhunter suddenly stepped out into the open, startling the fisherman! This action caused him to stumble backwards and fall to the ground, dropping his knife as he fell.

 When the fisherman raised his head, he saw an undernourished, unclothed, pale man standing before him with the appearance of someone who hadn't belonged. The fisherman had been slightly stunned by the stranger's appearance as he scrambled back to his feet, for the oddity of the stranger had alarmed him so much that when he finally began to speak, words of nonsensical gibberish spilt from the fisherman's mouth. In addition, in a fumbling way, he took a lengthy item of clothing from around his shoulders, which he then offered to the stranger to place over his naked body. While doing that, the fisherman secretly scoured, looking for his knife, using his eyes to the area from where he had fallen.

 Meanwhile, after three unsuccessful attempts at wanting the stranger to take hold of the clothing, the fisherman decided to make him decent looking by throwing the item over the stranger's shoulders. Then, after bending down to the ground and snapping a length of creeping vine from it, he cautiously tied it around the stranger to keep his clothing in place.

The fisherman liked to think he could tell a lot from a person by the look in their eyes. Still, the long matted dark hair of the stranger had prevented him from doing this, but the fisherman did manage to get a slight glimpse, and what he saw was nothing more than a deep space looking out from behind the stranger's eyes.

Still feeling uncomfortable with the stranger, the fisherman still managed to show concern towards him and did that by pointing toward the basket of fish he'd caught, but the stranger didn't respond. By now, the fisherman realized that the stranger wasn't sound of mind, which probably was why he had lost his way! So, while keeping a close eye on the stranger, the fisherman turned towards the stream while coaxing him to follow. Soon after, the stranger began to follow but only took a few steps when he spied something shining from beneath the foliage and quickly bent down to pick up; what was the fisherman's fish knife. Then, immediately after the stranger picked up the blade, the fisherman turned again and gestured for him to follow, not noticing.
The stranger had picked up his knife. The fisherman continued making his way to the stream, and the stranger quickly caught up; his nearing footsteps behind surprised the fisherman into turning sharply. The fisherman instinctively threw his arms up into the air to protect himself, and as he did, a shocked and puzzled expression fell upon his face, for he looked down to see blood dripping from the blade and the stranger's hand. The fisherman was bewildered to see the stranger tightly clasping hold of the fish knife by its blade rather than the handle, causing the stranger to cut deeply into his hand. Quickly, the fisherman began to pull at the stranger's arm

to lead him toward the stream's edge, where he washed it and wrapped the wound with a piece of rag he had torn from his clothing. Throughout the ordeal, the stranger's expression had not altered, and its deep empty stare remained; there was no sense of pain or word to speak, and the fisherman was sure that the stranger had lost his mind! He then began to wonder how he had ever survived at all.

Time passed, and the fisherman had just coaxed the stranger into sitting. While resting, he began to try and communicate further with the stranger, but he could not get any other response from him, for the stranger sat motionless and still! And so, the fisherman began to prepare a fish for them both to eat and while preparing it, the fisherman continued to speak of anything that came into his mind, for the strangers' silence made him feel uncomfortable. Nevertheless, the fisherman continued by placing the fish on a slate-like stone, and before lighting the fire, he poked and prodded at the fish with a stick whilst keeping a keen eye on the stranger. Finally, the fisherman noticed how the stranger seemed interested in watching how he was preparing the fish, so to keep the stranger interested, the fisherman talked any old nonsense whilst gathering a small amount of dry grass before placing three or four dried twigs above it. Then, after reaching into a small pouch he'd had tied to his waist, the fisherman took out two pieces of dark stone and began hitting them together just beneath the small mound of dry grass and twigs.

The stranger sat and watched! Flinching occasionally each time the sparks flew from the dark stones into the dry grass, it continued to watch until suddenly, the sparks turned into a flame. The stranger, not knowing any other, snatched one of the dark stones from the hand of the fisherman, thinking they must hold magical powers like that of the Emerald Green Acorn. Although slightly startled, the fisherman laughed as he passed the other dark stone to the stranger and wondered why he'd made such a fuss.

 After building up the fire with broken pieces of wood, the fisherman placed the fish upon it to cook; he again reached into his pouch and took two more pieces of dark stone out from it, and with them, he attempted to show the stranger how to make fire.

 Moments later, the fish on the fire had cooked and were now ready to eat, but after many unsuccessful attempts to offer the stranger some food, the fisherman finally gave up. So, while sitting alone, the fisherman began to eat his freshly cooked spoil. In doing so, he watched in disbelief at the malnourished stranger, who looked like he had never eaten nor drank and seemed contemptuous in creating many a small fire.

 The day moved on, the daylight quickly began to fade, and the fisherman had grown tired, so before resting his back against a small tree, he lit another fire to warm the bottoms of his feet.

 Sometime later, the buzzing flies awoke the fisherman from his slumber as the flies fought for a place on the skewered fish he had left for the stranger; suddenly reminding himself, the fisherman hastily sat up and looked around. Still, there was no sign of the stranger; after spending some time looking for him, the fisherman gave up and was quietly thankful that he'd gone; but several hours later, when he'd just finished washing in the river, the stranger suddenly appeared.

 The fisherman's expression after seeing the stranger wasn't happy but was dismayed, for he was thankful that the stranger wasn't around and was ready to set back on his journey alone.

 So, after greeting the stranger with a wry smile, the fisherman attempted to communicate to him by miming his actions and that he was leaving the area and continuing his travels alone. Curious to know whether the stranger could understand him, the answer arrived as the fisherman bent toward the ground to pick up his belongings. At that moment, the stranger approached and shoved him to stop him from leaving.

The abruptness from the stranger caused the fisherman to stand up against him and stare directly into his eyes; the fisherman suddenly looked bigger, taller, and more challenging against the stranger, leaving the stranger feeling intimidated and nervous.

The Woodhunter hadn't had this feeling before and wasn't sure how to deal with it; its first instinct was to lash out, but it knew the fisherman was too much of a challenge for it, so instead, the Woodhunter reluctantly backed off.
The fisherman looked on and couldn't help but feel sorry for the stranger, so he decided to stay instead of leaving.
The following day the fisherman was busy showing the stranger how to hunt by using many different kinds of weapons, snares, and cunning traps, which greatly irritated the stranger. For in the stranger's mind lived the Woodhunter, for it now knew that humans could threaten and stand in the way of its plans.

The stranger was becoming angrier and angrier and began showing signs that violence towards the fisherman wasn't far from his mind.

Meanwhile, the fisherman gave up on showing the stranger what hunting techniques to use, and sat beneath a leafy tree, thinking instead about the stranger and how the longer he was in his presence, the less he trusted him; from there, he quietly planned to leave at his first opportunity.

The fisherman briefly dozed off to sleep and awoke to

find the stranger peering down at his face, prodding him with his finger into his chest and muttering the words' Humans to him.

'Humans, humans,' he muttered in a strange, croaked voice. The fisherman quickly manoeuvred himself from beneath the stranger and was speechless as he stood. The stranger kept repeating himself, humans, while prodding hard at the fisherman's chest while frantically throwing his arms out in all directions. The fisherman kept calm while trying to figure out why he was saying the word humans when it suddenly dawned on him that the stranger wanted to know how many humans there were.

After studying how to answer the stranger's question, the fisherman took hold of a handful of sand and reached out to open the stranger's hand. Then, using his finger and thumb, the fisherman took a pinch of sand and sprinkled it bit by bit into the stranger's opened hand. The stranger watched on and looked at the tiny amount placed into his palm, and he then looked up at the fisherman with a pleasing look on his face.

The number of sand grains in the Woodhunters' hand was very few; if counted, there would only be around twenty or thirty pieces, which suddenly left the Woodhunter feeling powerful that so few humans lived on the new planet.

Meanwhile, the fisherman then sprinkled some more grains of sand, and the stranger looked on, puzzled, as more sprinkles of sand kept pouring from the fisherman's hand until the fisherman picked up two handfuls, which, if counted, would be the equivalent of tens of thousands of humans. The fisherman did not stop there; he continued to scoop many handfuls of sand using both hands and threw them into the air until he grew tired and eventually pointed to the stranger at the sandy beached area from where they stood.

After looking around at all the scattered sand, the stranger instantly realized that the new planet was home to countless millions of humans; with that realization, the expression on the stranger's face began to change. The fisherman could see darkness peering out from behind the stranger's eyes, and before he could prepare himself, the stranger charged at the stunned older man and grabbed him by the throat.

Quickly, the fisherman threw the stranger off, which gave him enough time to gather his senses just before the stranger went to attack him again. The fisherman promptly swept his foot across the top of the sand, bringing a cloud of sand into the stranger's eyes as he approached him. The fisherman then tightly clenched his fists and struck the stranger to the side of his head twice, causing him to stumble backwards before the fisherman moved forward with another heavy hit which caused the stranger to hit the ground and fall unconscious. This sudden attack allowed the fisherman to gather his belongings before he left; still, his conscience told him to check and see if the stranger was seriously hurt before he did. With that, the fisherman threw his sack across his shoulders and walked to where the stranger lay; he leaned forward to listen and take a closer look; he could hear that the stranger was stirring and beginning to wake, so the fisherman decided to leave the area hastily.

Meanwhile, the Woodhunter recovered, and the fisherman long disappeared into the hills and safety of the forests; the Woodhunter was still in its human form, and its encounter had left it with a bitter taste of revenge on the humans and the new planet.

The Woodhunter had learned all it needed to learn from the human, and its encounter only made it more determined than ever to make the new planet its own. Still, after learning of the number of humans there were, the

Woodhunter realized what two things it would need to be successful: was to build the tunnelled kingdom and plan for more Terror Flights. With that thought the Woodhunter uncovered the buried Emerald Green Acorn and the Emerald Key, and it again had to fight hard to gain its request to change back from the human it was. Still, when successful, it briefly searched for the areas for fisherman before returning to the forest of a million trees and the Green Planet where its army awaits.

14. THE SULPHUR SHELF BREED

The Woodhunter made its long journey back to the Green Planet, and once again, its baron lands were a stark contrast from the rivers, lakes, and forests from which the Woodhunter had recently left. More so, it was hundreds of years since the Neplèns first mysteriously arrived on the Green Planet, and during that time, they had achieved an impossible task of the death and destruction of the whole earth. Initially, the thought was that the Neplèns had become blinded by greed and that their desire to ruin a planet would have undoubtedly led them to their deaths! However, the real reason for the Neplèns' arrival would become evident that their real purpose wasn't to create an environment for themselves but for a new breed of Neplèns instead.

Upon stepping out from the Woodlock, the Woodhunter was suddenly distracted by a heavy stench of sweat and musk! Which seemed to drift out from every crevice of the valley's four corners. The air on the planet was warm, and its colour was reddish; the Woodhunter began tasting the foul stench from the reddish mist, which the breeze carried in the air until the Woodhunter distracted again, this time

by the thunderous noise of the stampeding Neplèn Army.
The noise of the Neplèns would typically only happen
when the Woodhunter called for a gathering, but that had
not happened, for on this occasion, it was different in
many ways. While the Neplèns continued to pour out from
the many tunnelled entrances, all the Neplèns, including
the Woodhunter, seemed to act out of instinct as they
wandered amongst mass groups, uncontrollably flicking
their tongues at the stench-filled air in what looked like a
bid to find a particular smell. This strange behaviour
continued for a lengthy period until it eventually stopped.
Something more unfamiliar started, for the Neplèns began
to act like stranded fish from the water, and each one
started simultaneously taking in deep gulps of air. Their
breathing became heavier, louder, and deeper until, after
another lengthy period, this too suddenly stopped, and
their breathing eased.

At that moment, the Carriers had appeared out from the
tunnelled entrances, forming long lines that stretched out
behind the gathered Neplèns.

Meanwhile, the Woodhunter had uncharacteristically crept
silently and cowardly-like between the Carriers and joined
more of the Neplèn masses; no sooner had it shunted its
way forward that puss-like fur! Yellowish in colour began
slowly seeping through the Neplèns bark-like shell's cracks.

The full scale of this bizarre event was yet to unfold, for
no sooner had the puss-like fur begun to seep through the
shells of the Neplèns than the Carriers then turned their
backs away from them and waited.

The eerie silence suddenly began to break as the
thousands upon thousands of Neplèns suddenly began to
move; while doing that, they cautiously but aggressively
crept around one another to locate a suitable area.

The bizarre behaviour lasted well into the night, and the
Carriers still stood with their backs turned against the
Neplèns.

Eventually, the Neplèns' bodies became so thoroughly covered in the yellowish fur-like puss that they could no longer move from where they had chosen to stand. The reddish mist had grown more potent as it steadily rose and hovered above the heads of the Neplèns.

The Neplèns were unrecognizable due to the amount of yellowish fur covering their bodies, and everything seemed to stop momentarily, and again there was an eerie silence. Suddenly the reddish mist began to fall from above the Neplèns' heads, and all but several thousand Neplèns started to stamp up and down on the ground frantically. The fur covering them began to crumble and roll from their bodies before coming to rest on the ground, forming a vast pile of ball-shaped pellets.

The Neplèns then tentatively began to make their way to the tunnels, cautiously walking around all the mounds of pellets in the hope of not destroying one.

Meanwhile, several thousand other Neplèns remained at the spot they had chosen. They waited for the reddish mist above their heads to fall around them, which it did and caused the yellowish fur not to fall like pellets to the ground but instead to run like liquid from their bodies. While the fur-like coats ran from their bodies, the Neplèns who once stood there were no longer Neplèns but now changed to become Carriers.

Meanwhile, the other Carriers waited, still with their backs turned against the army of Neplèns, and it wasn't until the last one had disappeared into the blackness of the tunnel entrance that they had turned. Before the Carriers began to make their way through the mounds of pellets, they stared out beneath the foul stench of the reddish haze and sniffed inquisitively in the air. Then, after only a short period, the Carriers hastily made their way to the centre, surrounded by umpteen million pellets, where they, once again, waited. Almost at once, the reddish mist that had hovered and fallen above the Neplèns' heads suddenly began to rise

again until it had submerged every one of the mounds.
 The morning sun had risen and somehow managed to
throw out some brightness from behind the dense smog,
but it shimmered pointlessly and aimlessly in the dim light
and had failed to throw any warmth down towards the
Green Planet's surface. But strangely! Beneath the reddish
mist which began to drift in and around the mounds of fur
pellets, temperatures had risen higher and higher,
becoming almost unbearable for the Carriers as they stood
and waited.
 As the reddish mist continued to drift in and around the
mounds of fur pellets, the temperature beneath stopped
rising, and the fur-like balls began to melt until they
became transformed into some pod-like cocoon covered in
a hardened resin-like shell. Then, quickly and suddenly, the
reddish mist dispersed, and so did the Carriers; in different
directions, they began to roam the area, and with great
care, they began examining each pod they had chosen.
 It had taken several days for the Carriers to examine all
the pods thoroughly, and the selection process began after
achieving this.
 Selecting the chosen pods was a slow process, but after
the Carriers achieved this, they would pick up their
preferred pods and place them into a sack beneath their
hardened shells, and the countless other pods were then
left.

 The hazy sun was about to set on the Green Planet, and
the bizarre, instinctive behaviour of the Neplèns and
Carriers had now ended. The Carriers had now made their
way back into the tunnels, where they would remain until
their pods spored, leaving a vast area of unselected pods
behind them.

 Meanwhile, the Woodhunter and the Neplèns began to
appear and spill out onto the surface of the Green Planet.
They frantically paced the area from where the mounds of

fur pellets were left and started sniffing at the rest of the pods as they tried to distinguish whether they would be the bearer of one of the Sulphur Shelf Breeds.

The Woodhunter didn't waste any time, for the time for spore had ended, so it immediately called for a gathering of all but the Carriers to attend, where it would tell them of its time learning about the humans of the new planet. It at once told them of the countless numbers of humans on the new world and how important it was to build the tunnelled kingdom beneath the forest of a million trees so that Neplèns, Carriers, and the generation of Sulphur Shelf Breed could make the world their own. The Woodhunter added that the third season was soon ending, and their year of two would shortly begin; with that, the Woodhunter opened the Woodlock before also opening the Silverlatch, reminding them that food from the new planet would have to be brought through the Woodlock so that the Carriers could feed.

Meanwhile, several weeks had passed, and while the Neplèns and Carriers fed from the forest of a million trees, the Woodhunter and the Terror Flights were planning hard for the eventual invasion of the new planet. However, plans to begin building the tunnelled kingdom beneath the forest of a million trees would wait until the Neplèns year of two had finished. During the meeting with the Terror Flights, the Woodhunter shared concerns about the number of humans who inhabited the new planet, how its weather was unpredictable, and how both could damage the trunk of the Rare Silver Oak during their year of two. So, the Woodhunter and two Terror Flights set about finding a safer place to shelter and hide the trunk and immediately set off across the skies of the new planet.

The Woodhunter and the Terror Flights' journey was relatively short and took them across a large ocean to an island surrounded by deep waters. The island had many hills and mountains, and it was soon that the Woodhunter found a suitable place to hide the Rare Silver Oaks trunk. The Terror Flights searched from the dark skies above the area from where the Woodhunter had chosen and were satisfied that there was no sign of human life. The hillside that the Woodhunter selected had rock and slate, and surrounded by it were leafy weeds, thorn-like shrubbery, and a small forest.

The Woodhunter ordered the Terror Flights to go with it to where the Rare Silver Oaks trunk would eventually become somewhat buried. From there, the Woodhunter ordered the Terror Flights to dig deep into the rocky hillside and prepare it for the arrival of the Rare Silver Oaks trunk before ordering them to return to the forest of a million trees and return with the oak.

While the Woodhunter waited for the return of the Terror Flights, it had made its way through the makeshift tunnels, which brought it further inside the hill to the area where the Rare Silver Oak would stay. The Woodhunter scurried around the insides of the cave, familiarising itself with the surroundings before tearing
through the rock and slate at the cave-like wall so that the Terror Flights could bring the oak directly through and into the cave they prepared. And it was not long before the Terror Flights returned and placed the Rare Silver Oak trunk inside its makeshift tomb, where it would stay for two years.

After placing the Emerald Green Acorn inside the Woodlock, the Woodhunter took one last look around the cave and ordered the Terror Flights through to the Green Planet. Then, briefly, the Woodhunter glanced out through the cave wall hole and peered out over the tops of the moonlit forest, and only then did it leave the Rare Golden Oak in the cave's darkness.

Back through the Woodlock and on the Green Planet, the

Woodhunter spent that final night staring into the Emerald Green Acorn, searching for anything else it needed to know before the year of two approached. Satisfied, the Woodhunter called for one final gathering before they retreated to the tunnels for their year of two. At the gathering, the Woodhunter spoke of times after the year of two, telling how everything was in place for the takeover of the new planet. It said how tens of thousands of Terror Flights would gain flight and how triumphantly, with the help of the sulphur shelf breed would help rid its earth of humans, change its environment to suit their needs, and make it their own. The Woodhunter then ordered them to their caves before spending its final moments in its den staring into the Emerald Green Acorn, continually searching for anything else it needed to know before finally falling asleep for the next two years.

Meanwhile, far across the new planet, a small cloud of golden mist gathered and steadily fell from the skies above, where the winds carried it across the mountains, valleys, and hills before travelling through the hole in the hillside and into the Rare Silver Oaks Silverlatch. Suddenly the trunk glowed a golden colour, and with it, a voice calling for it to wake up was Mother Nature. She told the Rare Silver Oak that all wasn't lost, that someone higher than herself had intervened and created the golden mist; she spoke of how the winds carried it through the Woodlock from the Green Planet and how it waited for Neplèns year of two to arrive. Mother Nature explained why she hadn't been in contact with the Rare Silver Oak because the Woodhunter was awake and still possessed the Emerald Green Acorn and the Emerald Key, and she didn't want it to know any part of the following plan. Mother Nature assured the Rare Silver Oak how through its ordeal, she never once left its side; and was with it the whole time. She then went on to add how she was given the golden mist as a gift for the Rare Silver Oak and that she was to tell it that the mist is the 'spirit of the acorn' and to let the spirit of the acorn guide you, for it is from the creator.

15. DESTINIES DECISION

The Wooden King had now finished and had, for the
time being, explained all he needed to explain; for now, he
waited for the silence within the cave to break before
asking them for their help to try and save the world.

Meanwhile, the girls sat speechless for a short while; it was
hard for them to understand what they'd learned and even
more challenging even to dare think of what would be
requested of them next, for there were still many questions
that needed an answer. They knew many and were
required to ask, and Melody was the first to begin.
'Would I be right in thinking that somehow you are, or
you were the Rare Golden Oak and that the trunk before
us is the Rare Silver Oak, and that it was brought here by
the Woodhunter and the Terror Flights'? She nervously
asked.
'Yes, Melody, you are correct in thinking that because I
am that of the Rare Golden Oak, or at least from it, and it
is also true that the trunk I am in was brought here by the
Woodhunter and the Terror Flights.'
'So, if it's true that the new planet is, in fact, this planet
and that it is the one the Woodhunter and the Neplèns are

to attack, then tell me! Before you ask us the obvious, how
do you suppose only three girls can stop them? It's
ridiculous', interrupted Holly arrogantly
Jasmine's outburst immediately caused the girls to fall out
with one another, and a confrontation between all three
nearly got out of hand.
Not once between the slurs and insults the girls were
throwing at one another had the Wooden King
interrupted, for he expected this and knew that emotions
would undoubtedly be running high. But at any rate, their
quarrel was short-lived and was soon over when Jasmine
asked the Wooden King about the golden mist.

The Wooden King's reply was immediate, for he answered
Jasmine's question quickly and explained how he had let
the spirit of the acorn guide him and how by doing so, it
led him to them. The Wooden King added that the only
way to stop the Woodhunter and its army from invading
the planet was only achievable with their help and that they
would need to accept the Spirit of the Acorn to do that.

The girls gasped at what the Woodhunter had just said,
and each took a moment to stare at the other while trying
to make sense of it all, and the Woodhunter took a
moment before continuing.
'Before I present to you the spirit of the acorn that I had
given me, remember I only ask for your help, so please
remember that you have a choice when deciding. When I
received the Spirit of the Acorn, it was another chance to
put things right and another opportunity to learn and
prepare for what was about to unfold, and I did this during
the Woodhunters' year of two. I wanted to avoid another
situation like that of the Rare Silver Oak, where there
needed to be more time to learn; I didn't want the same
mistake to happen again. Since receiving the Spirit of the
Acorn, I have learned all I can from it and planned all that
is left to prepare, for the Woodhunters' time to wake is

almost here. So, your time to decide before it does have to come quickly, for my learning has now ended, and yours could be about to start. So, my plans are why you are here and why I received the Spirit of the Acorn.

The Wooden King paused momentarily before continuing, but long enough to gauge the girl's reactions before he did. However, they seemed content to listen some more as he explained what they would need the spirit of the acorn for and how it would help them, should they choose to offer their help. So, the Wooden King continued by showing them the spirit of the acorn.

'Here it is,' said the Wooden King, opening up his hands to display a golden silk-like mist travelling around his branch-like fingers.
The girls watched as it floated out from his hands to where they sat on the hovering leaves, where it gently swirled around their faces and made playful wisps at their hair, almost like a gesture or a greeting. The girls laughed as they tried to shoo it away several times, but their fingers passed straight through it before the spirit left them and returned to the hands of the Wooden King. The Wooded King then continued to explain, and the girls listened whilst continuing to watch as the golden mist moved like a soft fabric between his fingers.

'Only when I tell you about the spirit of the acorn will you understand how magical its power is, and only if you accept the challenge to stop the Woodhunter can I pass it to you. There are many wondrous things that the spirit of the acorn can do, and those things are there to protect and help you in case things don't go according to plan, although it is the hope that won't be the case. However, if you wish to accept the challenge and the spirit of the acorn, you will only need to open your hands, and it will disappear through the pores of your skin and travel around your body like that of your blood. After receiving the spirit, you and it will become one, although you will not notice much change within yourself. If at any time you doubt being without the spirit, you can request to see it, and it will appear within your hand in the form of a golden acorn; this is solely for reassurance so that you can trust it will remain with you at all times and that its magic won't have to be requested, for the sake of knowing you have it. However, there is something vital that you should know! After the acorn appears in the palms of your hands, you cannot place it anywhere, nor can it be thrown or exchanged with one another, nor can it be forcibly taken, and therefore it is impossible to lose. The only way you will be without the spirit of the acorn is if you pass it to another by using your own free will, but there would be no need to do that, and besides, the Woodlock will only remain open to those who have the spirit of the acorn with them.

The spirit of the acorn will hold different magical powers, enabling you to change for short periods into countless creatures, large and small! Any beast from past and present times, the spirit of the acorn, will also grant each of you to become an element of the weather; although this request is only allowed for minimal periods, it can serve well if used correctly. During your transformation into something other than yourself, nothing can harm you; however, the animal or creature you choose to become is real and will act on your instinct; it will defend itself, and if threatened and has the ability, it will kill. But remember, whichever animal or creature you choose can become hurt and even die! And should that happen, your true self appears and will be open to attack, and you could be hurt if you don't quickly transform into something else; remember, the spirit of the acorn will not grant the same request twice, for instance, if you request to be that of a bird, you can choose many of different types of bird, but not the same.

The magical powers you receive will be the same strength, and although your capabilities will differ from one to another, you will be all taught equally, and to that of such a level that it will almost feel like you have been born with this gift. One last thing you should heed is that the more requests you need, the more tiresome you will become, which could lead to confusion, so think carefully and use the spirit of the acorn wisely. Finally, should the time come that you have decided to receive the spirit of the acorn, then there will be no purpose left for my present being; I will have to go. But what will remain is this trunk, the hollow, and the Silverlatch, which will remain open, allowing you the passageway through and back from the Green Planet.

If you decide to help, It is essential that the timing of your arrival on the Green Planet is within several days and before the Woodhunter and its Neplèn army awake from their year of two; however, that should not matter for neither the Woodhunter nor any Neplèn would know of your arrival for you will leave no trace or scent of you being there, for Mother Nature will take care of that, you will also not need food or water while time on this planet has stopped. After you have arrived on the Green Planet, and if it is safe, the spirit will guide you directly to the Emerald Green Acorn and the Emerald Key, which the Woodhunter will be wearing from around its neck; all you must do is request the spirit to lead. Once achieved, the plan will be to remove the Emerald Green Acorn and the Emerald Key and hastily make your way back through the Woodlock, leaving the Woodhunter and the Neplèns imprisoned on the planet they destroyed.

From the moment you return from the Green Planet, the Woodlock and this Silverlatch will close, and this trunk will crumble to only dust; within that dust, I would ask you to bury the Emerald Green Acorn and the Emerald Key. Immediately after you have done this, you will all feel a pleasant though strange sensation, and that will be the spirit of the acorn leaving your mind and body to join with the Emerald Green Acorn and the Emerald Key. Soon after, the dust pile will glow a warm golden colour until everything disappears, leaving a rare golden acorn in its place. You will then take the golden acorn on its final journey to where we shall replant and leave it to grow, but the location to which you take it will have to remain a secret, a secret that will have to be kept, even from you. The final part of the journey won't be through any Woodlocks or suchlike but through a rainbow, which will take you on a short journey to a place where the new Golden Oak will live.

So that was that! The Wooden King had now explained everything he could to the girls and waited through a short spell of silence for their answer.

'I can't pretend I'm not frightened, but at the same time, I think we all want to help! But why us? Is all this easier if dealt with by the adults, say the army or something? Holly asked.

The Woodhunters expression suddenly changed from apprehension to vague, and his reply came with a strong hint of disagreement.

'It's not for me to judge, although sometimes specific issues like this need addressing, but, Holly, you have asked a reasonable question; countless others would have asked the same thing, but! Adults and armies are equally as destructive as the Neplèns, for they continue to pillage, ravage, waste, and destroy the only planet they have. It wouldn't be fair to blame everyone, and that isn't what I intend to do because I know most people are kind, loving, and unselfish. Still, a small minority cares for nothing other than greed and self-interest and are more like the Neplèns than we dare to think, the kind who will stop at nothing to tear down what they inherit until nothing is left. That small minority believes they are not a part of anything around them, not even when nature screams out at them to see and hear it; they hear and see nothing because they do not see it as a living, breathing thing. Inviting such kind to see tools like the Emerald Green Acorn and everything surrounding that would be unimaginable beyond comprehension. So, Holly, that is why it can't be armies or suchlike and must be the three of you because you see it, hear it, and are one with it; for each one of you owns inner energy, and that energy attracted, not only me to you but the spirit of the acorn also.

The Wooden King continued to reassure the girls by answering as many questions as they cared to ask, but time outside the cave had now stopped long enough, and so came the moment for the girls to answer the Wooden King's question.

'Have you all reached your decision, and are you now ready to help and receive the spirit of the acorn,' asked the Wooden King.

The girls nervously looked at one another; Jasmine reached out for the other two to take hold and led them to the opening of the cave wall; silently, they stood and stared out before Jasmine reminded them of what was worth saving. Jasmine and Holly then noticed a slight nod of the head Holly was making; they turned with a little glint of something in each of their eyes as they turned towards the Wooden King, and instantaneously, their reply came.

'Yes, we will help, and we are ready,' replied the girls, laughing nervously to deal with their mixed emotions.

A wry smile appeared on the Wooden King's face, and instantly the dark hollow shone brightly with a golden colour.

'Then I thank you, although your answer has somewhat surprised me, your courage, love, and strength don't, and so it shall begin.'

The Wooden King reached out his hands to again display the spirit of the acorn; he then requested that the girls close their eyes, and it was at that moment when they heard the gentle voice of Mother Nature whispering words into their ears.

'Children,
you are so precious, so honest, so true,
and with god's love, I give to you,
this mothering message,
to be etched in your hearts,
to be carried along with you,
and never apart.

From the woodlands, fields, and all that grows,
to the streams, rivers, and seas that flow,
from the insects, mammals, birds, and bees,
from the sun, moon, and all in between.

For all that is your future,
and yesterday your past,
tomorrow lays in your hands,
for it has yet to pass.

So, go with strength and courage,
and fight for all that you love,
shine a light on the darkness,
and never give up.
Open your hands, hearts, and minds,
and let the Spirit of the Acorn guide.

Then no sooner had the voice from that of Mother Nature left the girls that a strange, indescribable feeling suddenly fell upon them! Their fears and concerns were no longer, and Mother Nature answered their remaining questions. The Wooden King then asked the girls to open their eyes, which they did, but only to find that he had gone. The girls didn't look surprised, nor had they questioned anything regarding this sudden disappearance, for they had already known that this would happen, even

though they hadn't realized it was to happen so suddenly.
'Oh look, he's gone,' cried Melody.
'Is that the last time we see him then' asked Jasmine.
'I don't know, probably not,' replied Holly, adding how
sweet Mother Nature and her voice were.
'What about this is a strange feeling I have. Do you two
have it also' asked Jasmine.
'I know I have the spirit of the acorn, but I can't feel it; it's
hard to make any sense of it?' replied Melody.
'Yeah, that's how I feel too; I'm not quite sure; I think my
spirit is telling me we should go,' replied Jasmine. 'What
about you, Melody? How do you feel?' She added.
'I also feel the same; we definitely should go; my spirit
tells me I'm hungry,' laughed Melody.

The noise outside the cave suddenly grew louder through
the girls' laughter, and the whole planet seemed to burst
into life. The girls then realized that the time outside had
started again, and now was the right time to leave the cave
and return home.

Through the girls' laughter, the noise outside the cave
suddenly grew louder, and the whole planet seemed to
burst into life. The girls then realised that the time outside
had started again, and now was the right time to leave the
cave and return home.

16. REALITY HITS HOME

Throughout the time it had taken for the girls to walk home, they had done nothing other than ask the spirit of the acorn questions; the questions they had asked were of all types. For instance, Melody learned some of the magical power she owned, for she could ask, amongst many other things, fifty million spiders or those of its kind, up to one thousand felines and those of its kind, and one hundred prehistoric animals of any kind. And Jasmine learned some of her magical powers, for amongst many other singular things, she could ask that of two thousand grizzly bears or those of its kind, one hundred mythical creatures, and the ability to clone herself. And lastly was Holly, who had also learned some magical powers. Among others, she could request that of a thousand woolly mammoths, two thousand Rhinoceros, and five thousand silverback guerrillas.

The more questions the girls asked, the greater their gifts seemed.

'This is just mind-boggling,' said Jasmine.

'Yep, it is; how does anyone even become a thousand woolly mammoths,' laughed Holly.

'Well, how about fifty million spiders? What about that? What can you do with that many' Melody jokingly asked.

The girls laughed and poked fun at one another about how they were already the things they spoke about, and throughout their journey home, their mood was excitement; before the girls realised, they'd approached their front garden gate.

'I never thought how a front gate could look so normal,' Jasmine jokingly said.

The girl's laughter and the rattling of the gate alerted Charlie, who began to bark from the back garden; this then alerted Dad, who was busily slurping his morning coffee.
'I don't remember expecting any visitors.' Dad muttered to Charlie while trying to make himself presentable by desperately trying to flatten his uncombed hair.
'Hello, I'm round the back; come to the back door.' He shouted.
'Hello, Dad!' replied Jasmine, 'It's only us'.
'Oh, right!' Replied a puzzled-looking dad. 'Where are you going at this time in the morning,' he added.
'Charlie,' screamed Melody as she raced past Dad.
'Easy,' Dad said while raising his cup up and away from Melody's head as she raced to greet Charlie. 'You're acting like you haven't seen him in a lifetime; what has gotten into you?'.
'We weren't going anywhere, Dad; we've just got back, said Jasmine, suddenly remembering when she received a sharp jolt from Holly's elbow.
'What! You've just got back,' replied Dad.
'I meant we've just got to the back of the house,' answered a flustered Jasmine.
'This is strange, isn't it, Jasmine? I feel we've been gone days,' said Holly. 'Come on, let's get some breakfast,' she added.

Throughout breakfast, the girls managed to gather their thoughts and had only just come to terms with what had happened, they were still excited but could see a sense of worry hiding behind each other's eyes, but neither spoke about it.

Dad came clattering into the kitchen with some tools from the garage and whistling some little ditty; the noise he was making added a sense of normality to an uncomfortable silence, which livened the place up a little and caused the girls to stop worrying.
'Dad, what are you doing today?' asked Melody.
'The garden and that back door handle,' replied Dad, pointing his finger at the kitchen door.
'No way!' added Jasmine.
'Yep, why, what's wrong with that,' he replied with a grin, for he knew what was coming.
'We've lived here for almost two years, and every day we've had to swing on that handle to open that door, and you ask us what's wrong with that,' laughed Holly.
'Let us help you in the garden, Dad,' requested Melody.
'Help me in the garden,' he shockingly replied, you never help in the garden.'
'Well, today we want to help,' replied Melody, acting like her request was not unusual.

In shock, Dad stopped what he was doing for a moment and scratched at his chin,
'Well, come on then,' he replied.
After everything the girls had been through, the garden was the last thing on their minds; however, they wanted a piece of normality, and helping Dad mow the lawn didn't seem like such a wrong place to start.

By now, it was just after lunch, and the girls had just finished helping out around the garden when Mum arrived to take advantage of their unusual offer to help by giving them piles of washing to hang out, a brush to sweep the path, and a cloth to clean the windows.

It was still early afternoon when the girls finished helping around the house and garden. The day still had plenty of sunshine to offer, so they spent the rest of that afternoon sitting outside, throwing the ball for Charlie, chatting, and quietly learning what they could from the spirit of the acorn, but that was proving to be too difficult.

'There's so much to see; I can't keep up with it all; no sooner have I requested to see a memory than the spirit shows me; it's all too fast, and I feel like my head will explode,' whispered Jasmine.

'Imagine if it did, just imagine your head exploded; then we'd be covered in sawdust,' laughed Melody.

'She's right, Melody, Holly said, and why do you always have to make a joke out of things; I think we should start practising how to use the spirit of the acorn properly; remember what the Wooden King said, we only have several days before the end of the Woodhunters year of two,' added Holly.

'Well, I'm ready when you are,' replied Melody; stop being so serious,' she added before laying back on the grass and squinting at the sun.

'That's just your problem, isn't it?' Replied Jasmine, jokingly pouncing on her, 'You never are serious, are you?' she added, as they rolled around the grass, encouraging Holly and Charlie to join in.

The day soon passed, and teatime came and eventually went, for it seemed to last an eternity! Because the girls' appetite was not near what it usually was, for they spent half their time hiding the cheese beneath the lettuce, sliding the tomatoes across the plate, and trying hard to bury everything else beneath an ever-growing pile of unwanted food. Still, there was one whose appetite never changed, and that was Charlie, for he was more than happy to continue to sit underneath the table and wait for his seemingly endless flow of sausage rolls and quiche.

Meanwhile, the house finally settled in the early evening, and Mum and Dad were busy watching TV. At the same time, Holly, Jasmine, and Melody made their way to their bedroom, deciding that the time had come for them to try and familiarise themselves with the spirit of the acorn, the Green Planet, the Woodhunter, and the magic they now possessed.

The girls made themselves comfortable on the bed, and for the benefit of Mum and Dad, they played some music to add a bit of background noise before they started. They each sat in the middle of Holly's bed; it was bigger, and with their backs leaned against the wall, holding hands, they requested the spirit of the acorn to show them memories of the Woodhunters' den. No sooner had they done this when the spirit immediately showed the dark path of the tunnel's entrance leading them down and into the darkness of the Woodhunters cave below.

'Stop! That is well spooky,' said Holly; 'hang on a minute, I'm not ready for that,' she added while shaking her hands and shoulders in readiness.

'Right, are you ready now, Holly? What do we ask for next' asked Jasmine.

'Let's see the distance between the tunnel entrance and the Rare Golden Oaks, Woodlock,' replied Melody. It'll give us an idea of how far and fast we have to run from the Neplèns,' she joked while Holly and Jasmine rolled their eyes at her.

In the meantime, when the girls settled, the spirit granted the request, and again the vision was instant; the girls watched the Woodhunter making its way from the cave entrance to the top of the hill and the Woodlock.

'Well, at least we now know it's not too far for us to

travel, right? Said Jasmine. It shouldn't take us long to take the Emerald Green Acorn and the Emerald Key and reach the Woodlock,' she added.

The memory requests went on for some time, and the girls were going backwards and forward, learning what they could from the spirit of the acorn and most of the critical things they needed to learn about the Woodhunter. After some time, the girls' attention went from trying to understand what quickest routes to take when on the Green Planet to how to work together in case things didn't go to plan.

'I'm going to request to talk to you both,' said Melody.
'What do you mean?' replied Jasmine.
'Shush a minute,' added Melody.

Melody closed her eyes and requested to communicate with Holly and Jasmine; she thought only the words, 'can you hear me?'
Both Holly and Jasmine instantly jumped from where they were sitting, which caused Melody to jump, too.
'That was so weird, so weird; I heard you; you were echoing inside my head,' yelled Jasmine.
'I heard you too; wow, that was a crazy moment,' exclaimed Holly.
'Come on, let's do some more,' asked Melody eagerly.
It wasn't long before the girls had lengthy conversations about all kinds of things without speaking; still, the novelty of having that gift wore off as they began to drive each other mad, with the sounds of each of their voices echoing inside their heads.
'Right, come on, we'll do a little more of something else,' requested Jasmine, 'I want to see the Neplèn army, and then we'll go down for supper; we can always do some more tomorrow,' she added.

So the girls sat back and again requested to see the spirit of the acorn's most recent memory of the Neplèn army. Immediately the girls could almost believe that they were standing on the hilltop staring down at the Neplèns, and their readiness to see such a sight was one they'd taken for granted, for the view was frightening and by far the worst they had seen. The visions the acorn's spirit then showed were of the menacing sights of the Terror Flights and equally those of the Carriers; although the Carriers looked equally as hideous to that of the Neplèns, the girls sensed from them no immediate fear.

All the visions the girls had seen were just what the Wooden King had already told them, but the images were far more significant than those of his words, and it wasn't long after that the girls had witnessed enough and had requested for the spirit of the acorn to show them no more.

'Listen, how about we take Charlie for a quick walk? It's only eight o'clock, and the sun is still out; when we get back, we'll have a bit of supper and watch TV in bed, and we'll not request anything from the spirit of the acorn until tomorrow,' said Melody. 'Because we've done enough for today, I'd like to spend some time with Mum and Dad,' she added.
'Yeah, you're right, Melody,' said Holly as she shuffled off the bed, 'I'm thirsty; I'm going to get a drink.' 'Are you coming'? She added before racing out of the bedroom and slamming the door shut.

All the while, Jasmine stared at Melody as she stood staring at the floor, for It wasn't often to hear Melody being serious, nor was it often that she'd be upset, but that was just what she was, for her eyes suddenly welled up with tears, and her chin began to quiver. But these were the times when Jasmine showed her true colours; for she had seen the signs and quickly threw her arms around the neck of Melody.

'Are you alright, Melody' asked Jasmine.

'Yeah, I'm fine'! 'It's just Mum and Dad; I wish they could come with us,' she replied.

'We don't have to go, Melody; we don't have to do any of this if you don't want to.'

'It's not that I don't want to go and help; I do, and it's not because I'm scared, because I'm not, well, not really,' replied Melody. 'It's just, I know I'm going to Miss Mum, Dad, and Charlie, that's all. What if something goes wrong and we can't get back,' she added.

It wasn't as though Jasmine hadn't already felt or thought the same way as Melody; for she kept the same concerns that Melody had hidden away in the hope that nobody would have to talk about them. But quietly, Jasmine was relieved that Holly was now talking openly and honestly about all their concerns.

'Melody, we'll discuss this properly when Holly returns, but let me tell you this! We'll be fine, all of us'. 'We'll be in and out of the Green Planet and back home before we know it,' Jasmine said.

Meanwhile, Holly returned to the bedroom, and teary eyes greeted her. Still, within moments they were all laughing when Holly exclaimed why she left the bedroom in such a hurry after Melody mentioned wanting to spend time with Mum, Dad, and Charlie, that she was upset and had to hurry out.

'You're not the only one worried or concerned, Melody,' Said Holly. 'It's only natural; if any of us decide we don't want to do this, we say so, are we agreed?

'Yeah,' replied both Jasmine and Melody.

The girls took a moment with their arms around each other, huddled together to support one another before carrying on with their evening the best way they could.

 It was hard trying to be as normal as possible and act like everything was the same as before, but it wasn't the same, for what lay ahead was hard for them to comprehend, and the reality of that had hit Home.

17. A RUDE AWAKENING

   The night had slowly ebbed away, and the girls were now fast asleep in their beds. They tossed and turned silently as they struggled to keep cool throughout a hot and humid night. Even the curtains and windows, open as they were, hadn't served many purposes, for the only things they had let in other than that of a slight breeze, were a couple of disorientated moths, distracted by that of the landing light which beamed through the gaps around the girls' bedroom door.
 The darkness outside was beginning to fade, the fluttering noises made by the moths had lessened, and all outdoors was peaceful and quiet. When suddenly Charlie stirred from his sleep and raised his head from the basket he lay in, his ears weren't the kind to point straight upward whenever he heard a peculiar noise, but instead, they would raise a little and slightly flicker.
 By this time, his head was moving slightly from one side to the other while trying to figure out what he was hearing; the only trouble was there was nothing to hear. Charlie then moved from his bed and climbed onto an old junk box that stood beneath the window, where he rested his two front paws onto the window ledge to peer out; while

doing this, he whimpered quietly and peered across at the sleeping girls with a sad expression on his face. He remained where he was for a short time before jumping onto the window ledge and poking his nose through the gap in the opened window, where he sniffed the air outside. What happened next was very unusual for a calm dog like Charlie, for his lips puckered upwards, baring his teeth as he began to snarl and growl at whatever he had sensed outside.

Although Charlie wasn't happy from what he had sensed, for anything else, the mood outside the window was calming, for the dawn chorus chimed, and a new day suddenly sprung to life, and with it, so did Melody, for she too suddenly awoke; and was soon followed by Jasmine and Holly.

It hadn't taken long before all three girls were sat up and awake in their beds; at first thought, it had seemed that the girls had either woken to the noises which Charlie made or because of the dawn chorus and the different sounds the birds made outside. Still, neither of those was why they had suddenly awoken from their sleep, for the real reason was that the acorn's spirit had acted on its own to purposely stir their rest to show them an untimely new vision. It seemed strange that the girls didn't request to see the images and more so that they could not help but see what the spirit of the acorn was showing them, for the visions appeared before their eyes like a projection used in a cinema.

The girls barely had time to wipe their sleepy eyes before seeing the sights of the Woodhunter, who had already awoken several days early from its year of two. They quietly continued to watch from their beds as the Woodhunter left the tunnels alone, and before any of the other Neplèns awoke, it made its way to the Rare Golden Oak trunk and stepped into the Woodlock. The following visions, which the spirit of the acorn had shown the girls, came as a shock to them and made them sit up, wake up and take note, for it showed the Woodhunter stepping into the green mist before stepping out of the Rare Silver Oaks Silverlatch, and into the cave from where the girls had been just the day before.

From that moment, the girls realized the significance of what they had seen and the reason behind their rude awakening, for it suddenly dawned on them that any plan they now had at retrieving the acorns from around the neck of the Woodhunter was now in tatters.

The visions continued to show that of the Woodhunter, creeping around the cave, examining the disturbed earth, and sniffing hard at the stale air as it steadily circulated throughout the corkscrewed tunnels. Suddenly the visions stopped and were replaced by a voice, the Wooden King's.

Before telling the girls about the Woodhunters' untimely visit to the cave, the Wooden King first exclaimed that there wasn't much time to explain what happened, but their readiness to act was paramount. The Wooden King then tried to ease the girls' minds by telling them that he hadn't thought the Woodhunter had suspected they had visited the cave and shouldn't worry.

However, the Wooden King needed to be clear about his main concern: could Holly, Jasmine, and Melody still try to retrieve the acorns from around the Woodhunters neck?

'This has come as a surprise for all of us,' said the voice of the Wooden King. 'However, the stark reality of the situation is it is now inevitable you will all have to come face to face with the Woodhunter to retrieve the acorns. The only way you can succeed is by using the magical powers the spirit of the acorn has given,' the Wooden King added.

The Girls looked across at one another with shocked expressions on their faces.

'How do we use the magical powers' Jasmine asked the Wooden King. 'We need more time to learn them,' she added.

'Remember to let the spirit guide you,' replied the Wooden King.

'But can't you slow the Woodhunter down to allow us more time' asked a worried-looking Holly, 'I remember you were saying we wouldn't need to use much magic because the plan wouldn't take long,' added Holly.

'I'm sorry, I can't slow the Woodhunter down, and I'm also sorry for getting it wrong, for it does seem you will need as much of the magic at your disposal; we haven't the time to correct things; the only chance we have at stopping the Woodhunter now is to visit the Green Planet and take the acorns from the Woodhunter and close the Woodlock for good,' replied the Wooden King.

The Wooden King's message had lasted only a short time, but before his voice left the girls, he told them again that their time was running out and that they needed to act immediately to stand any chance of stopping the Woodhunter and its army. He said to them that the Rare Silver Oak would probably be taken from the cave and brought back to the forest of a million trees and that their chance to do anything to stop the Woodhunter would be lost forever, and with that, the Wooden King's voice disappeared.

The girls knew from this moment that things would be difficult and that it wouldn't matter how they approached the situation. They still had to decide on a plan without knowing if the Woodhunter was one step ahead and had already planned for their arrival on the Green Planet.

'What shall we do' whispered Holly.

'Well, I say we do what we were going to do, and that's to help the Wooden King,' replied Jasmine.

'I was hoping you would say that,' said Holly, 'And what about you, Melody? You've been quiet; what do you think?' she added.

'I think,' replied Melody while rubbing her sleepy eyes, 'we should get up, get ready, have some breakfast and kick the Woodhunters ass.'

It was the oddest thing that the girls began to laugh, given the circumstances they now found themselves in, but they seemed surprisingly confident, unafraid, and fearless.
Quietly the girls began to get washed and dressed, but no matter how careful, they could not help but stand upon the squeaky landing floorboards outside the bedroom doors, for every time they stood upon them, they squeaked and caused mum or dad to shuffle around their bed. Eventually, they managed to creep onto the staircase, but it was like the house had taken on a life of its own, for each step seemed to have a new louder squeak than any time before. It wasn't until they'd crept downstairs and sat around the dining room table that they realized all their sneaking around wouldn't account for much because they wouldn't be able to leave the house at such an early time anyway, for it wasn't even 5 am. So, wondering what to do next, the girls continued to sit and ponder their next move. The kitchen's silence met with the clock's ticking and Charlie's nails as they hit against the hardwood flooring of the kitchen floor, for he seemed to have other ideas as he made his way back upstairs to sleep in Mum and Dad's room.
'I've got an idea,' claimed Melody, 'we'll write a list of things we should take with us.'
'Things like what, Melody?' asked Jasmine.
'I don't know,' replied Melody. 'Things like,' she added, unable to finish what she was saying.
'Like what, Sandwiches, Pop, Sweets, and Biscuits! We're not going on a picnic, Melody, or hadn't you noticed' laughed Jasmine.
'Listen, we have to be serious about this; we have to sort something out; we can't just sit around waiting and doing nothing, scowled Holly, aiming most of the responsibility at Jasmine.

'What can we sort out? What reason do we give Mum or Dad for wanting to go out at five o'clock in the morning'? Jasmine yelled. 'And, let's be honest, it's not like we are going on some fantastic day out, so excuse me for not doing cartwheels across the floor in excitement or being the overly frilled creator of a master plan on how to save the world,' she added.

'Nobody said you had to be Jasmine; this plan has to be decided by us all; we either agree to go ahead with this, or we don't; we need to be sure, and it doesn't look to me that neither of you two is bothered,' snapped Holly.

'We are bothered, but we can't do anything until at least 10 am.', exclaimed Melody; even then, we'll have to explain the need to go off so early.

'We first need to make sure that this is what we all want to do, and when deciding, we've got to remember that we have no idea what to expect, so think carefully before answering,' Holly said before asking Jasmine. 'Do you swear that you want to go ahead with this'?

'Yes, I swear it is what I want to do,' replied Jasmine.

'And Melody,' Holly again asked, 'do you also swear that you want to do this.'

'Yes, I swear this is what I want to do; now, does this mean we can get on with it because? I want to return as soon as possible, climb back into bed, and stay there for a week'.

The girls' giggles were interrupted suddenly by the Wooden King's voice; unbeknown to them, he had been waiting, for he also needed to know whether they were sure about what they were about to do. He told them they need not worry about waiting, for the time outside had once more been stopped.

The girls raced to the living room window to view for themselves the sight outside; they then ran up the stairs and across the landing before peeking their heads into Mum, and Dad's bedroom, not that it mattered much to

Mum and Dad because for them, time to had also stopped. The girls giggled loudly at the sight of Charlie lying at the foot of the bed with his paws in the air, his head tilted to one side, and his tongue sticking out.

'He's a comic, that dog,' said Jasmine. 'Should we make him more comfortable' she asked.

'No, he'll be fine,' whispered Holly, worried Mum and Dad may still hear them.

Holly, Jasmine, and Melody decided not to waste any more time, so they left the bedroom and went back down the stairs. Then, just before joining them, Jasmine popped back into the mum and dads' room and whispered, 'We love you.' She then turned to leave, and before doing so, she took hold of the door handle and pulled upon it, but the strangest thing happened! For the door wouldn't move.

'You two, come up here a minute,' shouted Jasmine. 'Take a look at this! It's strange.'

Immediately Holly and Melody raced back up the stairs and were greeted by Jasmine, heavily swinging on the bedroom door in her vain attempt to try and close it.

'What are you trying to do?' asked Melody.

'Just come here and try close this door,' replied Jasmine.

'I'll do it, Melody; I'm bigger than you,' claimed Holly as she walked confidently towards the door.

Holly soon realized that she, too, could not move the door, for it seemed the more she pulled and tugged at it! The sturdier it became.

'Oh, I give up,' exclaimed Holly. 'Why do you think we can't close it'?

'Who knows' replied Melody.

The girls had eventually decided to take some things with them, so before leaving the house, they had one last check on the items in which they thought they might need, only this hadn't consisted of much other than a few chocolate bars, some bottles of water, and a phone! But, of course, one would render useless while the world outside had now stopped, and they were about to venture to another.

Meanwhile, the girls had left their home and made their way to the back garden gate when Melody suddenly stopped and turned to look back at the house; a vague expression fell upon her face as she thought she had seen Charlie at their bedroom window.

'What's wrong, Melody' asked Holly.

'I could have sworn I have just seen Charlie at the bedroom window,' exclaimed Melody.

'Come on, Melody, you know the time has stopped; that's impossible,' replied Jasmine.

'But I swear, I have just seen him; I'm certain of it,' added Melody, with a shrug of her shoulders and a hint of uncertainty in her voice; the window is open; what if he tries jumping out?

'That can't happen, Melody; come on, let's go and get this done,' asked Jasmine.

Nature showed them an incredible scene throughout the girls' short journey through the woodlands. It was like something from a beautiful dream; they witnessed many animals and insects who would typically flee at their sight, but now they were captured in their movements, allowing the girls to share their beautiful moments with them.

The girls' wonder and awe at the sights they passed during their journey were dampened slightly by the pitiful sight of a beautifully coloured butterfly within a very short striking distance of being snared by a spider's web. But remembering what Mother Nature had previously said about the two rules she couldn't break, Jasmine felt she was in a position to help. So, despite the two rules, Jasmine intervened by trying to move the doomed butterfly away from the spider and its web. Still, sadly this wasn't to be; for the butterfly and the web, and like everything else around them, were protected by what seemed to be an invisible force, and any attempt to move either couldn't happen.

Reluctantly, the girls decided they could do nothing more, so they continued their short journey through the forest, leading to the cave where their journey had first begun.

Before entering the cave entrance, the girls stood silent for a minute; Jasmine turned to look at what they were leaving behind and also to remind herself why they were willing to fight. Then, as she looked around at the shrubs, bushes, and trees, some activity caught her eye; she looked puzzled, for she knew everything had stopped and couldn't understand why there should be any movement. Jasmine looked closer at the area that caught her eye, and again she saw a little flutter of activity from behind the leaves on a tree.

'Hey, you two,' whispered Jasmine to the others, 'look over there; something is moving from behind the leaves of that tree; that's twice I've seen it move; I think it's a bird,' she added while pointing toward the direction.

'I can't see anything, replied Melody.

'I can,' said Holly as she moved closer to the area, 'you're right, Jasmine; it is a bird, it's a Robin, but it's not moving, look for yourselves,' she added.

Jasmine and Melody moved to where Holly was standing to take a closer look, and sure enough, it was a Robin, but much to Jasmine's disappointment, it certainly wasn't moving.

'I saw it move,' exclaimed Jasmine after waiting a short time, hoping to prove herself right.

'That moment was the same as mine; when I said, I was sure I had seen Charlie at the bedroom window,' replied Melody, confidently reminding Jasmine and Holly. 'All is not what it seems,' added Melody.

'Come on, let's do this,' requested Holly.

Once again, the girls were standing at the cave entrance,

side by side, they held nervously onto each other's hand, and without speaking a single word, they stepped into the cave. At the same time, the hearty Robin turned its head and watched as they entered before tweeting and flying off.

Meanwhile, Jasmine and Holly were keen on casting their eyes across the cave, hoping that the Wooden King would be waiting for them, even though they knew that wouldn't happen. In the meantime, Melody was busy casting her eyes toward the ground in her last desperate attempt to find her toy thingy, the stretchy and sticky alien, but she also had no luck.

Nether-the-less, the girls made their way to the cave that homed the trunk of the Rare Silver Oak, and cautiously they walked across to where it stood.

The three girls stared at one another, each sharing the same thought that the Woodhunter had just visited the very same cave they were now standing in, and that was enough to remind them that a story once told by the Wooden King was now real life, and how they dealt with it; only time would tell.

The girls' hands held tight and were sweaty, as neither wanted to let go; they stared upwards and into the darkness of the Rare Silver Oaks Woodlock when it suddenly illuminated a brilliant golden colour, and the voice of that of the Wooden King echoed around inside. A sigh of relief followed as the girls breathed before waiting to hear what the Wooden King had to say. The message from the Wooden King was short and to the point! He first apologized for the little time they had to prepare; he quickly continued by telling them that all the Neplèns and Carriers had also awoken from their' year of two and that the Woodhunter was now preparing its army to invade. The Wooden King told them that courage would be with them throughout but warned them to be alert and ready.

Then, once after the Wooden King had spoken of courage, the girls suddenly felt unafraid and confident. The Wooden King reminded them to work closely with the spirit of the acorn, one another, and to have faith; with that, his voice fell silent.

'Well, Melody and Holly! That's it, exclaimed Jasmine confidently, 'Are we ready'?

'Yeah, let's do this,' Melody and Holly replied.

'Remember! If we have too much difficulty, we make our way back here straight away, and for our sake, let's try to keep together, added Holly.

The girls then took a moment to gather their thoughts; still, with no plan of what to do next, they fumbled inside a small backpack before awkwardly sharing a drink of bottled water and placing the bag in a little nook at the foot of the trunk.

'We can do this,' said Melody, feeling the tension building within the cave, 'Anyway, remember the lyrics in Dad's favourite song, the Impossible Dream, that should encourage us to see this through to the end.'

'Your right, Melody; come on,' replied Holy as she held open her arms to encourage a hug.

Then a short moment later, the girls looked up toward the Hollow of the Rare Silver Oak, gave one last nod of acknowledgement to one another, and simultaneously spoke the words! 'We are ready.'

Suddenly a brighter-than-usual golden colour shone out from inside the Woodlock and shuddered its way down toward the feet of the girls, leaving a glowing trail of golden steps behind it. The girls watched on; their faces were radiant from that of the golden glow, and before they began to climb the golden steps, they turned, and with smiles to melt the coldest of hearts, they held on to each other's hands and climbed up into the Hollow, and into the rare oaks Silverlatch.

18. THE LESSON

The Woodlocks green pool of rippling mist dispersed, and In a blink of an eye, the girls' found themselves standing silently inside the huge Woodlock; the air surrounding them left a taste of staleness in their mouths, and although it'd been two or so years since the lightning struck the Rare Golden Oak the smell of burnt wood was still evident. The girls' quickly scanned the area of the Green Planet; it wasn't yet full daylight, or at least it was hard to tell, for the yellowish smog-filled skies blighted their view. Before they even had any chance to gather their thoughts, they received a message from Mother Nature. She quickly asked them to step out from the Woodlock and not to go forward towards the hilltop but instead to make their way around the back of the golden oak trunk and to move down the hillside where they would see a nook in which to hide.

 The girls moved around the giant trunk and scrambled upon and over the remains of wooden debris surrounding them; suddenly, they felt slight vibrations beneath their feet, and with every second, the vibrations grew heavier, causing the girls to somewhat hide with their backs pressed hard against the trunk of the Rare Golden Oak.

'What is it,' whispered Jasmine while Holly peeked around the giant trunk.

Before her, and across toward the hilltop, Holly could see a massive figure; it was hard to see, but it was clear enough for Holly to make out that the darkened figure had its back turned against her and was displaying enormous wings, like those of a flying insect. Something inside Holly told her that the suspected figure belonged to the Woodhunter, and she took that feeling as the spirit of the acorn telling her.

'It's the Woodhunter, and it is massive; here, take a look, be careful; we do not want it to see us.'

Jasmine was the first to look and share the same reaction as Holly; for the Woodhunter, even at a distance, its size was something the girls hadn't expected. So next to look was Melody.

'Don't you be doing anything stupid, Melody,' whispered Jasmine.

'Give me some credit, Jasmine; let me see.'

No sooner had Melody peered from behind the trunk than the Woodhunter turned and seemed to look right at her. Melody didn't want to move, for she didn't want any sudden movements catching the Woodhunters eye; instead, her grip on Jasmines' hand grew tighter as each second passed. The Woodhunter then slowly began to move forwards and in the direction of the girls. Then, as it neared, the sounds of ticking and snorting noises grew louder; Melody spotted a brief opportunity to pull back out of sight as the Woodhunter briefly removed its stare.

'The Woodhunter is heading towards us; it was staring right at me,' whispered Melody.

Holly pressed her finger to her lips for nobody to make a sound.

The noise of the Woodhunter became louder as it grew closer, and it was so close that the girls could now hear the sound of its breathing. All they could do for now was hope that the Woodhunter was making its way toward the Woodlock, not them. Suddenly the sound of the Woodhunter stopped, and the girls, still with their backs pressed against the trunk, stared open-eyed at each other as they waited.

Suddenly the noise started again, and this time it neared the back of the trunk from where the girls stood. The first thing they saw was the Woodhunters' giant claw-like hand as it reached to take hold of the side of the trunk, and then it appeared and walked straight past them, for they were not there.

Holly, Jasmine, and Melody had requested the spirit of the acorn to transform them into something petite, Holly, a mouse; Jasmine, a cricket; and Melody, a frog.

Melody remembered the night before when they were in the bedroom and how she spoke with Holly and Jasmine through their mind and attempted to do it again. She silently called out to them, and the spirit of the acorn granted her request for them to begin talking.

'Can you hear me,' asked Melody as she called out to the others.

'Yeah, I can,' replied Jasmine, great work Melody, I would've never remembered that.

'Yeah, nicely done, Melody, said Holly, jokingly adding, 'I never thought I'd be happy to hear your voice.'

'Where are you both, and what are you?' Jasmine asked as she looked around.

'I'm just where I was, but I'm tiny; you'll probably have to look down.'

'No way, you're a grasshopper,' laughed Holly.

'Get your facts right; I'm a cricket, not a grasshopper; I'm not sure how I even managed it, forget that anyway; we

need to move from here,' replied Jasmine.
'Excuse me, you two; I am still here, you know, cried
Melody; 'so how do I look' she added.

Jasmine and Holly looked around, still slightly
disorientated by their size, until they saw Melody peering
over at them as the frog she chose.

'A frog,' they said, laughing.
'Of all the things you could've been, you chose to be a
frog,' laughed Holly.
'Yeah, a frog; not sure it was my choice either, but I'm
glad I am because I've always wanted to do this,' replied
Melody as she flicked out her long tongue and slapped
Holly on her mouse nose.

Given their circumstances, it was hard to imagine for the
girls to find humour, but they were safe for now and
buried beneath all the fallen debris and well out of sight of
the Woodhunter.

It was almost two minutes since the girls transformed, and
they were beginning to wonder how long it would last, for
they needed the Woodhunter to move away from the
hilltop and make their way down the hillside and to the
nook. As small as they were, they needed more confidence
to head straight past, something they needed to gain at the
moment, for it would be unlikely the Woodhunter, given
its size, would even notice them pass.
'I think we're changing back,' exclaimed Jasmine.
However, just before they did, the Woodhunter took off
from the hillside from where it stood and disappeared into
the hazy sky, leaving behind a vast dust plum covering the
three creatures the girls became. No sooner did the
Woodhunter leave that the girls returned to their usual
selves.

'That was mad,' whispered Melody.

'Forget that for a minute, and let us get down the hillside,' Holly demanded.

The distance from where the girls set off to where they were going was pretty close, but the ground beneath them was full of obstacles.

'Hold on, you two,' said Melody. 'I can't move around for all this; it's like a war zone,' she added while pointing at the wooden obstacles in her path.

'Tell me about it,' replied Holly. 'I'd have thought all this would've been polished up and eaten by the Neplèns already.

'Yeah, but remember the size of the Neplèns; all this may seem big pieces to us, but to them, they'll be mere scraps. Didn't you notice the size of the Woodhunter?' added Jasmine, 'anyway, where is the ending to this hilltop? I can hardly see anything for this haze.'

Suddenly, the girls heard a voice.

'Hurry, and don't speak' were the words the girls heard Mother Nature saying, and no sooner had they listened to this than they heard another sound; this time, it was the heavy thumping of footsteps. Moments later, the girls finally made their way to the edge of the hill and began making their way down its hillside, and while doing so, the sight before them cleared to give them a clearer view of the vast area surrounding them.

'Wow, this is unbelievable,' exclaimed Holly. 'It's all but desertland.'

'Ruined is what it is, and to think this is what they want for our earth,' replied a sombre voice Jasmine.

'At least now we know the true meaning of why we're here,' added Melody with a strong hint of defiance in her voice.

Meanwhile, the girls made their way to the nook buried within the hillside, where the voice of Mother Nature again greeted them with a message of better news and one which would allow them some much-needed time. She told how she had learned that the Woodhunter was added to the army in the skies by creating twenty thousand Terror Flights. She said doing it would take time, but it would allow them time to plan and, more importantly, learn how to use the spirit of the acorn magic correctly. Mother Nature then commended how well they managed by using the essence of the acorn.

Jasmine looked slightly puzzled and wasn't sure Mother Nature would answer her question, but it regarded her using the spirit of the acorn and how she wasn't sure how she even managed it.

'I'm not sure if you can hear me, but I have a question; I never asked the spirit of the acorn to grant me that of a cricket, I never felt anything, nor did I hear anything; it just happened, but I didn't request it neither of us did.'
'Hello, Jasmine, and yes, I hear you; I'm happy to say that I can guarantee that you all did request what the spirit of the acorn granted to you.'

Mother Nature went on to explain how a request isn't spoken only in the quietness of one's mind, but it is also a feeling that comes from deep within oneself.
'Girls, for your first attempt, your use of the spirit was exceptional under the circumstances, which is why the Wooden King chose you to help, and you are already proving that you are the ones needed to do that. The essence of the acorn is there to trigger your instinct, and when you act on that instinct, the spirit will grant whatever action you choose, and instantaneously it will happen before you have time to think. So you are letting the spirit of the acorn guide you; it is up to you to do the rest.'

Mother Nature didn't know how much time she had left, and she worried that the Woodhunter and the Neplèns would move the silver oak trunk to the forest of a million trees. So, she set about with a plan to help the girls fully understand how to use the acorn's spirit in short, intense training.

Firstly, Mother Nature asked that the girls pit their wits against one another by using the spirit of the acorn's magic against each other.

The girls listened as Mother Nature explained how she wanted them to request a small animal or creature from the spirit of the acorn to begin their training. During their time transformed, they would have to outwit one another by subduing the animal or creature that the other had become; to do this, they would have to change into something bigger and stronger than their opponent's choice. Mother Nature then spoke of some rules she had set aside, one being that they could not choose anything they wanted, for the spirit had already decided that for them. And it was done to encourage the girls to listen to their instinct and to follow what the acorn was telling them. The second rule was that their time spent transformed was much shorter than before, encouraging quick thinking, and with that in place, she led the girls to a quiet area at the bottom of the hillside so that the short training exercise could begin.

'Well, I didn't expect this; this is going to be the strangest thing we've ever done,' exclaimed Holly.

'I know, this will be a bit weird,' replied Melody; how do you both feel about everything? She added.

'Well, we've got a job to do, so let's do it right,' replied Jasmine.

'That's just how I feel, Jasmine,' added Holly.

'Well, it sounds to me that we're all on the same page, so

let's get this done because you two are going down,'
claimed Melody, pointing suggestively at the ground.
 The girls arrived at the clearing at the foot of the hill and
waited for Mother Nature to explain what to do next. Still,
after several minutes her instructions never came, for this
was all part of the training; they didn't need instructions,
for they already knew what to do; they just needed to listen
to themselves and the spirit of the acorn.
 'I have a feeling that this is part of the plan; I think we
should continue,' Holly requested.
 Before agreeing, the girls each looked at one another.
 'After three,' said Jasmine.
 Each of them counted, and upon reaching three, Holly,
Jasmine, and Melody transformed as they each listened to
their instinct guided by the acorn's spirit. Holly requested
that of a spider, Jasmine that of an ant, and Melody that of
a cockroach.
 Immediately they began to fight, not to harm or injure,
but to try to hold the other down until their time ran out
or they failed to transform into something different within
their time. A short mini-battle ensued as each one tried
grappling with the other. Although the girls' insects made
much movement to try and stop each other from getting
the upper hand, it was slow, awkward, and non-
meaningful, and no sooner did the battle begin did the girls
transform back to themselves when Mother Nature
interrupted them.

 'You need to follow your instincts and work with the
spirit of the acorn; it is guiding you. When you feel you
might be losing, dig deep within yourself and find what it
is you need to overcome your opponent, think fast, and
feel at one with yourself,' explained Mother Nature.

 Again, the girls transformed into what they were before
Mother Nature interrupted, and the little battle continued.
The struggle was more purposeful, and the strength of the

insects they became was clear. The spider tried using its strong legs to spin its web to hold and subdue the ant, but the cockroach was heavy and robust and restricted the movements of both the ant and the spider as it lay heavy on both. Suddenly, both Holly and Jasmine heard the voice of Melody in their minds.

'I've got you both; I told you that you were going down,' claimed Melody as she bore down on the two trapped beneath.

'Ha, that's what you think,' replied Holly while listening to her instinct and the spirit which led her.

Knowing she was about to lose and that her time to change was running out, the acorn's spirit hurriedly guided her to request something more significant: that of a black-footed ferret and a highly skilled hunter. Her sudden change led the others to pursue her, and Jasmine quickly became a honey badger renowned for their fearlessness; finally, Melody was that of a mink, quick-witted and aggressive. The battle continued, and it was closely decided between them as they tumbled wildly around the sandy earth beneath them. It was quick and close, but the badger had the upper hand.

'They say the quiet ones are often the ones to watch out for; well, it's my turn now,' Jasmine claimed as she wrestled hard against both the others.

'Don't bank on it, Jasmine,' replied Melody.

The girls were now becoming familiar with listening to themselves and the spirit of the acorn as it continued to guide them.

Melody was the next to change and requested to change by becoming a Wolverine, a powerful animal for its size. Holly speedily followed and became a mean and aggressive bobcat, Jasmine, a coyote, an intelligent predator.

As each transformation grew, so did the battle, and the

girls were now also becoming one with the animals they became, leading to one of the most challenging battles yet.

The training exercise continued, and although the animals may not have been equal in size, strength, and speed, it taught the girls what they needed to do when they came up against something bigger and stronger than themselves, and they were learning fast.

As the battle continued, they requested to become something more significant, and with it, Holly became a tiger, known for its almighty powerful swipes of its paw. Jasmine transformed into a gorilla, a mammal with the strength of many men, and Melody, a bear, a big brutal animal who can be unforgiving. This battle proved to be a titanic clash between three very tough challengers, and it was that battle which brought the girls training to a close, for the requests ended, and the girls transformed back to themselves.

Mother Nature was not too surprised with the quickness that the girls learned from the spirit of the acorn, for each one had unique qualities, and that special gift would help see them through to the end, for soon, the Woodhunter would test their abilities to the fullest.

'You now know how the spirit of the acorn works,' said Mother Nature, 'and you all did tremendously well, better than I anticipated; however, I would have liked a little more time to prepare you, but unfortunately, we have reached the time, for there will be no more pretence, for the time to remove the Emerald Green Acorn and the Emerald Key from the Woodhunter is now upon us.

'How soon is now,' asked Holly.

'The Woodhunter is now selecting a further twenty thousand Terror Flights; we can't wait too long, for the more Terror Flights there are, the harder the battle will become,' replied Mother Nature. Therefore, we should make plans of our own, she added.

'Won't the Woodhunter know our plans already? Won't it be reading from the memory of the Emerald Green Acorn,' asked Jasmine.

'No, Jasmine, replied Mother Nature. 'You see, the Emerald Green Acorn only holds the memories of what it witnesses, for as long as it doesn't see you, then there would be no need for concern'.

'So, will you be helping us take the acorn and the Emerald Key back from the Woodhunter,' asked Melody.

'No,' replied Mother Nature, remember my two rules I must uphold; I can help in small ways, but taking back the acorn and the Emerald Key remains with all of you unless something intervenes, of which I yet know nothing about, or I have no control over.

The conversation suddenly stopped, for above their heads, they saw many Terror Flights awkwardly flying in the skies above them, but these weren't the original Terror Flights belonging to the Woodhunters most trusted; these were the new ones that it had recently selected, and in total, there were already around three to four hundred of them.

Mother Nature told the girls how the Woodhunter might, at any moment, move from creating more Terror Flights and concentrate on removing the Rare Silver Oak from its current place and returning it to the forest of a million trees. She went on to say how they couldn't give the Woodhunter any more time and that they had to act immediately. Lastly, she asked the girls to request something small and fast-moving, like a bird, so they could go unnoticed back to the nook in the hillside, which they did.

There, where they hid inside the nook of the hillside, the girls prepared to face the Woodhunter and its army and take back the Emerald Green Acorn and the Emerald Key.

The Wooden King

19. THE PLAN

Everything that had happened had now brought the girls to this very moment, for they sat within the small nook at the side of the hillside, staring out across the ruined landscape of the Green Planet.

'Do you think we'll manage this,' asked Jasmine while she sat staring at the spirit of the acorn in her hand after she requested to see it.

'Of course we will, Jasmine; why do you ask,' replied Holly.

'Just asking, that's all; where should we start?' asked Jasmine.

'I think wherever we start, we need to be quick; we need to create a distraction and surprise the Woodhunter,' replied Holly.

'I don't think that'll work; the Woodhunter would only protect what it had all the more added Melody, 'we need to be crafty and sly; the problem we have is how we get the acorn from around the Woodhunters neck without it noticing.'

'Why don't we wait until the Woodhunter opens the Woodlock? It'll have to remove it to do that,' said Holly.

Suddenly the voice of Mother Nature interrupted the

conversion with a thoughtful reminder for the girls; she explained the consequences of incorrect choices and told them how they would need to keep the Woodhunter from getting anywhere near the Woodlock and how if it and the Neplèns ended up in the cave with the trunk of the Rare Silver Oak, they would see that the world had stopped. The dilemma it would bring is that time would have to start again because the Woodhunter and the Neplèns could do anything while everything else had stopped, and that can't be allowed to happen. Also, she added that by starting time again, the girls' parents would wake up to find them not there and how that would cause untold problems. Again, she reiterated that the Woodhunter must be kept away from the Woodlock at all costs.

'Right, so, our plan has to involve leading the Woodhunter away from the Woodlock,' exclaimed Holly, 'but how do we do that' she added.
'I have an idea,' yelled Jasmine.
'What is it,' asked Melody.
'We lead the Woodhunter away by allowing it to see one of us.'

Jasmine seemed to come up with the first feasible part of the plan, which led the girls to then develop it further by adding how Holly would preoccupy the Woodhunter by allowing it only to see her and not the others and by using the spirit of the acorn she would request and use various small animals to lure the Woodhunter away from the Woodlock. During this time, Melody would choose her moment to transform into an insect with powerful jaws; she would aim to land upon the body of the Woodhunter and quietly cut through the thick root-like string which bound together those of the Emerald Green Acorn and the Emerald Key until it fell to the ground. Jasmine would be waiting for Melody to tell her when the thick root-like string was ready to snap, and her job would then be to quickly transform into a strong bird, able to carry the large acorn and Emerald Key through the Woodlock, where Holly and Melody would soon follow before the Woodhunter had even noticed.

The girls agreed upon the plan and were now ready to venture out of the nook and return to the top of the hill where the trunk of the Rare Golden Oak stood.

The air grew heavy as the girls neared the top of the hill, and as they did, loud sounds made by the Neplèns and the wafting of wings followed. A cloud of yellowish dust steadily rose from the valley below, and although they tried, it was hard for the girls to see much of anything beyond it, for the dusty smog blighted their view. They waited for a short while, hoping for the dust to settle, but it didn't; it just continued, and every several seconds, a new plume of yellowish smog bellowed upwards toward them, reminding them of a volcanic eruption. Suddenly swirls appeared and were likened to those of whirlpools within the plumes of dust, and for a moment, there was a lull of stillness and quiet before the Terror Flights emerged, rising out from and above the plumes that they created.

Quickly the girls took cover by requesting something small from the spirit of the acorn, and they did this as more and more Terror Flights took to the skies surrounding them; the earth beneath their tiny bodies began to shake as the winds grew harder, the nearer the Terror Flights became. The girls realised that their request would only last for a while and that they would need to be ready to constantly change into something other while the Terror Flights patrolled the skies above. However, the skies continued to fill with Terror Flights, and the force of the winds and the power they created blew them and the surrounding debris about the barren land, which was something that they and the spirit of the acorn hadn't accounted for it. The girls felt they needed to request something heavier by transforming into small animals fast on their legs, like a shrew, a mouse, tiger beetle, so they could hope to find refuge quickly.

Eventually, the girls found a large rock to hide behind, and although it was suitable for them in their current form, they would need to transform to remain hidden constantly.

'This is hard work,' exclaimed Holly, 'having to request and change into something so often tires me out; I didn't realise for it to be so testing.'

'Me neither,' replied Melody, but at least we can rest for a minute, she added.

'Well, the Wooden King warned us that it would be tiring,' said Jasmine. Anyhow, listen, the Terror Flights are moving away.

The girls listened, and the noise from the Terror Flights grew less; they weren't sure why they'd suddenly stopped, but thankfully they had, for this gave them a chance to return to their usual selves. Then, as they did, they each lay on the dusty surface of the hilltop and watched the last Terror Flights fly out of sight and back through the yellowish-looking smog in the valley below.

'Thank goodness for that,' exclaimed Melody as she rolled onto her back.

Holly looked on with a smile.

'What's the matter,' asked Melody, slightly confused.

'You, doing that,' replied Holly, 'It reminded me of the other day, back home in the garden, you and Jasmine began to wrestle, and Charlie and I joined in.'

'Oh, Holly, don't get me started,' said Jasmine, worried she'd get too emotional.

Momentarily the girls lay and pondered at the little things they missed when suddenly and before they'd even had a real chance of gathering their thoughts, Mother Nature whispered to them a warning that the Woodhunter had called for a gathering. She told them they needed to hurry and hide somewhere more suitable, for the Woodhunter was to speak with the Neplèns from the top of the hill.

The girls quickly decided between them to request something with wings so they could fly fast toward the Rare Golden Oak trunk and hide behind it, and no sooner had they chosen did the spirit of the acorn grant their request.

The girls speedily made their way just before the Woodhunter appeared in the skies and landed at the top of the hill to address its army below.

Before the girls transformed back to their former selves, they waited, for the first thing they couldn't help but notice was the sudden thunderous noise made from the trampling feet of the Neplèns as they spewed out from beneath the tunnels of the Green Planet below.

'This is insane,' whispered Jasmine, unsure if the other two had heard her.

The girls were now back where they started, each with their backs pressed against the massive trunk behind them. There was a difference this time, though; the girls had time to learn from the spirit of the acorn and were now more prepared than ever before.

The noise of the stampeding Neplèns lessoned, and near silence surrounded the girls; it was in that moment when the girls seemed a little more unsettled, for at least in the noise, they could feel where it was coming from, but in silence, they didn't know if anything was sneaking about them.

The following sounds came from the Woodhunter as it began telling the Neplèns of its plans. Still, the girls looked at one another with confused expressions, for they couldn't understand what it was saying until Mother Nature began to translate it for them. She started by telling them how the Woodhunter boasted of the Terror Flights, speaking about how from the Green Planet, it would secretly increase its army in the skies from two thousand to tens of thousands and how, when the tunnels within the forest of a million trees were ready, they would invade the new planet. Mother Nature didn't wait to tell what the Woodhunter went on to say after she heard it telling how it was to select three Terror Flights to cross through the Woodlock and back to the trunk of the Rare Silver Oak before returning it to the forest of a million trees.

The girls shared with Mother Nature the same concern and immediately set their plan into motion.

'Holly, this is it; you need to distract the Woodhunter and move it as far away from the Woodlock as possible,' Jasmine said. 'we'll try and stay right behind you, but if we can't, don't wait for us; we'll catch up with you.'
'What are you requesting, Holly' Melody asked. 'It doesn't want to be anything too big just yet; you just need something big enough to catch the Woodhunters eye,' she added.
'I know, but it needs to be fast; I'll only have several minutes before I change again. I will need that time to get myself as far away as possible,' replied Holly.
Holly knew what to do and what request she needed to make, but she allowed emotion to cloud her judgment.
'Breath for a second, Holly,' whispered Mother Nature. And she did, and with that, Holly transformed into a brown hare, an animal that relies on high-speed endurance running and having long, powerful limbs.
The other two, Jasmine and Melody, waited, hidden behind the trunk of the Rare Golden Oak, preparing themselves to transform into a Dragonfly and a Hawk-moth, both known for their stealthy flights.

Holly ventured out from behind the trunk; and made her way toward the back of the Woodhunter, who was still addressing the Neplèns, and while it did, Holly started talking to the girls through their minds; she described to them the direction of where she would run when the Woodhunter had seen her, Holly also shared with them her concern that the Woodhunter might not see her, for her size was considerably smaller to it. Nevertheless, she knew that if she didn't hurry, her time to request another transformation would soon be here, so she moved more quickly from the back of the Woodhunter to the side of it and began scurrying around within clear sight of its view.

She was about to use her strong legs to scuff the dirt up from the ground to try to catch the Woodhunters eye when it stopped what it was doing, and stared, puzzled at what it could see below. The Woodhunter began to sniff at the air to try and figure out what it was seeing before baring its teeth at Holly. That was Hollys' moment, for she wasted no time leading the Woodhunter away from the top of the hill and toward the Woodlock.

'Quickly, you two, change; I'm coming passed,' cried Holly.

The Woodhunter didn't need to fly, for the strides it was taking were good enough, but the Hare, which Holly became, was an excellent runner, for she upped her speed and began to outpace the Woodhunter. She ran straight toward the trunk of the golden oak and carried on straight past it, turning her head as she did to ensure the other two weren't there.

'Where are you,' called Holly.

'We're right above you, Jasmine replied, just keep going forward,' she added.

'I will; I'll try to lead the Woodhunter to the clearing at the bottom of the hill, where we practised, Melody, be ready,' shouted Holly.

Meanwhile, the Woodhunter was preparing to fly as the edge of the hill grew closer, but Holly was already down the other side, and the Woodhunter was about to lose sight of her as it flew into the air. Holly approached the nook they'd visited earlier; she quickly looked over her shoulder and spied the Woodhunter flying from the edge of the hill; she soon realised that the Woodhunter had lost sight of her.

Holly needed to get the Woodhunter down to the clearing and hopefully slow it to a point where Melody could transform again, land on the Woodhunter and begin the second part of the plan.

'Are you two still above me,' called Holly.
'Yes,' replied Melody.
'The Hare I requested is about to go; I'm requesting something larger to make the Woodhunter see me; it needs to be down here,' cried Holly.

With that, Holly requested a Grey Wolf, an animal known for its incredibly far-reaching howl. Hollys' plan wasn't to run but to attract the Woodhunters' attention, which she did when the wolf began howling at the skies above. The Woodhunter immediately turned in the skies and glared down at the spot where the wolf was standing, but it didn't do anything; it just continued to stare.
'What is it doing,' asked Holly, slightly confused by the Woodhunters' constant glare.
'I'm not sure, Holly, but we're going to request to change again now,' replied Jasmine. 'Just keep howling and stay put; we'll be ready.'
'Well, it'll have to hurry, or I'm going to have to change again also,' exclaimed Holly.

Suddenly and without warning, the Woodhunter flew speedily down toward the grey wolf; it was seeing, and it was evident in its approach that the Woodhunter was going in for an attack. Holly stood firm, waited until the last second before the Woodhunter attacked, and transformed from a wolf into a small fly. It seemed insignificant at the time, but the Woodhunter, with its muscular limbs and claw-like fingers, reached out to swoop the grey wolf up from the ground but met nothing; this caused the Woodhunter to somewhat stumble in mid-flight before crashing heavily to the ground. Holly manoeuvred quickly and watched from a small rock as the Woodhunter lay seemingly unconscious on its back.

'Quick Melody now's your chance,' called Jasmine.
'Just a minute, I think we might have killed it,' exclaimed Melody before deciding to take advantage of the situation by transforming into what is known as a "Bulldog raspy cricket," an insect known for its powerful jaws and spiny legs that it used to trap its prey.
Meanwhile, Melody made her way onto the shoulders of the Woodhunter; and the cricket she became wasted no time in attempting to chew through the thick stalk-like root which bound both the Emerald Key and the emerald acorn together.
Jasmine and Holly felt the need not to transform into anything else, so they returned to their original selves; by doing so, they decided to move closer toward the Woodhunter to check and see if it was breathing.
'Is it alive,' asked Jasmine, steadily holding herself back and ushering Holly in front of her.
'I can't tell,' replied Holly, now peering directly over the Woodhunter.
Melody was about to move that little bit closer when the Woodhunter spluttered and began to stir; quickly, Holly and Jasmine transformed again into small animals and hurried away before the Woodhunter had a chance to see them. Remembering what had happened, the Woodhunter quickly came to its senses and angrily called out with a loud warlike cry, like something not heard from any Neplèn before. Then a sudden movement made by the Woodhunter as it limped onto its feet caused the cricket to

fall from its neck and to the ground; Melody was about to request another strong biting insect when the Woodhunter flew into the sky and in the direction of its army of Neplèns.

'We came so close,' Jasmine yelled, feeling slightly disappointed. 'How did you get on, Melody? Did you manage to cut through any of the roots,' she added.

'I made a difference,' she replied, 'I did manage to get almost halfway through it; if only I had a bit more time, we'd have done it.'

'Jasmine and I could've stepped in and helped sooner,' Holly said, disappointed in the missed opportunity.

'Never mind that; what now,' asked Jasmine.

With the Woodhunter seemingly unaware of the girl's plan to cut the acorns free from around its neck, they decided it was still the best idea and that they would push forward with it; all be it to have changed slightly, for they hoped that next time Holly would be joining Melody in stealthily removing the acorns. However, the girls were also unaware that in the Meantime, across the hilltop and past the trunk of the Rare Golden Oak, in the valley below, thousands of Terror Flights circled the smog-filled skies above, and the countless army of Neplèns were making their way toward and up the hill. Hordes of others awaited the command from the Woodhunter to set out and surround it.

20. THE SPIRIT OF THE BATTLE

Loud booming noises echoed around in the distance, growing louder, bringing the Neplèn army ever-closer toward the valley from where the girls were last seen, for since their last encounter with the Woodhunter, they had made their way further from that area and to another hillside, for the terrain they chose was rocky with many hidden nooks which more suited them and allowed them to watch a wider area and the hill from where the Rare Golden Oaks trunk was. From there, the girls received a message from Mother Nature telling them how the Woodhunter had gathered all the Terror Flights and the Neplèns telling them of its encounter; it warned how it had seen animals with seemingly magical powers, giving them the ability to appear and disappear. She went on to tell how the Woodhunter had ordered as many Neplèns as possible to surround the hill and the trunk of the Rare Golden Oak and how many others would seek the area to find any trace of the animals it told of. Lastly, Mother Nature told the girls how she didn't know what the Woodhunter was going to do next and that they could not wait to find out, reminding them again about the importance of keeping the Woodhunter from the

Woodlock and the trunk of the Rare Silver Oak. The next part of what Mother Nature said to the girls reminded her of her last encounter with the Rare Golden Oak and how she asked it for self-sacrifice, for now, she was about to ask the girls something similar, and that was to prepare themselves to battle the Woodhunter for the sake of the Emerald Green Acorn, the Emerald Key and everything associated with them, and that included their world.

'So that's it', exclaimed Melody, 'we go straight from here into battle with the Woodhunter, with all of them, right now,' added Melody without fear.

'Yes,' replied Mother Nature, 'there is only one other way to avoid it, and that is not to take part'.

'We're not doing that, are we girls,' asked Jasmine with a strong hint of defiance.

'We're all ready,' Added Holly, her comment aimed at Mother Nature.

Mother Nature was calm but to the point as she asked the girls to think carefully of their plan, to watch out for one another and to use everything that the spirit of the acorn had given them. She told them how they would have to fight hard to remove the Emerald Green Acorn and the Emerald Key from the Woodhunter and how they wouldn't get a second chance to do that. She reminded them how the Woodhunter had proven itself in the past to be clever and skillful and how they shouldn't take it or anything for granted. Mother Nature went on to say how she would try to help where she was able and try to stop the Woodhunter and its army from moving forward with any plans it might have from this point on. One last thing Mother Nature shared with the girls before they went into battle with the Woodhunter was to tell them how brave they were and how they already had their spirit, which was more substantial than any magic. She spoke of the inner light they carried and how their light would consume any darkness surrounding them; she told them how fear is evil and that they should not let it in, and that God had not given them the spirit of fear; but of power, and love, and a sound mind. With that, Mother Nature created a soft breeze that she wrapped around them, and with it, she kissed each of their foreheads and, for now, was gone.

Meanwhile, back across the valley and down the side of the adjacent hill, the Woodhunter had ordered all the Neplèns to search the area for clues and to help find the animals it had seen. At the same time, the Woodhunter took to the skies before choosing a place from where it was to request to see any memory which the Emerald Green Acorn may have.

From there, the Woodhunter held the acorn and stared at it while requesting to be shown what memories of the animals it had seen. Soon after, it showed images of the brown hare running in all directions across the hilltop. With that, the next memory showed that of the grey wolf and how it disappeared before the Woodhunter took hold of it, but other than that, the Emerald Green Acorn's memory held nothing more of the Woodhunters' animal requests. The Woodhunter didn't give up, it was hoping to see something within the background of the images it was seeing, and so it continued requesting various other memories; one of those memories shown was the image of the sky and the surrounding hills from where the Woodhunter lay on the ground after crashing mid-flight. It continued to watch as the memory only showed movement from passing clouds above the Woodhunters' head when suddenly the image of the clouds was interrupted by the appearance of Holly standing above the Woodhunter as it lay injured on the ground.

Like the times before, and after witnessing something important, the Woodhunter broke free from its trance-like state while muttering the words human several times before racing into the skies and toward the Rare Golden Oak Woodlock.

Once there, the Woodhunter revealed the news to all the Neplèns, telling them of what it had seen and how it believed that the human was powerful like that of the Emerald Green Acorn, but added how it didn't know how many other intruders there were. The Woodhunter didn't spend much time explaining before ordering hundreds more Neplèns to prepare themselves by moving to the top of the hill, where it instructed them to stay and to protect the trunk of the Rare Golden Oak. Soon after, it ordered all the Terror Flights to comb the skies, search all surrounding hills, valleys and mountains, and seek out the human Intruder it had seen.

The Woodhunter didn't fully understand what it was searching for, nor was it aware of what the human wanted; however, its instinct was telling it that the animals and the human it did see were all connected, for the Woodhunter remembered back to its encounter with the lone fisherman, and the time when itself transformed into a human. During that moment of thought, the Woodhunter suddenly paused whilst staring into the direction of the trunk of the Rare Golden Oak before unexpectedly making its way toward the Woodlock, when there it stepped through the Woodlock and out from the other side and into the cave on the new planet. Still, before doing so, it had removed the Emerald Green Acorn and the Emerald Key from around its neck, and unnoticed by the Woodhunter, the root which bound them both together frayed and somewhat loosened.

Meanwhile, Immediately after the Woodhunter stepped through the Woodlock, Mother Nature quickly spoke to the girls, telling them that the Woodhunter had requested the Emerald Green Acorn to show its memory, and by doing so, it had seen the image of Holly. The girls listened more as Mother Nature went on to tell them the further bad news of how the Woodhunter had stepped through the Woodlock and into the cave on the new planet. She went on to say that she didn't know why the Woodhunter had returned to the cave but presumed it would be to search for clues as to what was happening. She then asked the girls to hold back and not worry, for Mother Nature on the new planet would send a message through the Woodlock whenever the Woodhunter reopened it. Lastly, Mother Nature wanted to reassure the girls by telling them she didn't think the Woodhunter was aware of the presence of Jasmine and Melody and how that would give the girls an upper hand to defeat it.

It was a worrying time for the girls, for they had no idea what the Woodhunter would do in a world where time had stopped.

'This isn't good, this is not good at all', whispered Jasmine, suddenly feeling slightly vulnerable.

'We'll just have to wait and see what happens and wait for a message; we can't do any other', replied Holly.

'What if we went through the Woodlock, the Woodhunter is by itself, we could do what we need to do there, and the world has stopped; we'd have time, and nobody would know', said Melody.

Soon after, Mother Nature spoke to the girls again; this time, it wasn't about the Woodhunter, it was about what Melody had said, for Mother Nature explained how Melody's idea seemed logical, but it couldn't happen and that there was too much at stake. She then explained what may happen if they failed and how the Woodhunter could roam freely across a world that had stopped. At that point, Melody interrupted to ask.

'But whilst the world had stopped, the Woodhunter wouldn't be able to touch or move anything; it wouldn't be able to feed, it would die eventually'.

'Eventually, Melody, how long would that be? 'The world cannot stop until the Woodhunter dies, the world would have to move again, and the consequence of time starting again in your world is too dangerous', replied Mother Nature.

Melody thought for a moment and understood how things could turn out, so all the girls could do for now was wait for a message to tell them what was happening.

Meanwhile, the Woodhunter prowled around the cave, quietly snarling and snorting as it sniffed hard at the air; there was still silence, which came from a world that had stopped, of which the Woodhunter was unaware. However, it was aware that Mother Nature would be watching, but still, it continued to search for any clue it could find, as Mother Nature presumed it would do. The Woodhunter began its search by looking in every small nook of the cave where the trunk stood, for it had even searched the weed-covered walls surrounding it and used its claws to tear at it to do so. The search was thorough, but the Woodhunter still moved quickly around the cave, only occasionally stopping on several occasions to briefly peer out from the makeshift window that the Terror Flights had previously smashed through and without noticing anything unusual outside. After venturing around the massive trunk of the Rare Silver Oak, it spotted a small something tucked away at the bottom of it: Holly's backpack. The Woodhunter toyed with it momentarily by poking and prodding at it as it tried to figure out what it was. Eventually, it went to grab it, but because of the size of the Woodhunters hands and claws, it struggled to handle it.

Nevertheless, it persevered and was eager to know what it was, or even if it was a living thing, for each time the Woodhunter fumbled with the bag, its contents rattled around from inside it, which intrigued the Woodhunter all the more. Eventually, the Woodhunter lost patience and didn't care if it was or was not a living thing, for it held the bag steady by stabbing its long claw into it to hold it in place and used its other to tear it apart. As the Woodhunter did this, the contents of the bag, including a phone, fell out onto the cave floor, causing the phone to illuminate after taking a knock to the floor. And as it lit up, it showed the Woodhunter a photo of the three girls from the cellphone screen; small though it was, in comparison to the Woodhunters size, the Woodhunter did recognise one of them, the others it didn't, which was Jasmine and Holly. The images the Woodhunter had seen aggravated it to the point where it smashed the phone before quickly sifting through the rest of the bag's spilt contents before making its way back through the Silverlatch and onto the Green Planet and no sooner had the Woodhunter done this than Mother Nature sent a message through also, and it was received instantly by the girls.

After hearing the message from Mother Nature, the girls were relieved to hear how the Woodhunter hadn't ventured outside the cave and, other than it seeing the image of them on their phone, nothing else happened, which did seem to them at the time, insignificant, and that they wouldn't worry and allow it to interfere with their plans, however, the girls were warned by Mother Nature not to take for granted the Woodhunter.

Meanwhile, after returning to the Green Planet, the Woodhunter, for some unknown reason, hadn't shared what it had seen back in the cave. Instead, it flew to a high rocky ledge and watched and waited for something to happen whilst its army of Neplèns gathered in mass, searching for Holly, the lone human.

Since the Woodhunters' arrival back to the Green Planet, the girls used their time to prepare and establish their plan and remained undeterred by the news Mother Nature had just delivered to them. Even as they prepared themselves, they watched hundreds of Neplèns gathering on the hilltop, countless others surrounding it, and the Terror Flights patrolling the skies above. However, while everything unfolded before the girls' eyes and the Terror Flights grew closer to where they were, they remained gallant.

'Just before we go, I've got an idea', claimed Melody with a little glint in her eye.

'Not now, we can't change the plan now, we haven't got the time,' replied Jasmine whilst rolling her eyes and slightly shaking her head.

'Let's hear it, Melody, be quick', added Holly scratching nervously at her head at what she was about to hear.

'We can see the commotion across there, the skies are full of those things, and the hilltop looks rammed with Neplèns; we keep to our plan, but why don't we confuse them? Holly, you draw the Terror Flights over here to us, and while we get as many of them searching here, we go there,' explained Melody pointing towards the Neplèns and the hilltop. 'The Terror Flights will be confused, and It will give us more time', she added.

Not surprisingly, the girls thought for a moment before agreeing to Melody's idea and set about getting the attention of the Terror Flights by Holly requesting and transforming to be that of a howler monkey, Known to be the loudest land animal in their world, with a call that can be heard several miles away.

Meanwhile, Jasmine and Melody remained out of sight, and Holly, the howler monkey, stepped out onto the sizeable rocky ridge of the hillside. From there, the howler monkey began to howl and screech and soon got the attention of the Terror Flights from far across the valleys. Before long and seemingly out of nowhere, the monstrous sights and sounds of the Terror Flights unfolded and headed straight to where the howler monkey and the girls were.

'Ready? After three, we all change, and then we go,' exclaimed Jasmine.

Each of them counted three seconds and vanished into thin air because that was what they requested, that of wind, and with it, they travelled unseen between the bodies of Terror Flights; silently and swiftly, they drifted, heading straight in the direction of the hilltop.

The wind, as they were, pierced through the yellowish smog-filled skies as they neared the hilltop, and in the not-too-far distance, the Neplèns wcrc seen massed together as they assembled and surrounded much of the surface of the hill. The girls planned to drift amongst the unsuspecting

Neplèns, and after they had reached the middle of them, they would transform into hordes of animals and creatures to ride in their wake as many Neplèns as possible from the hill and surrounding areas. The girls wanted to create an element of surprise, and by striking the very heart of the Neplèn army, they hoped to create chaos and confusion amongst them.

The girls had listened to their instinct and let the spirit of the acorn guide them, and it was that instinct which told them that the Woodhunter wouldn't be where the chaos was about to unfold. Nevertheless, the wind that the girls requested arrived at the hilltop, and through the marauding bodies of the Neplèns, it drifted toward the middle of the hill from where in their many hundreds, the Neplèns patrolled. The girls hurried the winds so that they would already be running at pace when they transformed.

'Are we ready' called Jasmine to the other two.

'Yes', they replied.

'Then after three, and remember, use these requests lightly; we don't have another chance at using the same ones again', added Jasmine, referring to the special requests the spirit of the acorn had given them.

Each girl counted, and after reaching three, they immediately transformed into their choice of being.

The transformation was instantaneous and likened to an explosion, as the immediate Neplèns from within the centre of the hill where the change occurred were amongst the first Neplèn casualties. For Melody became those of one thousand Lions, known for their courage, strength, and power, Jasmine became those of a thousand Grizzly bears, known for their Brawn, their claw length and, surprisingly, their speed, and Holly two thousand silver back guerrillas, known for their extraordinary strength, intelligence, and their absolute protection of their group.

The battle for the hill and its surrounding areas unfolded as the thousands of animals, all with one shared purpose spread out at speed; the surprise attack caught the Neplèns off guard, and they didn't have much time to respond, but as the noise of the battle grew so did the amount of Neplèns as they quickly began making their way from the valley below to the top of the hill. And in the meantime, the Woodhunter, apart from sniffing hard at the air, remained otherwise still as it watched the extraordinary battle below.

In such a short time, the number of Neplèn casualties began to increase, but so did the others, for as vital as the girls' choices were, the Neplèns were tougher, as in many cases, it was taking two and sometimes three to battle against one Neplèn. But never the less, the fight was fierce and bloody, and the combined speed, strength and agility of the girls' choices of animal were phenomenal, and the Neplèns quickly became exhausted.

The battle had seen the top of the hill covered with injured and dead Neplèns; the other animal fatalities simply vanished once their struggle had ended.

The fighting had since spilt over, down, and across the bottom of the hillside; above, the skies darkened with a seemingly endless swirling number of confused Terror Flights readying themselves after returning from the rocky hill.

'The time for the animals will be over soon; we'll need to change again,' called Melody to the others.

'Look above; we need to head for the sky,' replied Holly.

'We'll use what remaining time we have left before we change,' exclaimed Jasmine, not wanting to waste the spirit of the acorn's resources.

Up to this point, the girls' plan had worked, but from now on, they didn't have another one ready, but as the battle continued, the acorn's spirit began to guide Melody's thoughts towards the Terror Flights and how to attack them.

'I've got an idea,' called Melody, 'I need to transform and fly above the Terror Flights, but I'm going to have to do it now, she added, but don't take the battle to the Terror

Flights or fly into the sky, in-fact keep away until I say', she firmly added.

'Why, what are you doing,' replied Holly.

'There's no time to explain; just wait, and don't come into the sky'.

Suddenly all that remained of Melody's lions disappeared, as she requested and transformed into a bird, and that being a Rüppell's Vulture, a bird known for the fantastic heights of thirty-seven thousand feet it can reach into the sky. The bird melody requested wouldn't easily be visible amidst the battle which unfolded below; however, her size meant she couldn't fly directly between the Terror Flights for fear of being seen. So instead, she took a longer route and went around the Terror Flights before flying above them. However, as she did and unbeknown to her, the Woodhunter, still watching from the rocky ledge, saw the unusual-looking bird flying past, and unbeknown to Melody, the Woodhunter followed but could only travel so far into the sky before being forced to try and watch from a distance below and just above the clouds. Melody needed to be as far as possible above the Terror Flights for the plan to succeed, so she soured as far as the bird she chose allowed.

Once there, she couldn't see much of anything other than the passing clouds beneath her, but it was from there that she requested to become those of fifty million Darwin's Bark Spider, known to weave the strongest silk amongst all other spider species in her world.

Again this transformation was instant, and the watching Woodhunter lost sight of the distant spec it was watching, which was that of the unusual-looking bird, and in its place came a giant dark plume of spiders which erupted and spread out across the sky as they began to fall, weaving their silk as they went. Again, the Woodhunter watched but could not see anything, for the plume dispersed soon after it appeared; not knowing what the plume consisted of, all the Woodhunter could do was watch and wait to see what happened.

 The high-altitude winds eased, enabling the spiders to disperse and cover a wider area. As the spiders fell from the sky, the battle on the ground had temporarily ceased, for the chosen animals had gallantly served their purpose and were now gone. Leaving Holly and Jasmine to see the devastation of the land below after requesting those of flying insects and making their way to a safe area within the rocky hills, from where they returned to their usual selves to watch the skies and Melody's plan unfold.

 'Melody, are you there' called Jasmine, 'me and Holly are hidden in the rocks on another hillside, near to where we were; we're watching the skies, but what are we watching out for'.

 'Watch and see; it shouldn't be long now; I'm not sure if you're going to be needed up here, but be ready to request something when I say', replied Melody.

 Holly and Jasmine were left wondering what Melody was doing. Still, their wait was soon to be over.

 Meanwhile, the spiders continued to fall, and as they did, the silk they had woven landed on the unsuspecting Terror Flights as they continued patrolling the skies. The spiders used the great web of interwoven silk to anchor onto their prey, and as it did, they used it to climb from it and onto the bodies of the Terror Flights. At first, the spiders and their webs were slightly irritated, and they hadn't noticed anything until the webs they wove began to restrict their movements. Eventually, they became encased like a fly trapped by the snare of the spider web. Within moments of the countless spiders making contact with the Terror Flights, the Terror Flights began to lose control of flying and began to fall from the skies and ultimately to their deaths.

 One after the other, the Terror Flights fell, and the watching Woodhunter witnessed what was a gruesome sight, as did Holly and Jasmine, as more and more fell uncontrollably from the skies above until very few remained. Such was the scale that the need for Holly and Jasmine to request a transformation wasn't necessary. Despite everything that the Woodhunter had witnessed, it seemed not to care about anything other than the magic it was seeing and was left feeling infuriated by wanting something it didn't have, and that is the power the humans had, for it was now sure that there are three of them and not just the one it had previously seen. So the Woodhunter waited no longer and set off and gathered the Neplèns and what remained of the Terror Flights to address them for the first time in the tunnels beneath the Green Planet.

In the meantime, Holly and Jasmine waited where they were before Melody was soon to join them, and from there and upon Melody's arrival, they hugged one another in silence; things for the moment seemed a little subdued, and they were each feeling a little worn from the battle. There were no congratulations on what they had achieved up to the press because there was more to follow, for they still hadn't had the opportunity to retrieve the acorns from the Woodhunter.

'What now' asked Melody, eventually letting go of the smothering hug she was under.

'We need to keep at them', replied Holly, 'we somehow need to get close to the Woodhunter,' she added.

'Keep at them; I feel like we've been doing that for days already when in reality, it's only been hours', added Jasmine.

'It hasn't even been a second back home; how crazy is that' exclaimed Melody.

'Home, I'm ready for home', replied Holly.

'Me too,' added the others.

Meanwhile, with no time to rest, Mother Nature interrupted them with a message, firstly by telling them of their bravery and loyalty to one another and then by describing how the Woodhunter was gathering the Neplèns and about to lead them into the tunnels.

'We have to go', cried Holly, 'we won't be able to fight

them down in the tunnels successfully'.

The girls agreed, and without a second thought, they requested from the spirit of the acorn to grant them those of flying insects, or sorts, to quickly get them to where they needed to be. And within moments, they arrived, and just before the Woodhunter was about to order all Neplèns and Terror Flights into the tunnels. From there, the girls again requested to be transformed, and they did this before the Woodhunter had a chance to know what was happening. Jasmine became the first by becoming a hundred mythical Werewolf and Holly two thousand Rhinoceros, whilst Melody waited until the last moment before requesting her transformation, for she wanted to stay as she was until the remaining Terror Flights had taken to the skies.

Like the times before, the transformation was instantaneous, and it exploded into tens of hundreds of animals and mythical creatures. With them, they brought chaos to the Woodhunter and the Neplèns, and a fierce battle ensued. Soon after and whilst the battle took place, the Woodhunter and all one thousand, two hundred and twenty-one of what remained of the Terror Flights took to the skies. And as they did, they began their attack by swooping down in pairs to take hold of the battling animals below before taking them up from the ground, dropping them from heights, and down upon the other animals below. The time came for Melody to transform, and by using her last special request: she requested that of a hundred Pterosaurs, a winged creature known to be a once powerful flier and predator of the skies with a giant wingspan. The pterosaur's arrival was frightening though spectacular to see, for even the battling Neplèns below were momentarily distracted by the sheer sight, loud screeching noises, and the winds created by the sudden movement of their vast wings above. It was there in the skies that the Woodhunter led the Terror Flights into battle, and quickly they became the most tactical, for the

Woodhunter began by showing the Terror Flights how to attack the Pterosaurs by occasionally outmanoeuvring them and slicing hard beneath their webbed fleshy wings, which proved to be an excellent way to defeat them. However, the Pterosaurs were heavy hitters, for they used their wing power for speed and their great beaks to fire at them like darts as they sped through the skies, and soon the Terror Flights began taking heavy losses also. However, in desperation, just as time was about to run out, the Woodhunter lashed out in all directions and managed to take hold of the foot of a passing Pterosaur.

Meanwhile, on the ground below, it was scattered with dead and injured Neplèns, and Jasmines' time in the battle finished for her request had ended, and although she had only one special request left, it wouldn't be helpful in the ongoing fight. So, after she transformed, she retreated to escape the battle safely and waited in the shelter of the rocky hillside. However, Holly had one last special request left to use, and by using it, she hoped to weaken the Woodhunters' army much more significantly, for she requested that of one thousand Mammoths known for their great size and large size tusks. Knowingly, the Mammoths of Holly's choosing weren't very fast, so she let the spirit of the acorn guide her, and by doing so, she created a great circle by using the thousand Mammoths; in doing so, she encircled a great majority of the battle-weary Neplèns and steadily closed in on them.

Above the ground, the battle was ending, and the Woodhunter still had a tight hold of the leg of the pterosaur; the pterosaur was screeching and trying hard to shrug off and loosen the Woodhunters grip, and other pterosaurs were also trying to help. However, for this to happen, the pterosaurs needed to get close to the Woodhunter, but because of the fast though out of control manoeuvrers in the mid-air battle, they couldn't get close enough to the Woodhunter to do this. Meanwhile, the Woodhunter remained focused and wasn't letting go, which would prove disastrous for Melody, for her request suddenly ran out, and the Woodhunter would soon become aware that it was her it was holding on to. At that moment, the Woodhunter watched Melody tumbling from the skies with a shocked look in her eyes as she fell at speed toward the ground. Quickly though, Melody came to her senses and transformed into a bird, which the Woodhunter saw. Upon changing, she became disorientated and didn't know what direction she was heading, but it was toward the cliffs, a distance away from the hillside from where Jasmine was.

 Meanwhile, the Woodhunter had its sights firmly on the bird Melody became and quickly followed it. In the meantime, Melody, still disorientated, was just aware enough to feel the Woodhunters' presence behind her, and because of that, she became flustered. At that point, the spirit of the acorn was trying to guide her. Still, she couldn't hear nor feel it, for the panic was setting in, which caused Melody to turn to see where the Woodhunter was and wasn't aware of the nearing cliff heading towards her. Before she turned back to see where she was going, the bird hit the rock face of the mountainside, killing it instantly; with that, Melody returned to her usual self and fell from where the bird had hit to a rocky ledge below, where she lay unhurt though unconscious. Soon after the event, the Woodhunter arrived and before scooping her up from the ground and taking her into a cave-like area from the side of the ledge she lay, it crept around her, hoping to see any possessions she had, like the ones that resembled the acorns it was wearing from around its neck, or any other sign of magic it could take from her. Unable to see anything, the Woodhunter took her and put her down inside the cave, and in the meantime, it simply sat across from her and stared, thinking of what to do.

 Meanwhile, the fight on the surface of the Green Planet ended after the Mammoths had fully closed in on the battling Neplèns, leaving the Woodhunters' army decimated and in disarray. And in the meantime, Jasmine and Holly were hidden out of sight within the rocky hillside, and with the help of Mother Nature, they were trying to get in touch with Melody and locate her whereabouts.

'It's been a while now,' exclaimed Holly, 'I'm getting worried'.

'Me too; it's like she's just not hearing us; something's not right,' replied Jasmine.

Between the concerned conversation Holly and Jasmine were having, the sound of Mother Nature interrupted and told the girls that they should try not to worry and that she promised them they would soon hear from Melody.

Despite Mother Nature's good intentions, Holly and Jasmine decided to go out and search for her and were about to request a transformation when in their minds, they could hear Melody talking to Holly from inside the cave she was in.

'Who is she talking to? How can she be talking to you when you here' screamed Jasmine, while frantically pulling at the arm of Holly.

'Calm down, Jasmine, you need to be quiet', Holly replied, smothering Jasmine's voice with her hand. 'there must be a rational explanation'.

Suddenly, Holly and Jasmine again heard the voice of Mother Nature telling them what she thought was happening and how the Woodhunter may have requested from the Emerald Green Acorn to be changed into Holly, reminding them that it had done the same thing before when meeting the fisherman.

The girls were shocked to hear what Mother Nature had just told them because it made perfect sense to them, but some questions remained, why Holly, and what could the Woodhunter achieve by changing into her?

The only explanation Mother Nature could give was how the Woodhunter would be hoping for an opportunity to use Melody and how it would take from her what it could.

Meanwhile, Holly and Jasmine kept calling out to Melody in the hope she would answer, while in the meantime, Melody was sitting in the cave looking unharmed but dazed and confused, for standing across from her was Holly. Melody wasn't sure if Holly was talking to her because all she could hear were muffled voices inside her head, and for the time being, the words she heard weren't making any sense. However, shortly after, Melody remembered steadily and started understanding what had happened. The voices inside her head were less muffled than before but still not entirely clear enough to hear them properly. Then suddenly Melody sat up from where she was and remembered the spirit of the acorn, she could feel it was trying to guide her, but she didn't understand the feeling she was getting. So, impulsively, she requested to see it, and there in her hands, it appeared and lit up the corner of the dimly lit cave she was sitting in. Melody looked up with a smile as she watched Holly coming towards her, and not thinking anything untoward; she started talking to her.

'I'm remembering again', said Melody, still sitting while holding the spirit of the acorn and watching Holly as she steadily moved closer toward her, but not yet realising that it was, in fact, the Woodhunter and not Holly.

The Woodhunter neared closer to Melody and gestured with its open hands for Melody to hand over the spirit of the acorn, and in the meantime, the voices grew clearer within Melody's mind. For she could hear Jasmine telling her that it wasn't Holly and that it was the Woodhunter, and she needed to get out of the cave. But everything was happening too fast, and the message and the feelings she was getting confused Melody all the more.

'What's Jasmine talking about,' asked Melody, whilst thinking she was talking to Holly and not knowing she was talking to the Woodhunter.

Again there was no response to Melody's question, just another gesture from the Woodhunter as it tried to snatch

out from her hand the spirit of the acorn she was holding.
'Hold on, Holly, you know you can't just take it and that I
have to give it away,' laughed Melody, thinking Holly was
playing around.

Just then, something caught Melody's eye, it was a
glistening object on the cave floor, and it was shimmering
as it flickered between the shadows from the light of the
spirit of the acorn and the light from outside the cave.

'Here, Holly, hold this,' and without realising it, she
handed her spirit of the acorn over to the Woodhunter
and made her way across to the shimmering object on the
floor.

Upon approaching the object, Melody knelt over it,
stopped abruptly, and stared at it.

'This can't be', she muttered to herself under her breath,
'How is this possible, Holly,' she asked, turning to look.
'It's my glittery alien,' she added whilst picking it up from
the dusty ground. 'Look, how did it end up here'.

Suddenly, Melody began to realise what had just
happened.

'No, this can't be; you're not Holly, are you? You're the
Woodhunter, aren't you?' She quietly asked.

Melody then began to get angrier with the Woodhunter
and wanted so much to stand and fight it.

'That's how this got here, isn't it?' she shouted. 'You
accidentally carried it here, didn't you, when you were
creeping around in the cave, in my world', she screamed.

Melody was about to show the Woodhunter her glittery
alien she found but decided not to, for she knew it would
stupidly think that too was magic and that it would take it,
so she hurriedly stuffed it into her pocket.

Unfazed, the Woodhunter left the cave to retrieve the
hidden Emerald Green Acorn and the Emerald Key before
returning to its former self and back to where the Melody

was. It was evident by how the Woodhunter behaved that it was a taunting melody, for after placing the acorns back over its head, with the root fraying more, the Woodhunter held out its hand to show Melody the spirit of the acorn, and she could only watch as it turned into green mist and spun its way from its hand and into the Emerald Green Acorn hanging from around its neck.

Melody suddenly slumped further back against the cave wall and held her head in her hands. Tears were now streaming down her cheeks, and each one followed the same route as the last, leaving a clear trace and a little glimpse of a lost and bewildered child beneath the dirt on her face, and then her eyes fell as though a thousand thoughts had suddenly just raced through her mind.

Meanwhile, Holly and Jasmine were still calling out to Melody, and eventually, Melody began to listen and heard their voices enough for them to talk to one another.

'Where are you, Melody? Are you ok? We've been trying to speak to you; why haven't you answered' These were just some of the things Holly was saying.

'I'm ok,' replied Melody, 'but I've done something stupid', she added while still resting her head in her hands and trying through her disappointment to explain.

'What do you mean, Melody' asked Jasmine; calm down and explain; we'll fix it.

'We can't fix it; the Woodhunter has the spirit of the acorn; it tricked me into believing it was Holly, I woke up in this cave confused, and it was standing there impersonating Holly', replied Melody; 'I handed over the spirit; I just had no idea'.

'We can fix it, and we will fix it', said Holly, determined to try to make things right and give Melody some hope. 'Where is the Woodhunter now' she asked.

'It's here in the cave with me; it hasn't left here since transforming back into itself; I think it's waiting for you two to come'.

'But where are you? Do you think you can direct us' asked

Jasmine while Holly thought.

'I have no idea; I panicked when I requested to be a bird and hit the side of a cliff, I don't remember much after that, but there were many cliffs, I remember that much, and I was heading in the opposite direction to where you are now'.

'Could you send a signal or anything? There are so many cliffs around, it'll be hard to spot you', exclaimed Jasmine.

Melody told Holly and Jasmine to wait and allow her time to try and think. Melody only had herself and relied on her instinct to guide her. She listened and heard the past voice in her memory of Mother Nature telling her as she did before they went into battle with the Woodhunter, how each of them already had their spirit and how it was more substantial than any magic. It was at that moment when the idea popped suddenly into her head.

'I know what to do,' cried Melody in her mind. 'The spirit travelled into the Emerald Green Acorn that the Woodhunter is wearing around its neck; it lights up the cave where I'm sitting because it's a bit dark'.

'So what's the plan' asked Holly.

'I'll get the Woodhunters' attention and come to where I am sitting; the cave will light up slightly. But before that, you two transform into a bird or something and fly around; you should be able to see the light from outside the cave'.

'That's a great idea, Melody', said Jasmine, 'we'll do it now', she added.

'When you think you are somewhere near to where I am, let me know, and then I'll get the Woodhunters' attention', requested Melody.

Within moments of transforming, Holly and Jasmine took to the skies as small birds and flew a distance to the other side of the valley from where they were and to where they thought Melody would be.

The area from which they were was abundant with large cliffs, and without the acorn's light, they wouldn't have much hope of finding Holly, at least not in the time they would like.

Meanwhile, Melody was still in the cave and hadn't moved from the darkened area she was sitting in. Then, the girls told Melody that they thought they were in the correct place and to go ahead with the plan. Then, Melody counted to three and told Holly and Jasmine to search the cliff face for a cave entrance.

Melody braced herself before waving her hands around and whistling to the Woodhunter like she would if she were whistling for Charlie, her dog. The Woodhunter turned and stared inquisitively at Melody, who continued calling the Woodhunter across the cave.

'Come on, you stupid thing', she said, knowing that the Woodhunter wouldn't understand her.

'Come on,' she again called, coaxing it with another whistle.

By this time, the Woodhunter was showing signs of anger, for it was snorting and snarling, and its fish-like gills were opening and closing and making clicking noises. Melody didn't know for sure if it really didn't understand her or if, indeed, it knew she was taunting it, but she continued anyway.

'Your gross, but you probably know that already, and that's why you want to destroy everything, so everything else can be gross like you', shouted Melody as the Woodhunter neared her. 'You make me sick,' she added.

At that moment, the Woodhunter lunged itself toward Melody, and she closed her eyes and hid her face, not knowing what it might do. She stayed silent and still and could feel the Woodhunters' breath against the back of her hands as she shielded herself from its menacing presence.

'One, two, three', she counted to let Holly and Jasmine know that the Woodhunter was in the right place to lighten up the cave.

Holly and Jasmine immediately began to search the area by looking in different places. Then, after a short time exploring and just before the Woodhunter was about to move away from Melody, Jasmine spotted the faint green light shining out from inside a rocky entrance of the cliff face.

'It's here, Holly; I've found it, called Jasmine. 'We know where you are, Melody, we're coming to get you'.

It was a time of relief for the girls to find Melody's whereabouts, but the question of how they would get her out of the cave was the first thing the girls spoke about. Nevertheless, they quickly agreed and devised a plan so daring that they were willing to sacrifice all they had if it meant not leaving Melody.

Holly and Jasmine had now requested several transformations from the spirit of the acorn. During that time, they had made their way into the cave and visited Melody, all be it as insects, but it was good for all three of them to be together, even though they had to hide as insects to do it. Then, after a short stay together, the time soon arrived for Holly and Jasmine to act and deliver what they hoped would be the final blow for the Woodhunter.

'Are we ready,' asked Holly.

'Yeah', the others replied.

'Good luck, you two; I love you,' sobbed Melody.

'Love you too', they replied. 'Don't worry, we're never leaving you', added Jasmine.

At that moment, Holly and Jasmine left the cave and out onto the cliff's ledge. Out of sight of the Woodhunter, they took a moment to embrace and wish each other luck before Holly returned to the cave as a Deathwatch beetle, known as the destroyer of wood. She planned to finish what Melody had started by allowing the deathwatch beetle to gnaw at the root which bound the acorns around the Woodhunters neck. And Jasmine she followed as a snake not of no in particular kind, just big enough for the Woodhunter to capture, which it did. The snake Jasmine became only half-heartedly put up a fight, for it was no match for the Woodhunter. The Woodhunter was aware of what it had caught, and it also knew the significance of what might happen should it die, for it had seen the bird when it died and how it transformed into Melody. So with that thought, the Woodhunter showed no pity and simply pierced it with its claw, killing the snake instantly, and as the Woodhunter suspected, Jasmine appeared in its place.

 The Woodhunter took hold of Jasmine and held her up by one of her arms so it could take a closer look at her; Jasmine immediately began to kick and lash out while screaming for the Woodhunter to let her and her sister go. The Woodhunter was not phased by Jasmine's struggle, for it was a brave but futile attempt. Still, its mood rapidly changed when Jasmine swung at the Woodhunter, hitting it twice to the side of its face with her unrestricted free hand, which the Woodhunter took hold of. The Woodhunter, angered by the attack, held her closer toward its face, and as Jasmine did, she also closed her eyes and felt its foul breath on her face as it fiercely snarled and snorted at her.

 In anger, the Woodhunter carried Jasmine across the cave before picking Melody up from where she was sitting. Melody peered across at Jasmine as the Woodhunter held them apart, and as it did, she heard Jasmine speaking in her mind.

 'Am I doing a good job so far,' she winked her eye across to Jasmine.

 'Yeah, you are, Melody replied. 'And thanks for punching it in the face', she laughed.

 At that moment, the Woodhunter looked at them both before letting go of Jasmine and keeping hold of Melody. It was clear what the Woodhunter was doing, for the girls had already planned for this moment. For they knew that it was a threat by the Woodhunter to Jasmine, for it suspected that she also owned an acorn, and it was giving her a choice, and that was to pass over the spirit of the acorn in exchange for Melody's life. Jasmine knew what she was about to do, but before she did, she spoke with

Holly, who had already chosen several insects to gnaw at the root around its neck.

'How are you doing, Holly' asked Jasmine.

'I'm going to have to stop; I'm almost fully through the root, and if I'm not careful, the acorns will fall to the ground before we're ready; it just needs the slightest of tugs,' she replied.

'Alright then, but give us a count to three when you're ready', requested Jasmine.

Meanwhile, the Woodhunter was becoming agitated by Jasmine's slow response and began lightly shaking Melody to coax Jasmine to hurry her decision. And so, Jasmine held out her hands, and the spirit of the acorn appeared, and she stretched out her arms for the Woodhunter to take hold of it, and quickly it did. The Woodhunter then let go of Melody, and she hit the ground with a slight bump before the Woodhunter made its way toward the cave entrance. There, it held the spirit of the acorn and waited for it to travel as mist into the acorn from around its neck. Still, nothing happened, for the spirit of the acorn vanished, and the Woodhunter didn't think anything of it, for it was too distracted in waiting for Holly's arrival and in the hope that it could then do the same to her by taking her magic also.

'Get ready, Melody', said Jasmine.

'I am, don't worry', she replied.

'Right, you two, it ends here, on the count of three', called Holly.

'One, two, three', they called.

Holly suddenly transformed from that of an insect to that of a Golden Eagle, known for many things, including being a fierce hunter and strong flier, immediately the Woodhunter flinched as it felt the weight upon its back and neck, but before it had a chance to react, the eagle snatched the root, the Emerald Green Acorn and the Emerald Key from around its neck, and flew at an incredible speed out from the cliff edge. The Woodhunter turned slightly confused and stared at the girls before bellowing an almighty screech-like crackle before realising that the acorns were missing.

Leaving the girls in the cave and thinking they wouldn't be able to escape without the spirit of the acorn, the tormented Woodhunter quickly perused the golden eagle. Meanwhile, back in the cave, Jasmine produced the final part of the plan by transforming from the clone she was back to her original self, complete with the spirit of the acorn.

'What a plan', cried Melody.

'I must admit it worked a treat,' replied Jasmine before adding how she didn't think it would.

'Come on, we've got a bit to do yet', added Melody.

With that, Jasmine requested the last of her special requests, which was one of anything of her choosing, and with that, she chose a Pegasus, an immortal winged horse with spiritual powers. And so, from where they stood, Melody climbed up and onto his back, and Pegasus bolted across the cave floor and out of the entrance and into the sky; it flew.

'Whereabouts are you,' called Melody to Holly.

'I'm flying around the hill where the Woodlock is,' she replied, 'I'll be changing again soon; I just need to keep out of the Woodhunters sight; oh, by the way, there's still quite a lot of Neplèns here', she added.

'We're on our way', replied Melody.

Meanwhile, the Woodhunter was frantically combing the skies looking for the eagle when it had a sudden urge to head toward the trunk of the Rare Golden Oak. Once there, and from a distance, the Woodhunter spotted the faint emerald green light of the acorns the eagle was carrying. The Woodhunter called on the remaining Terror Flights to help, but for the first time, they refused his command, for too many of them were battle weary and didn't care to help. The raged Woodhunter didn't have time to deal with them and dismissed their behaviour, so instead, it continued in its pursuit of the golden eagle. Meanwhile, the Terror Flights were ordered to keep their distance until the Woodhunter was about to attack. Then, the Woodhunter flew as far above the eagle as possible before it came in, shooting down, almost in free fall, and like an arrow, it headed straight into the direction of Melody's golden eagle.

At that moment, Mother Nature warned Holly to prepare herself and warned them that the Woodhunter was about to attack but wasn't sure where or how. The spirit of the acorn was leading Holly, and her instinct was telling her that time was running out for the eagle and that she should prepare to transform.

Meanwhile, Pegasus and Melody reached where they needed to be, and in horror, they witnessed the Woodhunter approaching the eagle from above and was about to crash into it.

'Holly, it is above you; watch out', screamed Melody.

The eagle turned its head to see and noticed that the Woodhunter was about to crash into it, instinctively the eagle turned its entire body toward the Woodhunter and loudly screeched as it spread its wings and pushed out wide its talons just before the Woodhunter made impact. The eagle seemed to be flying backwards when the Woodhunter hit it, as it delivered a heavy blow. Amid the battle, several Terror Flights closed in on Holly's golden eagle, and through her struggle, the eagle lost grip of the root it was holding, and the acorn and the Emerald Key spiralled down towards the ground of the hilltop. And moments later, Holly was forced to transform into a small bird to help her reach the surface safely.

'I've lost the acorn, it's falling towards the top of the hill, and it's going to land in the middle of all the Neplèns', screamed Holly.

Immediately Jasmines Pegasus raced towards the ground, closely watching; the Woodhunter realised after seeing the Pegasus that it had been duped and had never received the spirit of the acorn. Angered, the Woodhunter watched as the Pegasus' wings clapped like thunder, causing the Neplèns below to crouch and shield themselves as it touched down. And he no sooner touched the earth with its hooves that great springs of water came gushing out from beneath the ground, knocking and washing away countless Neplèns, alive and dead, over the hillside to leave a somewhat clear path leading to the Woodlock.

Meanwhile, the Emerald Green Acorn and the Emerald Key landed, hitting the ground hard and becoming partly buried in the wet earth caused by Pegasus. Soon after it hit the ground, the Woodhunter and the Terror Flights followed close to where it landed. Holly then arrived as the bird she became and was about to transform again, but waited until the final moment, for at that moment, there was a brief stand-off, lasting only several seconds as each party waited to pounce for the acorn. The girls were so near and yet so far from reaching the trunk of the Rare Golden Oak and the safety of its Woodlock, and besides all other challenges, their biggest concern was with Melody, for she had no spirit of the acorn to help her. No powers of her own to call upon, and they knew at that moment that this was their final chance to claim the acorn and the Emerald Key, for if they failed now, they would have no choice but to leave everything with the Woodhunter forever.

'What do you want to do' asked Jasmine to the others.

'We fight, said Melody, just this once; if we fail, then pick me up somehow and get me to the Woodlock', she added.

'Then after three,' instructed Holly.

'Melody, hold tight; you are on my back again; you'll have to try to protect yourself from behind its ears', requested Jasmine.

'Ears', replied Melody, confused, before counting', One, two, three,'.

Holly immediately transformed into the only thing large enough to fight, and that being a Crocodylus Porosus, a

Crocodile known for its great size and strength and its heavy bite. As for Jasmine, she transformed into an African savanna elephant, known for its sheer size and aggressive behaviour if harassed, which she hoped to use to pave the way and retrieve the acorn.

Immediately after the girls reached the third count, a battle commenced retrieving the acorn and the Emerald Key from soddened earth it lay in. It was a gallant attempt by both the crocodile and the African elephant to reach the acorn before the Woodhunter or the Neplèns had, but with the help of Holly's crocodile, the elephant was the one to get the acorn first; however, no sooner had it reached that both became overpowered as more Neplèns joined the Woodhunters fight to regain the acorn.

The elephant stood firm, protecting the acorn beneath it; whilst it constantly fought off the Neplèns, it frantically searched the ground with its trunk to locate its whereabouts. Meanwhile, the crocodile stood little chance against the Neplèns as they continued to throw themselves over the top of it until it was unable to move, and their sheer weight began to suffocate it. During that time, the Woodhunter already sensed victory, that the Humans didn't have enough magic to win, and that it was only a matter of time before it regained the acorn and Emerald Key. However, that still wasn't enough, for the Woodhunter also wanted what the other two humans had, and that was their spirit of the acorn. And so, the Woodhunter decided again to threaten Melody's life in exchange for what they had and tried to pluck Melody up from the elephant's back that she rode. The elephant tusks and its huge ears did serve some form of protection for Melody as the Woodhunters' first two attempts failed; however, the shelter was never going to be enough, for the Woodhunters' final effort did manage to spike hold of her clothing and lift her from the elephant she was sitting on.

'Melody, what's happened,' Jasmine screamed.

'The Woodhunters got me', she replied in a panicked

voice.

'Melody, the Woodhunter wants us and the spirit of the acorn; try to stay calm and try not to panic; it won't harm you', yelled Holly.

Suddenly Jasmines' elephant became overpowered by the Neplèns and was forced to the ground as the Neplèns closed in to finish it off; meanwhile, Melody kicked and wrestled until her clothing ripped, and she freed herself from the Woodhunters claw and fell a short distance to the ground, cushioning her fall as she fell against the elephant. Melody was left amidst the confusion scrambling amongst the feet of the Neplèns as she tried navigating her way between the Neplèns trampling feet and toward the Woodlock. Meanwhile, the Woodhunter was busy following the same course as Melody but couldn't see where she was, for her small size became hidden by the amount of Neplèns she scrambled beneath. Things were about to get worse, for the Woodhunter was briefly interrupted in its search for Melody when a Neplèn stood on the top of the downed elephant holding both the Emerald Green Acorn and the Emerald Key above its head for the Woodhunter to see. The Woodhunter wasted little time in flying across and taking hold of the root which still bound them before returning to where it left off, only this time it stayed air-bound, and from there, it spied Melody scrambling towards many Neplèns who were still grappling with Holly's Crocodile. The Woodhunter then flew down towards Melody, who in the meantime had neared a mass of Neplèn feet, of which she wouldn't make it through when suddenly a pair of eyes opened beneath the wet mud caused by Pegasus and the great springs of water it unleashed.

'Holly, stay where you are; I'm going to transform into a Python; get ready to hold on; I'm getting you out of here', said Holly.

'Hurry,' replied Melody.

Immediately, Holly transformed and became a Reticulated

Python, known to be the largest snake in their world, and the python slid beneath Melody just before the Woodhunter and arrived; it scooped her up onto its back and slid its way slowly beneath the feet of the unsuspecting Neplèns and for the time being away from the immediate danger of their trampling feet. However, the confused Neplèns soon turned their attention away from the crocodile that they fought they had and turned instead to the slow-moving python. And no sooner had they done this; than the python was surrounded and pounced upon, causing it to coil itself around Melody to try and protect her. Meanwhile, the Neplèns killed Jasmines' elephant. At that moment, Jasmine knew she couldn't take on the Neplèns alone, so she requested a Buffalo, just so that the buffalo could make its way across to where Holly and Melody were, which it did, and that too was pounced upon by the Neplèns.

'It's no good, Jasmine, we can't carry on like this; we can't go any further,' said Holly, 'We're going to have to hand our spirit of the acorn over to the Woodhunter; we have no choice', she added.

'But what if the Woodhunter doesn't let us go' asked Melody, 'what then'.

'That's a chance we'll have to take; we have no other option', replied Jasmine.

For the moment, there was a lull of subdued silence, and within that silence came the sound of wafting wings brought by the Woodhunter as it landed before the Buffalo and the Python, and with its appearance, the Neplèns suddenly stopped their attack, and retreated.

Meanwhile, Holly and Jasmine agreed that there was nothing more they could do and that their only hope was to be released after they chose to hand the Woodhunter their spirit of the acorn. So, with that, they transformed back into their original selves.

No sooner had the girls done this had the Woodhunter stepped forward; the girls looked about them, they could see the trunk of the Rare Golden Oak behind them and were still hoping to find a way out, but instead, they found themselves surrounded by the Neplèns. The Woodhunter approached by first peering meaninglessly down at Holly before moving on to Jasmine and then Melody before snatching her up from the ground as she screamed.

Holly and Jasmine glanced at one another before hearing the voice of Mother Nature calling to them.

'Hold tight; we haven't quite finished yet', said Mother Nature.

Meanwhile, through the Woodlock and into the world that had stopped, perched on a tree branch was a hearty robin peering in through the makeshift window of the cave and at the Silverlatch. The hearty robin, who had already made fleeting visits to the cave, gave several faint whistles before flying off and in the direction of the girl's home. And in the meantime, a strong, commanding voice echoed around the inside of the cave; the words were calling to the Wooden King,

'You know what you must do'.

In the meantime, and after arriving at the girls' home, the hearty robin flew straight through the girls' open bedroom window and passed the already open door, which led to Mum and Dad's bedroom before coming to rest at the foot of the bed from where Charlie was still laying. Once there, the hearty robin whistled words into the ears of Charlie, and immediately he opened his eyes, which were brightly shining the same colour as the Emerald Green Acorn. Charlie then raced off the bed, through the girls' bedroom and out through the open window before transforming into a golden wooden arrow, with the shaft being that of heartwood, its tip being that of an acorn, and the fletching being that of oak leaves. And from there, it flew in straight toward the cave and the Rare Oaks Silverlatch.

Meanwhile, on the Green Planet, the Woodhunter held Melody by her leg and upside down; its frantic behaviour led the girls to believe that even by giving up the spirit of the acorn, their chances of being allowed to leave the Green Planet were now non-existent, for it was now more evident than ever before that the Woodhunter would let nothing stand in its way. However, since the girls heard Mother Nature's message, they felt sure that somehow things were about to change, and they didn't have to wait long for this to happen. Suddenly, a loud foghorn-type noise echoed inside the Woodlock, causing the Woodhunter and its remaining army to watch. And what followed was a brighter-than-usual golden light emitting from the Rare Golden Oak trunk, for everything across the hilltop shone the same colour even in the daylight. The golden light then suddenly began to flicker as though something was moving from within it and casting shadows as it did when out from behind it; the arms of the Wooden King appeared from inside the Woodlock, then his head, until he fully stepped out and onto the Green Planet. In the silence surrounding the hilltop, the Wooden King stopped briefly and turned to look at the tree he once was; he placed his forehead and his hands against the vast trunk of the Rare Golden Oak before closing his eyes. Then a beautiful thing appeared, for it was a mirage of the Rare Golden Oak as it once was, complete with its branches, leaves, and golden bark-like colour, a reminder to the onlooking Woodhunter and the Neplèns of what they took away.

The Wooden King then opened his eyes, and the mirage was gone; he turned and looked around him at the devastation before casting his eyes at the Woodhunter. Anger was building up in the Wooden King when suddenly he screamed for the Woodhunter to let the child go, the Woodhunter glared without emotion at the Wooden King, and emptiness filled its eyes.

The Wooden King then gave a short whistle, and out from the Woodlock, the golden wooden arrow appeared;

the Wooden King looked at the golden arrow and gave it a slight nod, and the arrow shot at the speed of light, leaving nothing but a golden beam of light behind it. The arrow struck the Woodhunter at such a speed that it didn't realise it had entered its left shoulder and out through the other side, forcing the Woodhunter to lose its grip on the acorns it was holding. They then fell to the ground, but before reaching it, the golden arrow returned within a split second and pierced the root, which bound the acorns and carried them far into the distance. The Woodhunter then grew unsteady and lost its hold on Melody, and she, too, fell to the ground. Again the golden arrow sped toward her, pierced her clothing and carried her, the acorn and the emerald key to the safety of the Woodlock before leaving and returning to the new planet, leaving Melody wondering what had just happened and what it was that made it happen.

Meanwhile, only several seconds had passed, and the spirit of the acorn was leading Holly and Jasmine to transform and fly their way to the Woodlock, which they did. From there, they watched as the Wooden King ran toward the Neplèns as he furiously battled with them to get to the Woodhunter, which he did, and the Woodhunter felt the full force of the Wooden King. Meanwhile, the girls were calling as loud as they could for the Wooden King to return to the Woodlock, as they could see him being eventually overwhelmed by the Neplèns, for that is what happened.

After some time, the Wooden King was sorrowfully brought down and was pinned to the ground by the sheer number of the Neplèns attacking him, he heard the girls calling for him, and he looked directly across from the ground he was pinned to and smiled, before saying 'thank you', the Wooden King told them that they must go, for he and the girls could see the injured Woodhunter limping towards them and the Woodlock. The girls were helpless as they watched the Wooden King's eyes close as his spirit faded. But then the girls noticed a flutter of something fly past them from inside the Woodlock and out toward the Wooden King as he lay on the ground.

Meanwhile, the Wooden King had no more to give as he lay with his eyes flickering to close and with the feeling of his spirit leaving him, for one last time, he opened his eyes to look at the trunk of the Rare Golden Oak, and what he saw was again, the beautiful mirage of what he once was, when suddenly, appeared in his sight was a hearty robin who was looking at himself in the reflection of the Wooden Kings emerald green eyes.

'Oh,' said the surprised Wooden King, 'you're the hearty little fellow I've seen before; the girls tell me you're a robin', added the Wooden King.

The hearty robin looked into the eyes of the Wooden King before whistling a little tune that spoke words to him, and the words told the Wooden King to 'get up', and with that, the hearty robin flew back through the Woodlock and passed the girls and out through the makeshift window of the cave into the forest.

No sooner was the Wooden King left with the words from the hearty robin had he suddenly felt a tremendous feeling; it was the same feelings he once knew when he was alive and rooted as the Rare Golden Oak, for now, the earth's vibrations where once again beginning to travel through and around his body. And immediately after, the Wooden King glowed a magnificent golden colour like that of the sun; he looked at his hands and his fingers before burying them deep into the earth, and as he did, his fingers spread out like those of roots, golden and green in colour which speedily travelled across a great distance and far beneath the earth of the Green Planet. The Wooden King then lifted his head and stared across at the girls peering back at him from inside the Woodlock before slowly raising himself from the ground, causing the Neplèns, who still clambered upon him, to fall to the ground. The Wooden King's forearms and hands remained rooted in the earth as he stood at the top of the hill from where he was first born; he looked across at the desolate valleys and screamed at the top of his voice several times the words 'Never again'. And with that, the Wooden King pulled his arms and hands out from the soil below and raised them high above his head, and by doing so, the roots which were still attached caused the earth within the valleys to crack and break apart like that of an earthquake. Great dust clouds spontaneously erupted across countless areas of the surrounding valleys, and the loud sounds of breaking rock grew ever closer as the mountains, hills, and tunnels began to crumble and fall in on themselves. Cracks in the earth grew wider and began swallowing up anything and everything in their path into the bottomless pit below. The Wooden King turned and watched as the Woodhunter continued limping its way toward the Woodlock in a desperate attempt to regain the power it once had. So, the Wooden King created a root and guided it across to the feet of the Woodhunter, from which it bound them before dragging the Woodhunter past the feet of the Wooden King and to the edge of the hill, where it would witness what it is like to have everything and then to have it taken away. With that, the Wooden King turned to look at the girls and closed his eyes before disappearing into a golden mist, which drifted across into the Woodlock and through into the Emerald Green Acorn.

 Meanwhile, the girls watched from inside the Woodlock and out at the Green Planet; in the distance and at the edge of the hill, they witnessed the Woodhunter struggling to break free from the root which bound it, and looking past the Woodhunter, the girls watched as the surrounding hills and mountains came crashing down around it. Suddenly, the trunk of the Rare Golden Oak and the hill from where it stood also began to shake, and the girls prepared themselves to step through the Woodlock and back home. But just before they did, Mother Nature from the Green Planet spoke to them by thanking them and telling them how she would never forget them and their bravery and that they should not worry about the Green Planet, saying how things have a happy knack of turning out right, and that it would eventually heal itself. With that, Mother Nature hurried the girls along and warned that the hill and the trunk of the Rare Golden Oak would probably fall, and with that, she and the girls bid farewell.

'Come on, are we ready' asked Holly, while shaking the others by the arm and excitedly jumping around inside the Woodlock.

'We are', shouted the others while sharing Holly's excitement.

With that and for the last time, Melody stepped through the rippling green mist; next was Jasmine, and soon after Melody, but before she did, she looked out one final time at the Green Planet and in the direction of where the Woodhunter was, and what Melody did see was the hillside collapsing toward her, so she quickly turned to step into the mist, and in her mind, she thought the Woodhunter must have perished and gone down with the hill when suddenly it appeared from the sky and headed straight toward her and the Woodlock. Melody screamed and went to pick the acorn up, but it was heavier than she had imagined, and it fell out of her hands. Then she heard Mother Nature shouting for her to hurry as the hillside and the trunk was about to collapse. As it did, Melody quickly managed to scoop up the acorn before jumping through the rippling green mist and back safely into the cave, leaving the Woodlock and the Woodhunter forever behind her. However, in her struggle to pick up the acorn, the Emerald Key had slipped out from the root and remained inside the Woodlock as the trunk and the hill tumbled toward the open ground below.

Meanwhile, Melody arrived back at the cave in somewhat of a state, and no sooner had she returned than the trunk of the Rare Silver Oak turned to dust, just as the

Woodhunter said it would.

'What's the matter, Melody' yelled Holly.

'The Woodhunter flew at me and nearly got me, it's alive, and the Emerald Key came off the root, look', cried Melody as she held only the acorn and the root for the others to see.

Suddenly, the calming voice of the Wooden King echoed around the inside of the cave and told Melody that she needn't worry and that the Woodhunter wouldn't be able to use the Emerald Key for anything, reminding her and the others that the Emerald Key that the Woodhunter used to cross through the Woodlock and through into the Silverlatch were now both destroyed. With that, the mood within the cave changed.

'Well, girls, it was a close call,' said the voice of the Wooden King, 'you certainly know how to exit,' he laughingly added.

'I can't believe all that just happened, screamed Jasmine, as she reached out towards Holly and Melody with her arms wide open.

'You two were awesome,' said Melody as she held them tight.

'Melody, you were there with nothing to help you', replied Jasmine.

'Wrong, I had you two, and I had this,' replied Melody as she plucked from her pocket her favourite toy, the stretchy glittery alien.

'What,' replied Holly and Jasmine.

'I thought you lost it; how did you end up with it on the Green Planet,' asked Holly.

'It's a long story; it'll keep,' replied Melody, smiling. And 'Hey, Wooden King, a few things are puzzling me'.

'And what are those things, Melody' replied the Wooden King.

'We'll, were we ever in danger? What was the thing with the robin, the root thing you did, and the golden arrow? What was that all that about,' asked Melody.

The Wooden King paused for a second to think how best he could answer the questions and began with the first.

'Were you ever really in danger? Well, things that weren't supposed to happen happened, and things got awkward for a second or so. Didn't you have a few of those moments, Melody?' asked the Wooden King laughingly.

'And what was the thing with the robin? As you put it, Melody? Well, the honest answer is, Mother Nature nor I was aware of it; all I can tell you is, It had nothing to do with the spirit of the acorn or any other magic, for it seems that the robin was a gift, here as a watcher and a messenger, sent by from the creator of everything good, I'm sure you know who that is Melody', smiled the Wooden King.

'Now the root thing, as you put it, again, I think you want to know how I did it, and again, the only answer I can give you is that it was in me to do that all the while; but I just didn't know. All I know is that I heard a voice, a message telling me that I knew what to do, and the hearty robin encouraged me to do that, and that was to believe in myself. So, I only did what all of you did, for you had the same message as me throughout this journey; however, you didn't need the hearty robin to encourage you, but instead, you encouraged each other.

And lastly, the golden arrow can keep for a bit longer, for I need to take you on one last journey. But before I do, we need to place the Emerald Green Acorn down into the silver oak dust pile and cover it. With that, Holly picked up the Emerald Green Acorn and placed it down on the mound of dust, but before burying it, each of the girls placed their hand on the top of it, simply as a parting gesture, before they covered it. Immediately after they had done this, they all began to feel a pleasant though strange sensation that was the spirit of the acorn leaving their mind and body, and as it did, it travelled from them to join with the Emerald Green Acorn. And after only a short time, they watched as a warm golden light shone out from beneath the dust, and from there, they uncovered it to display the golden acorn beneath. No sooner had that happened than a rainbow travelled through the makeshift window, and into the cave, before stopping at the feet from where the girls stood. They reached out to it, for the rainbow was unlike anything the girls had seen before, for it was real to touch and moved like that of water when they did.

'Is this it? Is this the time we step into the rainbow' asked Jasmine.

'It is, the Wooden King replied, 'but only after you have placed the acorn inside the rainbow', replied the Wooden King.

The girls stood for a moment, looking at each other with tears welling up in their eyes as a sudden sense of deep sadness suddenly fell upon them.

'This is it.' 'The final part of our journey', sobbed Holly and Jasmine.

'Yeah, but just think, Mum, Dad and Charlie, those cosy nights and play days,' said Holly, reminding them of the other most important journeys to come as she wiped away her tears.

The girls took a moment to compose themselves before they each played their part in placing the acorn down and into the rainbow.

'What now,' asked Holly.

The Wooden King asked the girls to step inside the rainbow, telling them that the rainbow would make them feel weightless, and all that they needed to do was to let the rainbow do the rest. With that, the girls held on to each other's hand and stepped into the rainbow of beautiful colours, and as they did, the colours suddenly poured like that of a waterfall, splashing imaginary droplets of water as they hit the ground. Then, immediately the girl's feet left the surface, and they began to float until steadily they sped up; the girls kept hold of each other as they watched the rainbow's beautiful colours speed by them; through their laughter, there was no sound; for it was just peacefulness and full of love.

After what seemed a long time travelling inside the rainbow, it was only a short time, for the girls suddenly began to slow, and their weightlessness ebbed away until they were eventually standing. The girls looked downwards at their feet to see where they had landed, and the ground they had placed their feet upon was grassy and full of buttercups and daisies. Then, before stepping outside the rainbow, they turned to each other with a look of wonder at where they might have ended up.

As the girls stepped out from the rainbow, greeting them were crystal blue skies and the sun glaring down upon them. Across the hill, a vast and varied amount of summer flowers danced within the tall green grass as they blanketed the ground, swaying to and fro in the warm summer breeze as it went. The Mountains, hills and valleys surrounding them were vast and mesmerising, for they'd never seen their world looking so beautiful.

'Where are we,' asked Melody.

'I don't know,' replied Holly, 'try asking the Wooden King or Mother Nature', she added.

So, Jasmine called out to both to ask where they were. Mother Nature reminded them it was a secret place, and nobody could know, as she appeared like the wind from the ground. And as she did so, the outline of who she was could be seen, and although Mother Nature appeared colourless and transparent like that of glass, it was clear that she was wearing a long flowing dress with her hair tied back with what looked like wildflowers.

'You look lovely,' said Jasmine, with Holly and Melody agreeing also.

'Thank you, and you all do too', Mother Nature replied as she thought about making them look a little more presentable, as she looked them up and down, staring at their torn clothes and mucky hands and faces.

'I certainly can't send you home in that state', She said, as

Mothers do.

With that, she plucked a slight whisp of a cloud from the sky and brought it down toward the girls before wrapping it around them, and for a short time, they disappeared out of sight and behind the cloud; Mother Nature then blew a slight wind and chased the cloud away to reveal Holly, Jasmine and Melody looking just like they did before the start of their journey, complete with their hair brushed, faces clean, their torn clothes mended, and even their bag and all its belongings intact.

After passing on some pleasantries to Mother Nature and each other, Melody asked if the Wooden King was still with them. Mother Nature replied by asking them to go and see for themselves, and by doing so, she pointed to the far side of the hill. With that, the girls turned to look, and suddenly the Wooden King appeared and was sitting on the side of the hill, overlooking the picturesque sight before him. The girls raced across and greeted him, with the Wooden King welcoming them also.

'It's beautiful, isn't it,' the Wooden King said, evidently talking about the creation displayed before him.

'Yes, it is', the girls replied, 'but where is it,' added Melody.

'I can't say, Melody; it has to remain a secret,' replied the Wooden King. 'But where would you like it to be,' he added.

Melody thought for a moment.

'Heaven,' she replied.

'Well, that sounds good enough to me, so if you like, you can keep that thought, Melody; in fact, you can all keep it, for that's where I'll be, replied the Wooden King.

With that, the Wooden King stood from the edge of the hillside and began to return to the rainbow, with the girls following closely behind.

'Oh yes, that reminds me', cried the Wooden King, stopping the girls in their tracks. 'You had one question that you wanted to answer'.

The girls looked at one another with thoughtful looks, for

it was hard to remember everything that had happened when suddenly Melody called out.

'I remember, it was the golden arrow'.

'Yes, the golden arrow, you wanted to know what all that was about', the Woodhunter replied with a heavy intake of breath to ready himself as he prepared to give the girls the answer.

I need you to think back a year or so and to remember that dreary night when you heard faint scratches on your door, and when you opened it, a little dog was standing there, remember the message he had in his eyes, and how the message was telling you that he was a stray, and how the message also asked for you to let him in. Well, that was his idea.

'What do you mean, his idea' asked Holly.

'I'll explain', replied the Wooden King.

So he continued, as I was saying, that was Charlie's idea; you see, before Charlie turned up at your house and Mother Nature needed to put in place a plan, we needed you three to help, as you now know, so for you to help, we needed to get the chance to meet you so that I could explain everything to you. However, Mother Nature and I couldn't figure out a way to make that happen, and that is where Charlie came in, for he created himself from me, for he is a part of me, and I of him.

'What,' cried Jasmine, 'Charlie is not a real dog', she added.

'I'll explain', replied the Wooden King; knowing that this was hard for the girls, he wanted to explain without complicating matters further and making things worse.

The Wooden King continued, Charlie is part of me and I of him; Charlie created himself after myself, and Mother Nature decided on an idea in the hope that we could meet. The idea was for Charlie to arrive at your door precisely when he did and to become part of the family, which he did. His idea was to lead you to the cave, but Charlie found it difficult to do, for you were all too good at capturing him before he had managed it, and we hadn't considered the leash and the protection you gave him by not allowing him to roam freely. So many failed attempts at leading you to the cave didn't happen, and all Charlie could do was persevere, which he did. For all the time Charlie was thought to be running to the farmer's field to pester the sheep, he wasn't; he was trying to lead you to the cave and me. To answer your question as to whether Charlie is a real dog is yes and no, for he wasn't, but during his time with you, he became more like one. For instance, I was calling for him to join me when I stepped through the Woodlock and onto the Green Planet. If it weren't for the hearty robin that somehow heard me calling him, he would probably still be asleep at the foot of your parent's bed; after all, that's why you found it hard to close the bedroom door on the morning that you were leaving, for he always was meant to be joining me. Still, he was just a dog enjoying his comfort at that moment.

The girls laughed, even though they found what the Woodhunter told them very hard to accept.

'So, what happens now,' asked Melody, with a worried look on her face, as she, Holly and Jasmine waited for the answer.

'Well, that depends on Charlie', replied the Wooden King.

'I don't know what you mean'. 'So is Charlie our dog, or isn't he?' 'Just tell us', cried Melody.

'Charlie has to decide for himself,' replied the Wooden King as he went on to explain.

'He is now immortal, he doesn't age, and he won't die, and as things are, he just can't go back home with you. However, Charlie can choose, and by doing so, he would become mortal, which would mean, that he would become a natural dog, and with the care you have shown him, Charlie should live a good life; however, he would eventually die, and that choice would be his'.

'So, how would we know what he wants' asked a teary-eyed Jasmine.

'We would ask him', replied the Wooden King.

With that, the Wooden King let out a loud whistle, and Charlie came running out from the foot of the rainbow and across the grass-covered hilltop, occasionally jumping above the tall grass to see where he was heading, and the girls cried as they watched him. Charlie made an instant fuss of the girls when he approached them, and they of him. Then Charlie stopped and slowly made his way across to the Wooden King, seemingly already aware of what he was about to be asked.

The Wooden King towered over Charlie, so he knelt on the ground to be a little closer to him; there, the Wooden King tickled Charlie beneath his chin and talked to him. Charlie listened, and as he did, he kept glancing up and across at the girls with a sad look before reaching up at the Wooden King to lick at his face.

'He made his decision', said the Wooden King.

Charlie stood for a moment, staring at the girls barking and wagging his tail fast before racing across to them to greet them for the first time as a real dog.

'He's chosen us,' screamed the girls while rolling around in the grass.

'whoa, hang about, Charlie,' called the Wooden King, 'aren't you forgetting something'.

Charlie stopped what he was doing and excitedly raced back to the Wooden King before sitting beside him, and almost proud and statue-like, he waited. There, the Wooden King held out his hand and from Charlie came an emerald green mist which travelled about him before disappearing into the Wooden King's hand. Then, before Charlie raced back to the girls, the Wooden King placed his mouth next to Charlie's ear and whispered some words to him before saying.

'That's between you and me, Charlie boy, you never know', he added before winking his eye.

Suddenly, the Wooden King stood upright and clapped his hands in readiness.

'It's time, girls, come on, let's get the acorn planted'.

There was a sort of acceptance from the girls that was it and that their fantastic journey was almost over, for they happily joked and chased one another, occasionally falling over Charlie as they ran and made their way to the foot of the rainbow to where the golden acorn sat.

'So girls, after all your hard work, it's only right that you decide where the golden acorn goes, but choose wisely, because where it goes, I go too', said the Wooden King.

'What, do you leave and go into it also' cried Holly.

'Well, yes, Holly, I can hardly walk around the hills forever looking like this, can I' laughed the Wooden King as he opened up his arms to reference himself.

'Well, yeah, I suppose', replied Holly, naturally feeling slightly disappointed at the thought.

'How about here,' said Jasmine, just at the foot of the rainbow.

'Sounds good to us,' replied Melody and Holly.

'Right, it's decided then,' agreed the Wooden King.

With that, the Wooden King placed his hand into the grass and down through the soil until he was satisfied it was the correct depth for the acorn before asking the girls to put it into the hole he'd made. It was a sad moment for the girls as they all placed their hands beneath the acorn and held it above the spot, but before they put it into its place, they each placed a little kiss upon it, for even Charlie managed to poke his head in-between the girl's hands to slather upon it. With that, the girls counted three before placing the acorn into its new home.

'Well girls, that's that', said the Woodhunter, as he lightly coughed because of a little sentimental croak in his throat and buried the acorn with the fresh soil he'd dug.

'It's now time to step back into the rainbow', he added.

'So, this is goodbye,' said Jasmine as she and the others ran toward the Wooden King to hug him.

'You're doing it again', said Holly, pointing at his face and the resin-like tear that welled in his eye.

'No', replied the Wooden King, 'Something must have

gotten into my eye whilst I was digging,' he laughingly added, wiping his eye with his hand.

After a long embrace, Melody and Charlie shuffled their way out from between the huddle, and Charlie began to bark, almost like he was instructing things to move along and that it was time to part.

In the meantime, Mother Nature had waited for them at the foot of the rainbow, where she whispered words into their ears, telling them how she would always be around and how she would miss them; Mother Nature then told them how she would start the world again, as soon as they arrived back, and to watch closely at their surroundings when they made their way home, telling them how she was allowed to leave a little surprise for them. The girls were left wondering what that might be when the Wooden King also told them how the rainbow would be different for their journey back home, telling them how little snippets of their thoughts and memories of what they held most dear and that if they requested to see or hear them, then the rainbow would show them as they travelled back.

With that, the girls and Charlie stepped into the rainbow and looked out at the Wooden King and Mother Nature as the colours began to pour like water before their eyes.

'One minute', the girls shouted before popping their heads through the rainbow.

'We love you,' they said.

'And we love you too,' replied the Wooden King and Mother Nature.

With that, they stood inside the rainbow, and the weightlessness returned as they waved, and Charlie barked through the colours as the Wooden King and Mother Nature waved back. At that moment, and as they began to travel through the rainbow, the area from where they left grew smaller and smaller until it and the Wooden King were gone. Suddenly, music started to play, for it was Jasmine who requested to hear the song 'Impossible Dream', and it was that which accompanied the various mixed images that they asked for, for what began to appear were memories of Mum and Dad, and of themselves, and Charlie, playing in the fields and the garden. The girls became tearful as more images flew past them as they travelled home, for there were even some images showing the simpler things like their bedroom and sitting having dinner. Other memories showed other things they held dear, such as the Wooden King, the Rare Golden Oak, the Green Planet, the spirit of the acorn, the Woodlock and many others. Suddenly the images faded, and the music stopped, and with it, their feet landed on the ground, and they found themselves and Charlie standing outside the cave, where the journey began.

'Wow, we're back home,' screamed Holly, as they all laughed and jumped around, hugging one another, as Charlie began to bark, and the forest burst into life.

'The world, it's started again', yelled Jasmine as she and the girls began to dance around again.

'Hang on, that reminds me', Melody yelled as she fumbled in the bag for the phone, 'It's not even 5.30 in the morning; what if mum or dad up out of bed? How are we going to explain'.

'I think after all we've been through,' laughed Jasmine, we can think of something to tell them on our way back.

And so, they continued with their short journey, and in the meantime, after looking through some pictures on the phone, Melody went to put it into her pocket and, as she did, felt her glittery alien.

'Oh, I forgot about this, she said, pulling it from her pocket while the others watched as she took it out.

'That's lovely, Mother Nature must have done that', replied Holly, as she and the others were shocked to see it looking brand new and complete with both its hands.

'I wonder if that's what she whispered to us before we left', asked Jasmine, 'she did say to keep a watch closely at our surroundings'.

'Yeah, that was probably it', replied Holly.

However, the girls passed halfway home and were walking through the same path they came when Melody suddenly stopped and stared at something that caught her eye.

'Hey, you two, come here, look at this', she said.

Holly and Jasmine looked at the thing Melody was pointing at.

'It's the butterfly, remember, we tried to free it before the journey', cried Holly.

'Oh yeah, we did, but how's that possible? It's like it was before, but time has already started', replied Jasmine.

'Not in there, it hasn't', yelled Melody pointing to the butterfly, 'that's what Mother Nature meant when she whispered to us; she's left it like that for us to save it'.

'But what about her two rules,' asked Holly.

'Mother Nature did say she was allowed to leave a little surprise', replied Jasmine.

With that, the girls reached out to help the doomed butterfly, and unlike the last time they tried, they weren't met with the invisible force preventing them from intervening. Instead, the butterfly was no longer captured in mid-flight and tenderly walked onto and across the girls' hands, and with that, they raised the butterfly into the air and watched as it flew into and between the bright beams of sunlight that flickered between the branches of the forest trees.

The End?

ABOUT THE AUTHOR

Hello all, and thank you for reading The Wooden King; hopefully, it was worth it.

Well, this page is about myself (I hate this bit), 'I smile'. My name is Ian Kelly, and this is my first publication; I set about writing this book a few years ago (it feels more like hundreds). I set out writing with all guns blazing; however, I ended up shelving it part way through. There it remained, gathering dust, until my youngest daughter, aged 9yrs at the time, suggested I read her part, which I did. She liked it and encouraged me to finish writing it, which I did. And here I am, writing my last little legacy about myself. On that note, 'the one about myself', I haven't got much to say other than I am very humbled.

I loved writing this book and living the lives of the characters within it, especially the Wooden King; I also loved the story's innocence and the love that the characters showed for the world they live in.

Each day, dream just a little,
keep every last one of those little dreams alive,
for one day, they'll grow bigger than you can
possibly imagine.

TWK

Printed in Great Britain
by Amazon

27905670R00142